SUNRISE KISSES

KRISTA LAKES

ZIRCONIA PUBLISHING, INC.

ABOUT THIS BOOK 1. ABOUT THIS BOOK ABOUT THIS BOOK

Ava Fairchild needed to get away.

After walking in on her cheating ex-boyfriend, she was delighted when her appraisal company was given a job in the Caribbean. A once-in-a-lifetime trip to appraise Sebastian Belrose's billion-dollar estate seemed to be exactly what she needed to relax and enjoy herself.

A walk to the beach at dawn gave her a first impression of the paddle boarding billionaire himself. He was reserved and mysterious, yet had a firey temper when pushed. His evasiveness and the fact that he forbade her from traveling to his Study just added to his allure, while simultaneously reminding her about the secrets that destroyed her last relationship. Still, every sunrise that they shared together made her fall more desperately in love with him.

But Bastian had a reason for keeping to himself. And as Ava saw the **scars** that criss-crossed his body, she knew that what she had found was a soul not unlike herself. A man who had been damaged. A man who deserved to trust. A man that deserved to love, and to be loved. Would this beauty be able to tame the beast, or would they be left with just memories of sunrise kisses?

~

"Thank you," I whispered. "You saved me."

I leaned forward and kissed him. It started innocently enough, but the adrenaline and fear mixed with gratitude and attraction overwhelmed me. I found my tongue pushing to enter his mouth, wanting his in mine and my hands pressing into his broad chest for more.

He pulled back, grabbing my wrists and holding me in place.

"I don't want to hurt you," he groaned, fighting with his own desire. "I don't want to take advantage."

I pushed harder against him, imploring with him with my eyes not to stop. "Please," I begged, unable to fight my attraction for him. His chivalrous refusal not to take advantage only made it that much harder. I wanted him even more. "Please..."

His brow softened. He picked at a loose strand of hair by my cheek, carefully tucking it behind my ear. His eyes absorbed me, trying to decide if I really was asking.

"Please, Bastian..." I whispered one more time. The sound of his name was his undoing. He kissed me just as the car pulled to a stop in front of the house. It was a short kiss, but full of raw passion.

He had my seat-belt undone in an instant, picking me up in his arms and carrying me up the steps to the main entrance. Elijah opened the door, but that was the last I saw of him as Bastian carried me up the stairs and to his bedroom, kissing me the entire way...

Don't forget to sign up for <u>my newsletter</u>! You'll be the first to see my new covers, comment on new books of mine, and always know when books are available for free or on sale!

CHAPTER 1

What the freaking hell?

I stood in the doorway and stared. This had to be a nightmare. A bad dream. There was no possible way this could be real. He wouldn't do this to me. He *couldn't* do this to me! And yet, there he was...

Banging the waitress.

While I looked on in horror.

I didn't know what to do. I had been so excited about the phone call for the most amazing job ever that I had literally ran the four blocks to Chad's apartment, the one I had a drawer and part of the closet at, to tell him the good news.

I had ignored the locked door and the strange sounds I heard inside, my excitement and eagerness at telling the news to my soon-to-be fiancé overriding everything. Well, now *ex*-soon-to-be fiancé.

She moaned, arching her back and flipping her bleach blonde hair around as he railed her from behind. They were both so busy cheating that neither one had heard the front door open. I had no idea what to do next.

Do I knock on the bedroom door and ask politely what was going on? Did I turn around and leave? Come back later after breakfast? This wasn't exactly something polite manners of society covered. So, I did the first thing that popped into my head.

I threw a lamp at them.

Glass shattered above the headboard. I hated that lamp anyway. The ugly off-white lampshade hit Chad in the head and I smiled. It had been a split second decision not to throw it directly at him, so I was glad something had at least hit him. The two illicit lovers froze mid pump, both of them turning at the same moment to see where the flying lamp had come from.

"You don't find her that hot, huh?" I asked, looking Chad in the eye. He at least had the decency to blush. He had, after all, told me several times that there was nothing going on between him and Charity. Nothing. They were just friends. He tipped her well because she was nice, not because she had a big rack.

"Ava, I can explain. It's not what it looks like..." he started, grabbing a pillow to cover himself. Charity scampered away from Chad, trying to wrap herself up in the tangled sheets and disappear. It didn't work very well.

I laughed, but it was more to keep from sobbing than actually finding the situation amusing. "It looks like you're banging the hot waitress two weeks before we were going to go look at rings. I'm not quite sure how it can look like anything else."

Chad scrambled off the bed. I used to like the way he looked, but today I couldn't stand him. He worked out regularly and had a great body. Nice arms, a great chest, the beginnings of a six-pack, but skinny chicken legs. The man really needed to not skip leg day.

"We're done, Chad," I stated, backing away. I was really proud that my voice didn't waver, even if tears were running down my face. "We're done."

"Ava, please," Chad begged, stuffing his legs into a pair of pants as I backed out of the room.

"I'll have someone come get my things." I looked over at Charity. She had made herself as small in the bed as humanly possible. I shook my head and considered throwing another lamp.

Suddenly I saw things in a new light. This wasn't the first time they had done this. Chad had missed too many breakfast meetings, explained away strange clothes in his apartment-- *had I actually believed that those panties were his sister's?* And I had believed him. I had believed every lying word. I was so stupid.

"Ava, please don't do this," Chad implored, struggling with the denim.

"Don't do what, Chad?" I snapped. "Cheat on you, all while pretending to want to marry you? Oh wait, you did that. I didn't do anything."

"Please let me explain." He held out his hands, asking me to just stay for a moment. "We're meant to be together."

I wanted to hit him so bad. I wanted to wind up and just clock him in his square jaw or break his handsome nose. I had thought I was so special because Chad Malin, the old high school quarterback and popular kid, liked me. Dated me. Had talked about going to look at wedding rings so he would know what style I liked. I had wondered how someone like him, someone who could have any girl in town, had picked me.

Now I knew. He hadn't picked me.

"Explain? You want to explain why you're wearing your new girlfriend's jeans?"

He looked down at his new skinny jeans with pink stitching and cursed. I turned to leave, but he caught my hand. Again, I nearly slugged him. The last person in the entire world I wanted touching me was that slime-ball. I wrenched my wrist out of his grasp, leaving him grasping at thin air.

"Ava, baby..." He flashed me his trademark smile, the one that had made me weak in the knees just yesterday. Now I saw how fake it was. How fake he was. "Baby, we have plans. We're going places..."

"Yup," I interrupted. "I'm going away from you."

With that, I turned and stormed out of the house.

He didn't try and follow me.

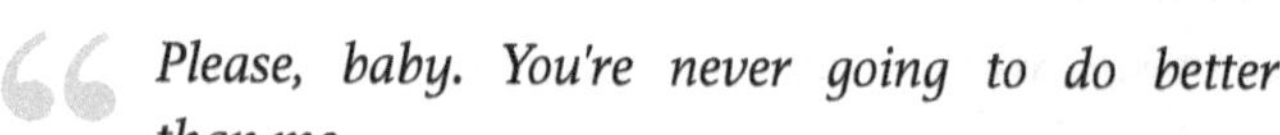

Please, baby. You're never going to do better than me.

You're just mad. You never respond well when I do something you don't like. Don't be this way.

Come on Ava, what are your friends going to say?

Delete text message, delete text message, delete text

message. I thought about calling my phone company and asking them to block his number, but that seemed like effort and I just didn't have the energy right now.

I sat on the floor and stared at the blank spot on my wall where a picture of Chad and I used to hang. The only sign that something had ever been there was the small hole where the tack had been to hold the frame. Other than that, it was as if the two of us had never existed.

The frame now lay empty on my desk, the picture torn to tiny shreds in the bottom of my waste basket. It had felt good to destroy something, but ruining the picture had only taken moments and then the desolation set back in. I had destroyed as many pictures as I could get my hands on.

He cheated.

I couldn't understand how it had happened. Two days ago, we were planning a trip down to the city to look for rings. Now, I was picking up everything he had ever given me, which was actually surprisingly little, and putting it out on the curb. I couldn't believe that he had betrayed me. With *Charity*.

"Ava? You in there?" Dad asked, knocking gently on my bedroom door. I sighed and wiped fresh tears off my cheeks.

"Yeah, come on in."

The door slowly opened and my dad peeked his head inside. He was a big man, but the way he chewed his lip made him look like a small boy. I knew he had heard me crying and had come to investigate. The downside to still living with my father instead of having my own place.

"What's wrong, sweetie?" he asked, sitting down at my desk. He ran a big hand through his graying hair and studied me. "Who do I need to go kill for my baby girl?"

I almost smiled. "Chad."

"Done. He's a dead man," Dad announced. When I didn't respond, he leaned forward, his glasses catching the last of the day's light. "What happened? You two have a fight?"

"I caught him cheating." The words were fire in my mouth. Each one burned just a little bit more.

Dad stayed silent for a moment before leaving the chair to join me on the floor. "I'm sorry, Ava. I really am." I could tell he was fighting the impulse to go bury Chad.

"It was with Charity."

"The waitress?" He frowned, tightening his fists and looking dangerous. Then he just looked tired. "That explains why he always insisted we eat there. I hate that restaurant. They never put enough salt on the fries."

"I can't believe I was so stupid..."

"No, no, Ava," Dad scolded me gently. He put his arm around me. I felt a little bit better. At least I had one man in my life I could depend on. "He's the stupid one. I can't say that I ever particularly liked him, but I knew how you felt about him. I'll fire him first thing in the morning."

"You can't, Dad," I informed him. I wished to heaven he could. I wanted that son-of-a-bitch as far away from me as possible. I groaned. I was going to have to see him at work. "He hasn't done anything wrong as far as his job goes."

"I'll ask your aunt. Heaven knows she can find fault in anything," Dad offered. He gave me a squeeze.

"She won't do it," I told him, wishing he could just squeeze the ache out of me. "He's her best auctioneer. Especially with the job coming up, she won't do it."

Dad sighed. He knew I was right. Up until now, Chad and I had been the perfect couple to take over the business when Dad and Aunt Jenny retired. Not any more. Everything I had planned on was now gone. I had no idea what was going to happen next.

"So, I'm not allowed to commit murder, and you won't let me fire him..." Dad mused, trying to make me smile. "Can I at least demote him to a crappy desk?"

I gave my best approximation of a laugh. "The smallest one. Away from the window."

"Done," Dad promised. I sniffled and he wrapped his other arm around me. "I wish I could make you feel better. I hate seeing you upset."

"I'm still tempted on letting you murder him," I replied. He chuckled and I rested my head against his big chest. "It's not fair, Dad. I had such good news and now it's all ruined."

"You can tell me the good news," he offered.

I fiddled with a strand of hair, playing with the dark red tress like a toy. Dad had once claimed the same shade, but now his was a distinguished silver. I sighed. Maybe telling Dad the good news would make me feel better, or at least distract me from the soul crushing betrayal that had me pinned to the floor.

"I got a phone call at the office today," I started. Dad nodded. He and his sister were the proud owners of Fairchild Auctions and Appraisals. Dad and I did all the appraisals while my aunt handled the auction side. "It was from Sebastian Belrose's assistant."

"Sebastian Belrose? One of the guys who run the Kindling Romance dating website?" Dad asked, sounding a little awestruck.

"Yeah," I answered. "How do you know who he is?"

"Just because I deal in antiques doesn't mean I don't know what is going on in the modern world," he justified. "I actually saw his name in the financial section of the paper this morning. What did he want?"

I wiped at my nose. This was good news, not news that I should cry about. "He wants to hire us."

Dad's eyes went wide with excitement. "That's fantastic!" Then he remembered why I was sitting on the floor crying and tamped his enthusiasm down a little. "And you went to go tell Chad?"

I nodded, a fresh wave of tears rolling down my face. "I was going to tell him that Mr. Belrose hired us to appraise his mansion in the Caribbean and to put it up for auction. It's the biggest job we've ever gotten," I said, still sobbing.

"Oh, sweetie, that's great" Dad whispered, hugging me close. "When does he want us to go?"

"Dad!" I wailed.

"Sorry, sorry," he quickly apologized. "You breaking up with your boyfriend takes precedence. Sorry."

He let me sob for awhile, just holding me and letting me get it out of my system. I knew he hated it when I cried, but I couldn't stop. I hadn't been enough for Chad and it made even my bones hurt.

"You going to be okay?" Dad asked when I finally stopped gasping for air. He brushed the hair out of my face and looked me over, checking my face for cracks like I was a valuable vase someone had dropped.

"No," I said shaking my head. "But you and I will be going to the Caribbean in two months, so that will probably help. Mr. Belrose, or rather his assistant, will be sending all the details tomorrow, but you and I will go out and appraise everything in the house and then Aunt Jenny will run the auction."

Dad grinned and then promptly tried to cover it up. He hugged me tight, nearly squishing all the remaining air from my lungs. I let him. This was the job that would save our business. He deserved to be happy for a moment, especially given everything that had happened in the past five years.

"It will work out, sweetie," Dad promised. "Things always do."

CHAPTER 2

I took a deep breath in, closing my eyes and taking it all in. The sun hung low in the sky, casting long palm-tree shaped shadows on the white sand walkway. Humid, warm air filled my lungs and it was like breathing in pure happiness. A trip to the Caribbean was exactly the thing I needed, even if it was a work trip. The sky was still blue, but the clouds were starting to bronze and crisp with color on the edges. The trees danced on a gentle breeze carrying the smell of ocean salt. I felt warm for the first time in weeks and like things were actually going my way.

That isn't to say I wasn't nervous. My palms were sweating and I was glad I had put on an extra swipe of deodorant before getting off the plane, but it was a good kind of stress. The kind that led to good things happening instead of feeling like I was constantly having to play catch-up.

I glanced over at my Dad, noticing he was just as anxious as I was. He rubbed at his shoulder, and despite the grin on his face, I could still see the tension in his jaw. I grinned back, knowing that my expression mirrored his.

The house in front of us was huge. *No*, I corrected myself, *house isn't the right word. Mansion is closer.* Even the word mansion still felt too small for the building in front of us. The entrance was immense and imposing with clean lines and a modern feel. Glass and soft white stone gleamed in the setting sun, promising a wealth of treasure past the huge wooden doors.

Huge seemed to be the word of the day. The private jet here had been huge. The limo to the house had been huge. Now the house was huge. Everything, including our commission and the boost to our business this job was going to give us, was huge. It would be the thing that would finally let Dad retire and leave the company in my hands.

Dad dropped his hand from his shoulder and knocked confidently on the large wooden doors. He was a big man, but his assured knock still sounded quiet against the might of the doors. I was sure that our driver was going to let us in, but my father was always one to take charge. It was something that had served him well over the years.

"Dad, come here," I hissed, hurrying over to him and straightening his collar. "We're supposed to look professional."

"Says the woman in shorts," Dad retorted, pulling away.

"They're dress shorts," I explained. "They are meant to be worn with a suit jacket, just like this. I look good."

Dad paused. He knew this was a sore subject for me. It had been for the past two months. I had to look my best. I didn't know if it was just because I was trying to convince myself that I actually was the best, or if it was just a way to hide my flaws. To me, looking good meant that I could take on the world and hopefully not look like I had been cheated on.

"You look great," Dad conceded. He smiled, his green eyes kind. "You always make our business look good."

And we needed this to the business to look good. The past few months had been rough. Like, thinking of selling the business kind of rough. I shook my head as he lowered his hand from knocking. Thank God he hadn't sold. Chad was the one interested in buying.

The door opened on silent hinges to unveil the biggest man I had ever seen. Huge, was again, the word of the day. I could of swore I heard the giant growl as he looked us over. I swallowed hard.

"Oh, good!" a female voice chirped as a pretty head peeked out from behind the massive doorman. She pushed him gently to the side, treating him like an overgrown puppy rather than the hulking beast he was. "You must be the Fairchilds. Please, come in."

The big man moved to hold the door open, letting us pass. I smiled up at him as we passed, but he kept a stern face. He was not a man to be messed with.

If I thought the outside of the mansion had looked grand and imposing, the entryway made it look dull. The room was more ballroom than entrance, with sprawling black and white tiles and two staircases that descended to meet at the bottom across from the door. The upstairs was open to look down on the main room, increasing the feeling of size. Everything about it screamed opulence and wealth.

Standing in the center of the room, looking tiny and young, was a well dressed brunette in a pencil skirt with a charming smile.

"Hi, I'm Charlotte, Mr. Belrose's personal assistant," she greeted us, and motioned to the big man still standing guard by the door. "This here, is Elijah, Mr. Belrose's private security."

"Please let me know if you see anything strange, no matter how small," the big man said. His voice was as deep as he was huge. He reminded me of a lion. With a polite nod to all of us, he promptly turned and disappeared into vast recesses of the house. It was almost unnerving how easily and quietly he disappeared, even with my eyes never leaving him. It spoke to his effectiveness and thus to the importance of Mr. Belrose. Who knew a dating website could make so much money?

"You can leave your bags here," Charlotte informed us with a smile. My father was trying to pull both our suitcases across the tiled floor and making a racket with the wheels. "Marcus will take them up to your rooms."

Marcus, our limo driver, came in behind us and held out his hands for the suitcases. Dad reluctantly gave them up, but only after Marcus cleared his throat. Despite his effort to carry the bags, Dad looked worn out and ragged from traveling.

"Mr. Belrose will be down after his meeting, but I'd be happy to show you to your rooms if you'd like," Charlotte offered. "I'm sure it must have been a long trip."

"Does Mr. Belrose usually work here?" I asked, looking around at the incredibly expensive room. I hadn't even met the man yet, but I had to wonder at his style. He must be obsessed with his own wealth. "I mean, does he run the dating website from here? I thought it was based in New York."

"He runs the logistics side of Kindling Romance, not the actual dating service," Charlotte explained. She crossed the black and white tiled floors to stand next to the massive landing at the bottom of the two stairs. "He usually does work out of New York, but this auction is incredibly important to him, so he is telecommuting until its completion."

Telecommuting? I looked down at my phone. I had it turned to airplane mode with wifi still active since we were now considered to be roaming. Super roaming. I didn't even want to contemplate what my phone bill would be if I left my data running for this trip. If Mr. Belrose was telecommuting, I could only imagine what his bill must look like. It was a good thing he was a billionaire.

"I'd actually love to go to my room for a bit," Dad said, finally answering Charlotte's question. I noticed his collar was crooked again. His big body sagged on his frame as he looked around, looking like he might just curl up on the stairs and take a nap. "Traveling always seems to wear me out."

Charlotte smiled and motioned us up the right hand side of stairs. "Your rooms are adjacent to one another and are on the second floor. If you'll follow me, please."

"I'm going to need a map of the house when you get a moment." Dad paused at the middle step, looking winded. It was a big staircase.

"I actually have some printed up. You wouldn't believe how many times I've gotten lost in this place." Charlotte answered with a grin. "You'll get used to it."

I shook my head, wondering just what kind of person would buy a house so big that they needed a map to get around. Add in all the opulence and wealth of all the furnishings, and it made me think that perhaps Mr. Belrose was a little too wrapped up with showing off his status.

"Before I forget," Charlotte said, pausing in the middle of the hallway. I nearly plowed into her. She pointed to a large double door on the opposite side of the grand staircase. "During your time here, Mr. Belrose will be working. The study is his office and bedroom, and he does not want anyone but himself in there. It's off limits to everyone."

"Is there anything that needs to be appraised in there?" Dad asked.

"A few things," she replied, "but Mr. Belrose will have you appraise those at his convenience. Until then, he requests that neither of you enter his study without permission."

"Of course," Dad assured her, nodding vehemently. I knew he wouldn't even look at the door to Mr. Belrose's study, his honor and integrity permitting him to do nothing less. It was one of the things I loved most about my dad. Me, on the other hand, I would probably try and peek in if I ever saw the door open. Making things off limits tended to make me curious, but I wouldn't want two random strangers poking through my bedroom without permission either.

Charlotte nodded, glad to see we understood and motioned us after her into another part of the monstrous house. The sunlight from the setting sun turned the room into a golden paradise as we worked our way down the hallways to our rooms. Every wall contained artwork and furniture that had my father and I drooling. In just the walk to our rooms, I already had a rough estimate of hundreds of thousands of dollars worth of antiques. This was going to be a massive job.

"Here are your rooms," Charlotte announced. They were side by side with one at the end of the hallway. "I thought Mr. Fairchild would like this one, as the furniture is all authentic Alexander Roux pieces."

Dad's eyes lit up. He nearly bowled Charlotte over to get into the room. I giggled. He reminded me of a kid on Christmas morning.

"I think you just made his trip," I told her. She grinned with childlike pride.

"I'm just glad they had certificates on them, or I never

would have known," she confided, then gestured to my room. "I'm afraid your room isn't anything special. I know your specialty is impressionist art, but most of the pieces aren't in any of the guest rooms..."

"This is perfect," I interrupted, stepping into the room. It was large, with a gaudy bed and overzealous artwork, but the real treasure was the big window overlooking the ocean. We were on the East side of the island, so I would be able to see the sunrise in the morning. "Thank you, Charlotte."

Her face split into a grin. I liked her. She had obviously taken the time to choose rooms for us based on what she knew about us. It was sweet.

"I'm so glad that the rooms are acceptable to you both," she said, slipping back into a more formal tone. "Dinner will be in half an hour in the kitchen."

"Thank you, again," I replied. I hoped I could get her out of her shell a little bit while we were here. She seemed like she could be fun if she wasn't working. "What are we having."

"Just some soup and finger foods," she answered. "Is that all right, Miss Fairchild?"

"That's perfect." I smiled. "And please, call me Ava. Miss makes me feel strange."

"I've never really liked it either," Charlotte admitted. We grinned at one another for a moment, feeling like we might be long lost friends after all. "I'll let you settle in."

I went to the window as she turned to leave and looked out, taking a deep, happy breath. The mansion backed out onto a small cove. The sand was perfect and white and the waves small and calm. The sky was turning a deep shade of purple as the sun set on the opposite side of the island, causing the deep blue of the water to fade with the sky as it approached the horizon. It was absolutely stunning.

That, I thought to myself, *not the house, is what makes this a billionaire's place.*

I was just glad that Mr. Belrose didn't know that, or I would be out of a job.

CHAPTER 3

I closed the front door carefully behind me, listening for the subtle click to indicate it had shut. Dinner had been delicious, even if Charlotte hadn't been able to join us. Dad hadn't eaten much of the conch soup, even though he said it reminded him of Boston clam chowder. I had eaten more tropical fruit than a monkey, stuffing my face with papayas and mangoes fresh off the trees. It was practically a dessert.

I stepped out on the big front porch, taking a deep breath of night air. It was humid and moist and everything I needed right now. It wasn't home. I could be someone else here. I wasn't the dumped ex-girlfriend, or the local library book-nerd, or the daughter struggling to save her father's beloved antique business.

As my father's only child, I was the proud heir to his legacy. I loved working with antiques and running my father's business with my aunt and cousins. Dad had been attempting to wean himself off the appraisal circuit, but a recent arson fire had set him back. Due to a faulty sprinkler system at our company's warehouse, over five million dollars of art and antiques had been destroyed. Sure, the insurance companies were covering all of the damage, but the blow to our company's image had been devastating.

It didn't matter that Dad checked the security systems and fire prevention units daily. It also didn't matter that the fire inspector had declared both the sprinkler system and the cause of the fire arson. As far as the public was concerned, Fairchild Auctions and Appraisals had let five million dollars burn.

But I didn't need to think about that now. My mind was already planning and preparing for tomorrow. A quick tour from Charlotte had revealed that the mansion was even bigger than I had suspected. A family of fifteen could live there and never see one another except at meals, and even then that was only if they wanted to use the main kitchen. Every room was full of antiques and art. It was going to be a fair amount of work, but work that I was excited about.

Several paintings stood out in my memory as ones I couldn't wait to get a closer look at. Every room had art that made my fingers itch to look closer at. I knew my father felt the same way about the furniture. Even though this was technically work, it was work we were born to do. Getting to study antiques and art of this caliber was practically a vacation. I would have appraised this house for free, just for the opportunity to work with what I had seen on some of the walls.

Furtive movement caught my eye. I was standing on the edge of the big front entrance, but I had a clear view of the nearby kitchen doorway, and someone was struggling to get something out. Whatever it was, the package was large and the person was trying very hard to be quiet.

I frowned. Elijah had said to notify him of anything strange, but standing here in the dark, I had no idea how to get a hold of him. I bit my lip, trying to figure out what to do next.

The figure stepped into the light coming off one of the security lights and I could see that he had what looked like a hastily-covered painting. The figure glanced anxiously from side to side, as if looking for someone.

I had seen that look before. The night the museum I was interning at was robbed, I had seen someone from an upper window. The way the painting was wrapped, the careful movements, even the shape of the man was exactly the same as that night. I knew I had to do something. That man was obviously stealing a painting from the house.

Be brave, I told myself. *Remember those self defense classes...*

I didn't think. I just took a deep breath, and yelled my scariest, most alarm-raising shriek as I ran at the figure. Using every memory of watching Sunday night football games with my Dad, I planted my foot and brought both my arms up and under his. I let my legs do the rest of the work, pumping hard to push him backwards and up.

It would have worked if he hadn't been well over six feet and outweighed me. And if he hadn't been pure muscle. Instead of flying to the ground like a sacked quarterback, he shrugged me off like a lineman, barely stumbling and still managing to hold onto the painting.

"What the hell are you doing?" the man yelled at me. I wasn't sure how he did it, but he somehow got bigger scarier. It didn't help that it was dark and now the light was behind him, completely hiding his face.

"You can't steal that painting," I announced defiantly, trying to regain my balance. *Where are you, Elijah?* I silently pleaded. I had been hoping my war-cry had gotten his attention. Now I just had to stall the robber until Elijah got here.

"Steal?" The thief sounded confused. "What in the world are you talking about?"

"You can explain whatever it is that you're doing to them," I said smugly, as flashlight beams came jogging toward us. I could see Elijah and three other security guards coming at us at breakneck speeds.

Elijah reached us first. "Mr. Belrose, are you all right? We heard a strange noise."

My stomach dropped straight to China. *Mr. Belrose?*

"I think so, but who the hell is this girl? And how did she get past you to fucking tackle me?"

He was royally pissed. And rightly so. I was so incredibly fired. My stomach dropped so fast, it went past China. It was falling to Pluto now.

Elijah shone the flashlight in my face, making me blink and blush. I couldn't seem to find any words now. I had been so brave two seconds ago, but now I was a stammering mess. I had just tried to take down a billionaire. I couldn't be more mortified if I tried.

"This is Ava Fairchild, Mr. Belrose," Elijah answered. He waved the other guards off. "She's the appraiser you hired. She's harmless."

I wished I still had enough courage to be angry about the "harmless" comment, but considering how easily I had been brushed off, Elijah was probably right. Mr. Belrose carefully set the painting down on the cement and looked at me. I didn't dare look up at him.

"You thought I was stealing a painting?" he finally asked, straightening his suit jacket. His voice was commanding and powerful.

I nodded, staring at my bare feet. Not only did I just try and tackle a billionaire, but I didn't even have shoes on. I was such a failure at life.

Mr. Belrose evaluated me for a moment and let out a sharp snort. "I suppose I should be grateful that an employee would feel so inclined to prevent theft," he said finally, sounding irritated. "Look at me."

I slowly rose my eyes to meet his. I had seen pictures of Sebastian Belrose on the internet, but in real life, he was gorgeous. He had light, golden-brown hair cut in a short, neat fashion that accented the strength of his jaw and broad shoulders. The thing that the pictures never conveyed was the strength and power that radiated off him in waves. It was like the difference between seeing a black and white picture of a painting and standing next to the real thing.

I could see the faint but distinctive scar across his cheek and eyebrow. I hadn't been able to find any information on where he had gotten it. It was just one of the many internet mysteries surrounding Sebastian Belrose. While the scar made him look dangerous, it was his eyes that gave him the aura of power and confidence.

They were a blue so light that they were almost gray, especially against the dark fabric of his designer suit. They reminded me of a misty sky just before the dawn. He looked at me, those eyes full of confidence, and I forgot to breathe.

"Miss Ava Fairchild," he said, as if testing out how my name sounded on his lips. I rather liked the way he said it, but it was a little overwhelming. "Would you like to see what I was stealing?"

I looked over at the wrapped package and fidgeted slightly. This was not a good way to meet one's employer.

"I'm so sorry, sir," I apologized. My voice cracked and I hated myself just a little bit more.

"I didn't ask for your apology," he growled. "I asked if you wanted to see it."

I opened my mouth to apologize again and quickly shut

it. That wasn't going to do me any favors. I knew I should say no, that it wasn't any of my business, but I couldn't. Now I was curious.

"Yes," I whispered, blushing a deep crimson.

Mr. Belrose's eyebrows raised. "Open it."

I looked up at him again, making sure I understood and he nodded toward the package. Cautiously, I went over and began to untie the string holding the wrapping to whatever was inside. Now that I was closer, I could see it wasn't a painting. It wasn't even shaped like a painting. The brown cloth wrapping fell away to reveal what looked like part of a broken surfboard. It was just the front piece, but it was obviously not a painting.

"Is that a painting?" Mr. Belrose asked.

I shook my head. "No."

"Do you still think I'm stealing it?" His voice was a little lighter this time, but not by much. I wanted to shrink into the sand and never show my face again.

"No, sir."

"Then we're done here," he said gruffly. He picked up the broken piece of surfboard and handed it to me. "Since you're so keen on me not having it, you can run it to the trash."

I nearly dropped it my hands were shaking so badly. Mr. Belrose's eyes went to mine again, capturing me in their dusky power. My heart pounded so hard I was sure I was going to need CPR soon.

His eyes are beautiful, I thought. I pushed away the thought and looked away. That thought was not even remotely appropriate for what was going on right now. I did not need to be noticing that my billionaire boss, who I had just tried to take down, had nice eyes. Or how broad his shoulders were. Or how nicely he filled out his suit.

"Yes, sir," I stuttered. But I couldn't help but look up at his eyes again. They drew me to him like a moth to a flame.

It was like he could see straight through me and knew exactly who I was and what I was thinking. It made me glad I wasn't thinking something inappropriate, like him in his boxers, though given the way he was filling out that suit, it would be a very nice sight. *Crap!* I thought, blushing harder. *Now, I'm thinking of him in his boxers!*

I looked down again, hoping that it was dark enough to hide my blush. When I peeked back up, his eyes were still on me, but with just the barest hint of a smile. As if he did know what scandalous thoughts were going through my mind. And that just made me blush harder. This was not my night.

"Good night Miss Fairchild," Mr. Belrose said evenly, turning to go back into the house. I just stood there, staring after him, holding the broken surfboard.

"Next time, just let me handle any thieves," Elijah remarked, walking past me to follow his boss. I nodded, waiting until they were both gone before going to my knees.

That had been a disaster.

I carefully picked up the broken surfboard nose and all the wrappings, finally noticing a trashcan just off to the side. It wasn't in the direct light from the house, so it was hard to see. That was why he had been looking around. If I had just waited thirty more seconds before turning into Sir Galahad, I wouldn't be in this mess.

I carefully threw everything away before turning to go back in the house. Except, I didn't want to go back inside yet. Mr. Belrose and Elijah were inside, and the very last thing in the entire world that I wanted just now was to run into either of them again tonight.

So instead, I followed the house around back to the beach.

THE FINE WHITE sand on the beach gleamed in the silver moonlight like a magical substance that only stayed on this world for a short time. I walked toward the calm, dark water, watching the waves whisper against the pale shore.

I hurried across the big, wooden back porch and down toward the water. Silver and black waves whispered to the shore as I approached, and I relished the squish of the warm sand beneath my bare feet. I took a deep breath in of delicious salty air and let it out slowly. This was a good place. Even if I was an idiot. At least he hadn't fired me.

The wet sand was cooler and more firm as I dipped my feet into the water. The ocean sighed and washed around my ankles, welcoming me to go deeper. In the distance, back on the island and away from the water, a frog croaked out a love song, filling the night with chirps that merged with the soft hush of the waves.

I glanced back at the giant house to see a light turn on in one of the upper windows, yellow and warm in the dark. I didn't recognize the position of the room from our tour and assumed it must be "The Study." I giggled. I was even thinking of it in quotations, like it was incredibly important and secret.

I wondered what the billionaire was doing this late at night, other than throwing out broken surfboards. I didn't actually know much about him. Sure, I of course had Googled him, but even the internet knew remarkably little about the reclusive billionaire. His two partners had several pages of information, but not him.

I knew he and his two partners, Leo and Gabriel, had started an online dating service together. *Kindling Romance-let us start the fires of love!* I had seen their advertisements everywhere. If I hadn't been with Chad, or burned so badly by Chad, I would have considered using them myself. They were apparently the best dating website around.

I stepped out further into the water, stopping when the water hit my knees. I wiggled my shorts up a few more inches to keep them from getting wet. It was so peaceful and calm out here. For the first time in months, I felt my shoulders drop from my ears and the frown ease from my face. Even after the debacle of trying to tackle a billionaire, I finally felt like myself again. Like I didn't have to keep up a happy face just because it was expected.

Squishing my toes in the bottom of the ocean, I let out the tension I hadn't even realized was there. I hadn't worried about the business at all today. I hadn't looked over my shoulder for my ex-boyfriend all day. I didn't worry about him showing up and ruining my good mood. Things were good, he was far away, and I could finally relax.

Dammit. I was thinking about Chad again. I needed to stop that. He would have called me stupid for trying to help a billionaire save money anyway.

I shook my head. This wasn't the place for thinking of people who didn't want me. This was a place to relax and recover. Here, I was free. The ocean was washing me clean so I could start over. The money and prestige from this job would get Fairchild Auctions and Appraisals back on track. It might even give me enough to book my ticket to Paris.

The thought of Paris made me smile. This could be just the thing I needed. The thing that would get me going again. Finding out about Chad had nearly ruined me, but I was strong. This job could pay for my Paris trip and give me the best fresh start a girl could ask for.

With happy thoughts buoying me, I turned around to head for bed. The giant mansion welcomed me back from the water as I reluctantly left the ocean behind me. The sand felt warm after the cool of the water.

The curtains over the lit window shifted and I saw a silhouette move away from the edge of the window. I shook my head. He couldn't possibly have been watching me walking out in the waves and moonlight. If he did, he probably thought I was an idiot for being out there in the dark.

Mr. Belrose's intense blue-gray eyes flashed through my mind. After our spectacular encounter, it was hard to imagine him helping people fall in love. *He must handle the business end*, I thought. *His partners must handle the romance. He probably wouldn't know love if it hit him over the head with a baseball bat.*

I giggled a little at the thought of a world-traveled billionaire watching me from his window like a love-struck teenager. *As if.* I was a small-town girl with no stamps in my passport and the exact opposite of high society class. I appraised things for high society, I didn't join them. Not to mention, I had just tried to tackle him in my bare feet. I had to be the farthest thing from interesting to him.

I shrugged and climbed the wooden steps back up to the house, collecting my shoes at the door. A yawn the size of Texas cracked my jaws. For now, it was time for bed, not for musings on what a billionaire found or didn't find interesting. Tomorrow would be a new day.

At least I'll know who my boss is tomorrow, I thought.

CHAPTER 4

The room was made of fuzzy gray shapes and indistinguishable shadows. My breath came in short gasps. I sat up, confused and panicked for a moment before remembering where I was. As soon as I remembered I was sleeping in a billionaire's mansion alongside the Caribbean ocean, I sighed and laughed a little at myself. Leave it to me to freak out about sleeping somewhere too nice.

I tried to lay back down, but just settling back against the perfectly-stuffed pillows made me antsy. The bed was too soft and the blankets too fancy to be comfortable. I didn't deserve three-million thread count sheets or sleeping underneath what I suspected was a Picasso. I was not billionaire material. I wasn't even Chad material.

Besides, I was ready to get started. I needed to show Mr. Belrose that I wasn't just a wanna-be football player who tackled random billionaires taking out the trash. The day was going to be full of exciting work and I didn't want to wait. Not that I could get anything done until Dad woke up, as we had to go over our plan for dividing up the work, but I still couldn't just lay in bed. It was like asking me not to peek out at the tree on Christmas morning.

I padded over to the window, the wood floors cool on my bare feet. My messy reflection greeted me in the glass. Auburn hair all tangled and messy fell over my shoulders and green eyes peered back at me. I frowned and pulled my red hair back into a untidy pony-tail to deal with later. Dawn was on her way, with the gray skyline lightening and heralding her impending arrival. The clouds were tinged with pink and reflecting in the quiet ocean waves.

I remembered how good the water had felt around my legs last night and grinned. Sunrise with my feet in the ocean was the perfect way to start a day. If the water had been beautiful in the moonlight, I could only imagine how amazing it would be in the first golden rays of the day.

I hurried down the stairs and out onto the wooden deck, pausing for a moment before going outside. I was only wearing a thin, white, jersey-knit t-shirt and a pair of old blue boxers covered in pale pink hearts that were once part of a pajama set-- not exactly appropriate attire for company. I peered out the window and didn't see anyone.

I shrugged and stepped out. If anyone saw me this early, they would most likely be in pajamas themselves. Besides, I didn't want to go back up and change and possibly miss the sunrise.

The sand was cool against my feet, but still just as soft. It was colder now that the night had the chance to cool the world, but it was still far warmer than the freezing temperatures of home. I considered getting a light jacket, but that would entail going back upstairs. Instead, I just wrapped my arms around myself and hurried to the water.

The sun wasn't up yet, so the water was dark and colder than last time, but I didn't care. It was still exhilarating. The sky was turning a vibrant shade of pink and every wave was tipped with the warming color. I was in for a magnificent sunrise.

A noise behind me made me turn. Coming down the beach, carrying a long surfboard looking thing and a paddle, was a billionaire. Wearing a skin-tight, full-body wetsuit that showed off just how in shape he was, he looked hotter than the sun that was supposed to come up any moment. His light brown hair was tussled with sleep, but his eyes were bright. And on me.

"Hi," I stammered as he entered the water, eyes still on me. "Good morning..."

What exactly was one supposed to say when meeting a billionaire in one's pajamas while standing in the ocean at dawn? After trying to tackle him the night before? Not to mention that my very sheer shirt was highlighting just how cold I was. I tightened my arms around my chest, hoping that I had myself appropriately covered.

"I don't usually see anyone out here this early," he replied, stopping a polite distance away. It was still closer than I felt comfortable with, especially with the wetsuit showing off his broad shoulders and toned ass. The wetsuit, if anything, accented his perfect build rather than hiding it. I almost would have preferred him to be wearing a normal swimsuit because it would have let my imagination stop putting him together. "Are you going to try and take my board again?

"No, not until later," I replied, blushing straight down to my toes. I wasn't going to let him get to me today, though. I was a strong, independent woman. Or at least I was going to pretend to be one. "I only tackle billionaires at night. I'm actually more of a morning person. I like sunrises, and long walks on the beach." I didn't mean to quote one of his commercials, but there it was. I really needed to learn to think before I spoke sometimes.

Mr. Belrose's brows raised and his eyes met mine. Butterflies started dancing in my stomach. There was no reason for me to feel this giddy nervousness, but I couldn't help it. For whatever reason, I wanted him to like me and standing out in my pj's quoting his company's commercials sounded incredibly lame. I was an idiot.

He half-grinned, thankfully finding me amusing.

He nodded toward the horizon. "This is a good place for sunrises." His gaze went past me and up toward the horizon and his grin shifted into an all out smile.

I turned my head from him to see a golden ball of fire rising up over the dark blue water. The sky was awash in blues, pinks, golds, and oranges that stole my breath away. It was possibly the most stunning sunrise I had ever seen.

I glanced over at him again. The sunlight was bathing him in total glory, accenting the strength of his cheekbones and the golds in his hair. His shoulders were relaxed as he soaked in the morning light, absorbing it's radiance. His smile was almost brighter than the sun and just as beautiful. When he smiled, it was better than the sun coming up. It made my heart beat faster and my stomach make strange knots.

I looked away, turning back to watch the bright ball rise further until I couldn't bare to look at it anymore. Feelings of hope and renewal flowed through me. *This is the way to start a day*, I thought to myself. *Almost better than coffee.*

After a moment, I shifted my weight in the water, feeling awkward. "So, are the waves any good for surfing?" I asked, looking over at the billionaire and motioning to the board floating in the water beside him.

He looked over at me surprised, as if he had forgotten

that I was there. The brilliant smile was gone, but so was the sternness I remembered from the day before. Out here, he looked like a young man excited for the day. Even the scar down his cheek was less pronounced. He was friendly in the morning light, as if he hadn't had time to harden.

"The waves here aren't big enough for surfing," he patiently explained. "I paddle-board." He grinned, threatening to reveal that brilliant smile again, as he held up the paddle. "Best way to greet the day."

I looked at his board. It looked like a surfboard, but just a little different. The fact that he had a long paddle that looked like it belonged more on a kayak also suggested something I wasn't familiar with.

"I've never actually done that," I said slowly.

"You're welcome to join me," he offered. "There's extra boards in the shed."

"I'm not exactly dressed for swimming." I blushed, looking down at my boxer shorts and seeing the pale pink hearts darkening on the hem from the ocean water. "Is that how you broke your board?

His eyes looked me up and down, taking in my thin pajamas and just how tight I was holding my arms close. I could have sworn his pupils dilated, and just thinking that they did made me blush harder.

"No," he said shaking his head. "That board got hit by a boat."

"I hope you weren't on it," I said when he didn't offer anymore information.

He regarded me quizzically for a moment before shaking his head slightly. "No, I wasn't. I was driving the boat."

"Oh." I smiled and nodded, hoping like hell that the pink sunrise was at least partially hiding my blush. It was really hard not to stare at his muscles under his wetsuit. Good lord, he was built. "Then maybe I'll take you up on your offer to paddle-board, but I'll remember not to go out on a boat with you. Or at least not be on a paddle-board when you're sailing."

I looked up to see the corner of his lips twitched, hinting at his own amusement.

"As long as you don't tackle me again, I promise not to hit you with a boat." He kept his face straight, but his eyes twinkled. I couldn't help but smile back.

He nodded politely and stepped away. Pulling his board close to him, he then lay down on his stomach and began paddling out into deeper water.

It only took a moment before he rose first to his knees and then up to standing in a graceful motion I knew must have taken months of practice. Even from where I was standing, I could see his abs and arms working with the strength needed to push him through the water. It was easy to see how he stayed in such good shape if he did this every morning. It looked like a full body workout.

I watched him for a moment, enjoying seeing his finesse and strength in the water, until I realized that I was staring again. Somehow I managed to blush even more, especially knowing that I could have happily watched him all day. I was a creep, but at least I knew it.

I shook my head, trying to clear my thoughts. Now that the sun was up, it was warmer but my pajamas were still thin and getting wet. My stomach rumbled, reminding me that dinner had been a long time ago and Charlotte had mentioned something about breakfast in the morning.

Reluctantly, I turned and headed back to shore. At the base of the deck was a little freshwater shower that I used to rinse the sand and salt from my legs before climbing the stairs back inside. I looked out at the water as I finished rinsing, surprised to see Mr. Belrose looking back at me.

He grinned, and the blush that had finally faded came roaring back. I bit my lip, determined not to make a complete fool of myself and hurried inside, nearly colliding with a giant wall of man. Elijah avoided me easily, making sure that I didn't run into him or the door in my attempt to stop the collision. He chuckled, shaking his head.

My face was burning now, knowing that not only was the stealthy body guard chuckling at me, but Mr. Belrose had seen the whole thing. I mumbled an apology and scurried up to my room to put on real clothes and hopefully fade my blush before my skin permanently matched my hair.

CHAPTER 5

I glanced at the map as I hurried through the maze of rooms. I was fairly sure that the kitchen was two more rooms to the right, but every room had the same opulent extravagance. Gilded frames and antique furniture all meshed together until every room looked the same. It was all about the display of wealth. It made it hard to distinguish what room I was in without physically checking the art hanging on the walls. Since the map didn't have that information, I had already gotten turned around once.

I finally just followed the smells of cooking and coffee. It was two rooms to the right and one to the left. Once in the kitchen, though, I finally felt like I was where I belonged.

The mansion's kitchen felt like it had been decorated by someone else. It's simple, rustic charm didn't match the rest of the house. That isn't to say that it wasn't luxurious, huge, or full of gourmet items, but that it didn't feel pompous or overbearing. Of all the rooms in the giant mansion, the kitchen actually felt like one that people lived in rather than a museum.

Leaning against the center island with a bright red mug that said, *"If this cup is full, don't bother talking to me"* was Charlotte. She was happily chatting away with a heavyset woman in an apron who was bustling around the kitchen cooking something that smelled absolutely divine.

"Good morning, Ava," Charlotte greeted me, a welcoming grin spreading across her face. Her dark hair was pulled back in a neat ponytail and she wore a crisp short sleeved, polka-dot shirt with the cutest skirt I had ever seen. "I wasn't expecting anyone up for a little while yet."

I grinned back. "I wanted to see the sunrise. I'm very strange and happen to like mornings."

"Just like her mother," added a very grumpy voice. I turned to see my father stumble into the kitchen and settle with his work bag at the heavy wooden table. His gray hair was rumpled, and he still looked swollen from traveling. His green in his eyes looked strange against the bloodshot whites. I knew he had slept because I had heard him snoring from across the hall, but he sure didn't look like it.

"It was the time for just Mom and me," I recalled, smiling at the memory. I could still recall with perfect clarity how Mom would always curl up in the sunny patch of the couch in the mornings, reading the morning paper or a dogeared paperback book. She was always sipping on tea or coffee and wore the same pink, ratty robe. I still had that robe, tucked away into my closet at home. Sometimes in the mornings, I would wrap myself up in it to read the paper just so that I could feel her presence again.

Charlotte handed me a full cup of coffee in a plain blue cup, pointing to the kitchen table where a pitcher of real cream and a sugar bowl sat waiting. I grinned and headed over to make my mug more cream and sugar than coffee.

"Coffee, Mr. Fairchild?" she asked, holding up a green

mug. Dad mumbled a barely coherent yes and she poured him a generous helping. Just as she finished setting the cup on the table in front of him, Elijah the Bodyguard bustled into the kitchen. Without missing a beat, Charlotte picked up two waiting travel mugs from the counter and handed them to him. *She's like Starbucks, but without the line*, I thought to myself.

"Charlotte," Elijah said, taking a big sip out of one of the mugs. "You're the best, you know that right?"

"Of course I do," Charlotte replied smugly. She held up a brown paper bag. "Make sure Sebastian eats something for breakfast today. He's got that meeting with the sales rep, and last time he nearly took off the poor guy's head because he was hangry."

Elijah went to reach for the bag, but she pulled it back, wanting a response before she would give it to him. "Yes, ma'am," the big man said, rolling his eyes. "As long as there's one in there for me, too."

"Have I ever let you down?" Charlotte asked, not letting go of the bag.

Elijah growled and she let go of the bag.

"What's 'hangry'?" I asked, not recognizing the word.

"You know when you haven't eaten, and it makes you mad at everything for no real good reason? That's hangry," Charlotte explained as Elijah nearly ripped open the bag and pulled out some sort of breakfast sandwich. He immediately began to devour it. She raised her eyebrows at the big man. "You'll make sure?"

"Yes, I'll make sure he eats. I'm the one he takes his temper out on if I forget," Elijah informed her, stuffing the last bite of his sandwich into his mouth. I kept waiting for him to comment to me about last night, but he never did. After finishing his sandwich, Elijah nodded politely to everyone in the kitchen and hurried back out carrying his coffees and sandwiches to Mr. Belrose.

I shook my head, unsure of how the tiny brunette survived bossing around the giant bodyguard. He certainly scared me a little. I sat down at the table across from Dad. He was staring into his coffee like it held the answers to the universe.

"You okay, Dad?" I asked, kicking him gently under the table when he didn't look up. "You don't look like you slept well. Or did you just stay up all night talking to Jackie?"

He narrowed his eyes at me, but took a sip of his coffee. He hated when I teased him about Jackie. As much as he insisted that the adorable woman from next door wasn't his girlfriend, the two of them spent an awful lot of time talking on the phone whenever they were apart.

"No, Jackie had to work today, so we didn't talk long." He took another big sip of his coffee and I smiled. He *had* been talking with her. I liked Jackie and I was glad that my father had someone in his life that cared for him. He rubbed his jaw and looked up at me. "Remind me to get a dentist appointment when we get home. I think I have something wrong with one of my teeth."

"If you'd like, I can have someone here on the island look at it," Charlotte offered from her spot against the center island. She came and sat down at the table next to me. "There are several doctors, dentists, and other medical services located on the island that Mr. Belrose has access too. As his guests, you would have access to them as well."

"Like, concierge doctors?" I asked, taking a sip of my perfectly sweetened coffee. I had heard of doctors that catered to the rich and famous, but I had yet to actually ever meet any. I didn't make anywhere near the kind of money that required.

Charlotte nodded. "Basically. Since this island is known for it's expensive tastes, the doctors here are all world class. The doctor on our retainer even has his own portable x-ray machine as well as a whole car full of medical equipment. He's like a driving hospital."

Dad took a sip of coffee and nodded. "If it's not a bother, Charlotte. I'd be very much obliged to have that dentist take a look at it."

I frowned. My dad hated doctors. Hated them with a passion, especially after what we went through with Mom. I knew he must be in a fair amount of pain to willingly see one.

"I'll see to it," Charlotte promised, pulling out her phone and making a note. She then looked over at the woman cooking and grinned. "Now, Lucia makes the best omelets and french toast on the entire island and it looks like she's ready."

I grinned as the apron donned woman came over with two heaping plates of food. She carefully set each plate down in front of my father and I, as if we were her children and she was feeding us breakfast. It smelled like breakfast heaven and had my mouth watering.

"Will Mr. Belrose be joining us?" I asked, trying not to sound too hopeful. After this morning, particularly the way he had smiled, I found myself hoping that he would come and sit next to me. I wouldn't even try to tackle him or anything.

"Bastian? No." Charlotte shook her head and picked up her fork. "He doesn't exactly do breakfast."

Lucia made a "harumph" noise as she placed more food on the table. "Not for my lack of trying."

"Oh," I replied, doing my best not to be disappointed. "I

saw him out on the beach earlier. I thought that since he was up, he would be here."

"He'll be out on the water until his first meeting," Charlotte answered, her eyes following Lucia as she put a steaming plate of food down in front of her. She was practically drooling on the table for her omelet. "If he could get decent phone reception out in the cove, he'd take all his meetings out on that paddle-board. Though, I swear, if he breaks another one, I'm going to have to strangle the man."

"Breaks another one?" I asked. My voice squeaked just a little bit, but luckily no one seemed to notice.

Charlotte sighed. "The things are not that easy to break, but he seems to enjoy destroying them. He can certainly afford to, but it's kind of an ongoing issue between the two of us."

"Oh." I smiled secretly to myself, waiting for my food. I now understood why he was sneaking out of the house with the board wrapped up. I wasn't about to tattle on him to Charlotte, though.

"Lucia, no french toast for me please. This looks even better than usual." Charlotte said, as Lucia put the food down in front of her.

The older woman smiled and wiped her hands on her apron. "Well then, get to eating before it gets cold."

I looked at my plate, unsure of what delicious thing I wanted to eat first. The omelets were cheesy and gooey with all sorts of perfectly cooked, fresh vegetables and the french toast was thick and steaming. I went for the french toast first, as there was real maple syrup on the table, and nearly moaned. The outside was the perfect level of crispy while the inside was melt-in-my mouth soft.

"Lucia," I groaned. "This is fantastic!"

She beamed and stood up a little taller. She wore her

apron with pride. "Thank you very much, miss. I'm glad you like it." She wiped her hands on her apron one more time and then went back to the kitchen, turning on the sink and washing dishes while she hummed a happy song.

The mark of good food, silence, sat comfortably around the three of us as we ate. I couldn't believe how good the food tasted here. I could tell that everything was fresh and of the highest quality. Charlotte finished her meal first.

"So what are your plans today? If you tell me your schedule, I can make sure there is food available for you," she said, getting up and putting her plate in the sink.

Dad pulled out his bag and placed his tablet and one of the maps Charlotte had given us the night before. He had color coded sections and a key on the bottom. "I thought I would take this room," he said, pointing to a room in canary yellow. He then moved to one in red. "Ava, you can start in this one. Then, we'll switch and double check one another's work."

"Thus, turning the room orange," I replied, quickly stuffing another bite of french toast in my mouth as soon as I finished speaking.

Charlotte peeked over my shoulder and saw my red colored room. "Ava, could I come watch you this afternoon? There's a picture in that room that I'm curious about." She paused, biting her lip, as if afraid I might say no. "It's an impressionist piece, but that's all I know about it. I'm hoping you could tell me more, if you have the time."

I nodded, trying to swallow my bite of food before talking. "I'd love to teach you, Charlotte. Impressionism is actually one of my specialties."

Charlotte grinned from ear to ear, her pretty brown eyes glowing. I could already feel the bonds of friendship forming between the two of us. Anyone who wanted to learn more about my favorite style of art had an instant in with me.

I reluctantly swallowed the last bite of food on my plate. I wished I hadn't gobbled it all up quite so quickly, but it was just so delicious that I couldn't help it. I glanced over at my dad's plate to see if he had eaten his as quickly as I had, only to discover most of the food was still on his plate. I was a little concerned since this was a man who usually ended up finishing my plates.

"You okay, Dad?" I asked, snagging a bite of his french toast. It was just as delicious as mine had been. "You've barely eaten."

He looked down at his plate in surprise. "I guess I still have some indigestion from last night," he admitted. Seeing the worry written all over my face, he smiled and put his big hand on mine. "Don't worry. I'll be fine. It's just this tooth."

I stood up, picking up my plate. Dad took a bite and then pushed his at me to take away. I frowned. Our dinner hadn't been anything that should have caused indigestion. I did my best to smile, though. He would be fine. He was as strong as a horse. There wasn't anything that ever got him down. When the rest of us were sick with the flu, he was always the one running around making soup because he didn't catch it. He'd be fine.

"That was delicious," I said to Lucia, putting our plates in the sink. She looked at Dad's plate and I shrugged. I didn't know quite what to think of it either.

"You ready to get started, Kiddo?" Dad asked, packing his colored maps and tablet into his shoulder bag. I nodded and grinned. I was more than ready.

CHAPTER 6

Charlotte walked with us out of the kitchen, leading the way to the main foyer. It was there that Dad and I were going to split up and start on our separate rooms. The foyer made a great middle point for us to base our attack around.

"Hold on a second kiddo," Dad said, eying a something along the far wall. "I know this room isn't first on my list, but I have to look at something."

I followed his gaze to see a small table pressed up against the far wall and I instantly knew why he wanted to look at it. It looked like an Alexander Roux piece. He had a definite fondness for the 1800's Rococo Revival style cabinet-maker. When Charlotte had given him the room full of Roux pieces, she had unwittingly given him one of his biggest dreams. The man had a Roux calendar on his wall, for heaven's sakes.

"Go for it," I said, shaking my head and grinning.

He nearly ran over to the small table, with me not far behind. Although paintings and art were more my thing, I knew a good piece of furniture when I saw one.

The table was small and made of rosewood and marble. Intricate designs covered the open spaces, highlighting the beauty of the warm brown wood beneath. My father's hand trailed reverently across the smooth surface of the table, his knowledgeable fingers gleaning information from just the touch.

"It certainly looks like an Alexander Roux piece," Dad said reverently. He went to his knees and looked underneath, practically trembling with excitement. "And it looks like it's signed. Let me get my glasses to check…"

He sat back, patting his pockets for his glasses. I shook my head, knowing that they were in his left breast pocket but that it would take him a good thirty seconds to find them. Instead of waiting, I just went over and looked at it myself.

"What do you think of the piece?" Charlotte asked. "Mr. Belrose had it appraised before at close to twenty-five thousand dollars."

"Well, it would be if it were authentic," I replied, snapping a picture of the engraved signature with my phone. "But, unless Alexander Roux forgot how to spell his name properly, the signature is false. I hope you didn't pay that much for it."

Sticking my hand out from under the desk, I handed the phone to my father and heard him sigh sadly as he looked at it. Despite the table's beauty, the mark spelled Roux as Row.

"A forgery?" A stern, deep voice echoed around the room, and I bumped my head on the desk. I wiggled free of the table and stood up to catch my first glimpse of the confident owner of a false Roux piece.

It was him. It was Sebastian Belrose.

I immediately wished I could duck back under the table and hide.

Mr. Belrose was descending the stairs, wearing a dark, three-piece suit that fit him like a glove. I remembered he had worn something similar last night, despite the heat. My mouth went dry, not only at the incredibly attractive way he looked, but at the fact that I had just flippantly spoken to billionaire Sebastian Belrose. Again. At least I hadn't tried bodily harm this time.

He reached the bottom of the stairs and I could see the scar again. It was dark against his stern face. He looked at me, his eyes like gray mist across the ocean and full of just as many secrets and I forgot to breathe.

Realizing that I was now staring, I quickly looked back and the table, hoping my blush wasn't too obvious.

"It's still a beautiful table, and it is in Alexander Roux's style. It could be that someone suspected he was the maker and wanted to increase the value of the piece, so they added the signature themselves." I was rambling now, trying to explain myself. It didn't help that I was now thinking very clearly of how I had tried to tackle him last night. How was I going to explain that to my father? And now I had just told him his table was a fake. I was the best employee ever. "Even with the fake signature, I would still expect it to fetch around ten thousand at auction."

When I looked back up, he had silently crossed the large room and was now standing in front of me. It was hard to be this close to such a powerful man and not shake, especially when I found him even more attractive up close. His frown was tight, as he must have been displeased with my findings.

"Miss Fairchild, I presume." His voice was stern and hard as he held out his hand.

I took it, giving him the firmest, most professional handshake I could muster. Unfortunately, my blush was searing up my chest and lighting my cheeks. I couldn't believe that I had just knocked off fifteen thousand dollars off one of his antiques and then stared at him like a star-struck teenager. It was looking like my second impression wasn't much better than my first.

"It's a pleasure to meet you, sir," I managed, feeling tongue-tied and awkward. He had so much class and poise that it left me fumbling for words. I wasn't quite sure what I was supposed to say. I had technically already met him last night, and again this morning.

He nodded, releasing my hand. My skin tingled from where we had touched, but if he felt anything similar, his face didn't show it. If anything, he seemed more guarded and stern.

"Carl Fairchild," my father said, extending his hand. "If your appraiser missed the signature, I do hope you found another before he got too far."

Mr. Belrose took his hand. "That's why I hired you. According to the head of the Society of Appraisers, you are the best at what you do. You and your staff come highly recommended."

My father's chest puffed out slightly in pride. "Thank you, sir. I'd like to think that we are." He wrapped a heavy arm over my shoulder. "My daughter here is certainly the best art appraiser I've ever met."

Mr. Belrose's blue-gray eyes went to mine again, entangling me in their smoky depths. I couldn't help but wonder what he thought of me. I was just glad that he wasn't bringing up last night. I glanced at my father, but Mr. Belrose gave me just the slightest of head shakes. I nodded. As far as anyone else was concerned, last night didn't happen. I didn't want my father to know, and he didn't want Charlotte to know.

"It is a pleasure to meet you both," Mr. Belrose said,

breaking off his gaze and looking at my father instead. "If either of you need anything, please let Charlotte know."

I wished I wasn't blushing so hard. I wished I had been more polite about dismissing the signature on the piece. I wished I hadn't tried to tackle him, though at least now we had a shared secret. I wished I had been able to brush my teeth after breakfast before standing in front of Mr. Belrose with coffee breath.

Unfortunately, there wasn't much I could do about any of those things at this point.

Mr. Belrose evaluated both of us for a moment, his gray eyes taking in every detail and filing it away. My stomach churned, wondering what he must think of the unkempt, flippant girl in front of him. I wanted to melt into the floor. He turned to leave, stopping to speak with Charlotte as he crossed the tiled floor.

"Miss Page, please remind them about the study," he said softly to his assistant. It was just loud enough for me to make out the words. I had a feeling that wasn't a mistake. The man didn't seem capable of making a mistake.

"Don't worry, boss," she told him with a grin. "Now, get going or you'll be late for your meeting."

He nodded and continued his walk to the front door. Without another word, he opened it and stepped outside, leaving me staring after him and trying to figure him out.

He had this fancy, over-the-top house that he was selling for some reason. No one had said why yet, and since it really wasn't any of my business, I hadn't asked. Yet, the kitchen didn't match and he had a secret study that no one was allowed in. The man was the CEO of a billion dollar company, but he paddle-boarded out on the ocean by himself every morning, and didn't want his assistant to know he had broken a board he could obviously afford.

He intrigued me. There was something about him that made me want to know more, something about the way he held himself and the self confidence he radiated that made me curious about him. I shook my head. He was a mystery, but one that I knew I should stay away from. He was a billionaire and way out of my league.

"Interesting fellow, your boss," my father said after the door closed. I couldn't help but agree.

"That he is," Charlotte replied, putting on a fresh smile. "But, you just impressed him."

"Impressed him?" I nearly laughed. "I just devalued a possible Alexander Roux."

Charlotte chuckled. "And you think he didn't know that? Why do you think it's sitting out here as the first thing you would see? It was a test and you passed with flying colors."

I opened my mouth and then closed it. It was a clever tactic, and one that had worked incredibly well. If he wanted to make sure we were going to do the appraisal correctly, putting the false signature was a good way to test our skills. I smiled slightly, suddenly proud that I had passed a test I didn't know I was taking.

"Well, well. I guess that's why he's the billionaire," Dad mused. He turned to me. "We better get working, kiddo. There's a lot to do."

I looked around at the big house, stopping at the door Mr. Belrose had just left out of. "Yes, we do," I murmured, but my mind wasn't paying attention to my father anymore. It was thinking of Sebastian Belrose and how I couldn't quite put him together.

He was a puzzle, but one I wasn't worthy of solving.

So, I smiled at my father and headed into my room to solve the puzzles that I knew I could solve. Time to appraise some art.

CHAPTER 7

The room I was starting in was huge, as was everything in the mansion. Three immense paintings dominated the walls surrounded by smaller ones scattered tastefully to complement the larger. It reminded me of an art museum rather than a house, but then I had only ever been in art museums this big, not houses.

The room had one window, and if I had been the interior decorator, I would have focused my attention on the view rather than the art. While the art was beautiful, the seascape out the window was more dynamic. Sheer curtains floated over the big window, and I was glad to note that a special film had been placed on it to block the UV light. At least whomever had set up this room had designed it to hold the artwork.

I stood for a moment at the window, watching the waves break against the shore and sea birds fly through the air. It reminded me of this morning's sunrise and that made me smile and wonder what Mr. Belrose was up to. I couldn't see him out on the water, which meant that he must have had his meeting.

"Why aren't you working?" Mr. Belrose's deep voice asked, distracting me from my thoughts. I turned around, startled, to see him standing in the open doorway. All the joy on his face from this morning was long gone.

"I was just getting started," I stammered, going to a table in the center of the room to lay out my supplies. I flushed, knowing I had only been standing at the window for a couple of minutes, but from his viewpoint it must have looked like I was doing nothing at all.

"I'm not paying you to stand around," he growled. I nearly dropped my tablet on the floor, but managed to catch it in the nick of time. He glared at me. "There are deadlines for a reason. If I wanted someone to stand and look pretty, I'd hire a model."

My face flamed to an even higher degree. I wondered if Elijah had remembered to feed him breakfast.

"Didn't you have a meeting?" I asked. All I wanted to do was snap at him to go take a long walk off a short cliff, but I didn't. He was my employer.

"It was canceled. Are you going to work or what?" He glared at me, daring me to sass back. But, I was a professional, despite the fact that I had enjoyed looking out the window. So instead of saying something I knew I'd regret, I put on my biggest smile and looked up at him.

"Of course, Mr. Belrose. I'll get right on it."

I cocked my head to the side, willing sweetness to drip off every word. I made syrup look bland.

He frowned, opening his mouth and then closing it. I had to hold in my sense of accomplishment at throwing him off. He had obviously been expecting a smart-aleck, defensive remark and my overly-sweet response was not computing.

"Now, if you'll excuse me, Mr. Belrose," I continued, still

smiling and forcing sugar sweet niceness from every pore, "I need to get to work."

With that, I turned back to my table and arranged my tools. I moved methodically and carefully, feeling his eyes on me as I went about my work. I ignored him, concentrating on what was now entirely my domain. This is where I was most comfortable. I was now entering my element.

Once my station was arranged to my liking, I went to one of the smaller paintings on the wall and carefully began my examination. It took all my willpower not to look up and say something snotty as Mr. Belrose kept watching me, waiting for me to do something he could criticize.

The first painting was small, only about a 10X8 piece of oil on canvas. It's something I could see my mother having painted and I immediately fell in love with it. It was of an impressionist piece of a boat floating in the moonlight. Blues and silvers dominated the canvas, with short brush strokes carefully invoking the feelings of a festive boat out on dark water.

I trembled taking it off the wall, not from nerves but because I could feel it in my bones that this was an important piece. It spoke to me. The frame was well made and I was glad to see that care had been taking in preserving and displaying the artwork properly.

"That came with the house," Mr. Belrose informed me, the tone of his voice dismissive. "I'm sure it's not worth much. You should start on the Degas."

I gritted my teeth and forced my face into a polite smile. I hated it when people told me how to do my job. If he was so sure the piece was worthless, then why the heck had he hired me?

"Thank you," I said politely, beaming my smile at him

before turning back to my original painting. "I'll be sure to let you know when I'm finished."

I would get to the Degas when I got to the Degas. I had a system, one that I had perfected over the years, and I would be dammed if I was going to let him tell me how to do my job. Even if he was a billionaire.

I took the frame over to the table, pointedly ignoring Mr. Belrose. I could feel his temper heating from across the room. He wasn't a man that was used to being ignored. He was a billionaire after all. I rolled my eyes. He probably had people begging to ask "how high" at just the thought of him saying jump.

But I wasn't jumping. I wasn't even bending my knees to prep for a jump. This was the one thing that I was good at. The one thing that I knew made me worth something. He may be a billionaire, but an art connoisseur he was not. The painting was far from being worthless. Very far.

I smiled down at the painting without realizing and heard him let out a frustrated sigh. I peeked up just in time to see his back stomping off down the hallway. I rolled my eyes and told myself to be nicer next time. He was the one paying my salary and he was definitely not pleased that I had ignored his suggestion to start on the Degas. But, if he wanted this done right, then he had to let me do what I was good at.

I pushed him from my mind and focused on the painting. If I was right, and I usually was, it was a Berthe Morisot painting and probably worth around at least fifty-thousand dollars. The last time I had seen her paintings up at auction, a painting of similar size and style had gone for over one hundred thousand dollars.

I hummed gently, starting my real investigation of the painting. I was at peace whenever I held artwork like this. I loved this part of my job. To touch things that were little windows into the souls of painters, to hold something in my hands that had moved the lives of others, was exhilarating. To have it all to myself for just a moment, to be able to see every brush stroke and every careful line of color filled me joy.

I loved the challenge of authentication and appraisal. It was a puzzle that never ended. I always imagined that it was a game to see if I could distinguish real from fake, and I loved having to use all my knowledge of art and painting to make sure that something was what it appeared.

This particular piece was relatively easy as it had a certificate of authenticity from a museum I knew and respected, though, I still had to double check it, and check the certificate in order to catalog it for the auction.

I opened up my tablet to begin putting in the details when I heard a loud thunk from the room next door. Frowning, I carefully set down the painting and went to investigate the noise coming from the room where my father was working.

"Dad?" I called out, stepping into the large room next door to mine. "You in here?"

Silence answered me. I frowned and then gasped as I saw my father's form on the floor next to a large wooden desk.

I screamed a sound of pure disaster and ran to his side. He was ashen and clammy to the touch, but I thought he was at least breathing. Panic welled up in my chest and my heart threatened to beat right out of my ribs. I could hear every beat echo in my ears, whooshing and rushing as I cried for someone to come help us.

Everything moved in surreal time. Some seconds, like the one where I waited for him to take that single shaky gasp, seemed to drag on while others flitted away faster than the speed of light.

"What happened?"

Mr. Belrose was suddenly filling my vision, his hands on my shoulders and shaking me. I looked down at my father, unable to move and unable to make my mouth work. *My Dad... Daddy...*

I looked helplessly back up at Mr. Belrose, focusing on his gray eyes. Something in them helped loosen the tightness in my chest making it hard to breathe. His hand on the bare skin of my arm was a tether back to sanity.

"I heard a thunk and I came in. I..." I stammered, the words sounding off-key and hollow to my ears. I knew there was something I should be doing, something I should have done by now, something that would help my father, but for the life of me, I couldn't remember what it was.

"Bastian?" Charlotte's soft voice echoed through the room. Her brown eyes went wide as she saw my father on the floor. "What's going on?"

"He's alive," Bastian said quietly, holding his fingers against my fathers throat and feeling for a heartbeat. Somehow, he was ridiculously calm, while silver cords of panic wrapped around me and threatened to strangle me. "Charlotte, please call Dr. Verner. Tell him we have an emergency that appears cardiac related. It will be okay, Ava."

The word "cardiac" resonated in my mind, reverberating and cinching the cords of panic even tighter. I couldn't breathe. I couldn't think. I needed my father to wake up.

"Ava." Mr. Belrose grabbed my wrist, his eyes connecting with mine. When I looked at him, the slender threads of panic holding me in place lessened. He knew how to be in charge and what need to be done. I was so glad he was taking control because I was freaking out. "Ava, I need you to go get the AED. It's in the kitchen next to the door. Lucia will know where it is if you don't see it right away. I need you to bring it to me, okay?"

I nodded, my head bouncing wildly. His words were my direction and I took off running the moment he let go of my wrist. I ran as fast as my legs could pump, skittering and sliding across the wood floors like an overgrown puppy all the way to the kitchen.

I stumbled into the bright yellow kitchen, panting and eyes wild. The smell of breakfast was still in the air. I looked for the AED, but since I wasn't sure what it would look like, I couldn't find it. The rush of having something to do, of doing something to help my father, quickly wore off in the face of my defeat. The panic from before returned full force as I had no idea where the AED was, yet knew my father needed it.

"Miss Ava? Are you looking for something?" Lucia asked, coming around the center island and wiping her flour covered hands on her dark apron. "You look like you've seen a ghost."

"The AED, I need it," I gasped. My voice came out squeaky, like I had forgotten how to use it.

Lucia's face paled and her eyes grew wide. She scurried over to the door, moving faster than I would have thought possible. Hanging on the wall to the side of the kitchen door was a small white and blue briefcase with a red cross on it. I couldn't believe I hadn't seen it. Lucia took it from the wall and placed it in my hands.

I nearly dropped it I was shaking so bad, but as soon as I told my fingers to wrap around it, it would have taken pliers to make me release it. "Thank you," I whispered, turning around and running before I had even finished saying the words.

"No, don't sit up just yet," Mr. Belrose scolded as I sprinted into the room. He had his hand on my father's shoulder, keeping him pinned to the floor. I didn't care what he was doing, my father was awake.

"Daddy!" I cried, rushing to his side and going hard to my knees. I was fairly sure I hit hard enough to leave a bruise, but I barely felt it. I threw the AED at Mr. Belrose so I could wrap my arms around my father's neck.

"For the second time, I'm fine," Dad said, giving me a weak hug back. I wanted to sob into his neck, but I knew I needed to keep myself under control. Tears could come later. Right now, I needed to be strong for him.

"Lift up your shirt, Mr. Fairchild," Mr. Belrose instructed, pulling several pads out of the now opened AED case.

"Why? What are you doing?" Dad asked with a frown. He didn't move to adjust his shirt.

Mr. Belrose didn't wait for him to actually lift his shirt, and instead just did it for him, placing the big square stickers across Dad's chest. "Just attaching the monitor and shock pads," Mr. Belrose replied, turning to the machine and pressing a button. He looked right at me and gave me an gentle smile. "Excellent job, Ava."

"Well, obviously I don't need a shock if I'm a awake, now do I?" Dad grouched, his eyebrows nearly coming together. I gripped his hand tight, holding onto him as if I could keep him here with me through that connection alone if necessary. He looked back and forth between Mr. Belrose and me like we were crazy. "I don't know what has the two of you all worked up."

"Daddy, you were out cold on the floor," I said quietly. I felt a tear trickle down my cheek and I wiped it quickly away with my shoulder. I couldn't cry right now. "You weren't waking up and you were barely breathing."

Dad's face went from ashen to ghostly white. "What do you mean?" He looked over at Mr. Belrose and the AED. "What's going on?"

Mr. Belrose turned the AED monitor to face Dad. "I'm not a doctor, but I'm fairly sure your heart isn't doing what it is supposed to."

Instead of the rhythmic peaks and valleys that I had seen on every medical show I could remember, the monitor was making strange patterns that only vaguely resembled the traditional ones on TV. My father's heart was obviously beating, but something wasn't right with it. I tightened my grip on my father's hand, even more determined not to let him go.

"Right this way, Dr. Verner." Charlotte's voice floated across the silent room as she escorted someone in. A man in a pale blue dress shirt with a stethoscope slung across his shoulders hurried through the doors. He was probably mid-thirties, with messy brown hair and sharp eyes, but he moved with confidence to my father. He had a large, black leather bag that reminded me of the old school bags doctors once used to make house-calls with.

Mr. Belrose moved back to give the doctor his spot next to my father. In doing so, he moved closer to me and put his hand on my shoulder. Just having someone else there was comforting and I took a deep breath. I felt like I wasn't holding up the weight of the entire mansion on my own anymore.

"He's in here, guys," Charlotte called down the hall, motioning to the thunderous footsteps I could hear coming. Two men dressed in paramedic gear entered the room. Mr. Belrose raised an eyebrow at Charlotte. She shrugged. "Dr. Verner told me to call them."

"Beat us to the scene again, Doc," said the first of the

paramedics as he came over to where Dr. Verner had just finished listening to my father's heart. "What do you need?"

Mr. Belrose squeezed my shoulder, giving me strength. His hand was warm and steady, keeping me from shaking like a leaf. He was helping me stay grounded instead of floating off into a cloud of panic. The small gesture meant the world.

"Health history, and let's get an IV going. I don't like the look of that EKG, so I'd like to have something ready if we need to push meds," the doctor replied, opening up his black bag and beginning to pull medical supplies out. I swallowed hard. There was nothing in that statement that I liked.

The other paramedic came over to my side. He had a pad of paper and an easy smile, but I was glad Bastian was sitting beside me. Even though I hadn't known him very long, I felt like he was on my side. Like he was there for me, supporting me and helping me find my own strength.

"I just have a couple of questions for you," the paramedic began. "I'll ask your father too, but the more information we have, the better it is."

I nodded, trying to gather my chaotic thoughts. "Okay," I replied.

The paramedic began his first question, and I felt like throwing up. Bastian squeezed my shoulder again and I felt stronger. I could do this. With a deep breath, I focused on the paramedic and began to answer his questions.

CHAPTER 8

I watched the sun rise from it's morning resting place to crest at high noon through a window in the bedroom adjacent to the one my father and Dr. Verner were in. Outside, the world was sunny and bright, full of bright green and cerulean that seemed at utter contradiction with what was going on in my world.

Daddy.

I had nearly lost him. I still could lose him. The idea of losing both him and my mother was just something I wasn't ready to come to terms with yet.

Bastian had helped carry Dad up to his room with the paramedics. He had even sat with me for a little while, but he had a company to run and couldn't sit with us all day. I had replayed it in my head for the past couple of hours.

"Are you going to be okay?" Mr. Belrose asked, putting his phone in his pocket and sighing. His eyes watching my face carefully.

I looked over at my dad, laying on the bed with the doctor watching the monitors attached to his chest. My soul was shaking.

"I'm not sure..." I whispered. "But you should go."

He hesitated. "Really, I can stay with you if you'd like. I can cancel meetings. They're just meetings."

For a moment I considered having him stay. I felt better when he was with me. He had practically saved Dad's life after all. When he was around, I couldn't help but feel like I was safe. Like he would never let anything happen to me. Like Dad would be okay as long as Mr. Belrose was nearby. It didn't make any sense, but then, nothing today made much sense.

"No," I told him, putting on my closest approximation of a smile. "You should go to work. I'll let you know if there's any updates."

He frowned, his dark brows coming to a beautiful point. I didn't know why he wanted to stay with me. Maybe he just felt sorry for me. Maybe he saw something of himself in my situation. I knew he couldn't possibly want to stay because he had any interest in me. That was just crazy thoughts. He was a billionaire with far better things to do than sit with a random girl who wouldn't do the Degas painting first.

"I'm fine. I was actually thinking of taking a nap," I lied. I didn't want to feel guilty about having him stay with me instead of running his billion dollar company. I wasn't worth that.

"If you need anything," he said, pausing to make sure I understood. "You let me or Charlotte know."

After he reluctantly left, my nerves had kicked into high gear again.

When I started pacing the floor, Dr. Verner and my father had kicked me out of the room so they could concentrate. Instead of sitting and fretting, I worked. I went through all the paintings in the hallway and started on an empty bedroom just to keep myself busy. While Dr. Verner with his van of equipment ran his tests and kept my father calm in his room, I let antique paintings and furniture distract my mind from the potential doom that could still fall upon my family.

I was sitting in the doorway of a bedroom, waiting for an update from the room at the end of the hall while I put in the details of a very nice Matisse sketch, when Charlotte came by with a tray with tea and some food on it.

"How's it going?" she asked, settling the tray of tea and cheese and crackers on the floor next to me before sitting herself. "Bastian would like an update as soon as there's any news. He's trapped in a meeting or he would have come down himself."

"Nothing yet," I replied, glancing at the closed door. I picked up the tea pot and poured a cup. It smelled wonderful, and a little bit like lavender. "Are you sure this is okay? I feel like we should be at a hospital."

Charlotte smiled gently and put her hand on my shoulder. "It's more than okay. Dr. Verner is the best." She shrugged. "Besides, why go to the hospital if you don't have to? Dr. Verner has all the same equipment."

"But..." I set the cup down in my lap and sighed. It just felt strange, but I supposed medicine could be practiced anywhere. It was just odd to think of her father getting lab work without having to go to the lab. Add on to that, that I was sure we couldn't actually afford Dr. Verner's services. I was fairly certain he wasn't covered on our insurance.

"It's one of the perks of working for a billionaire," Charlotte assured me, as if reading my mind. "Don't worry. These kind of things are why Dr. Verner is on Bastian's payroll. Your dad's in good hands."

I played with my teacup, spinning the delicate china around in my fingers. If I dropped it, it would shatter and the similarity to my father's life frightened me.

"You need to eat something," Charlotte coaxed, handing me a cracker with cheese on it. "Or you'll get hangry."

Her reference to this morning made me smile and I took the cheese. Despite knowing that it was probably the best, most expensive cheese on the whole island, it was tasteless to me. I chewed automatically, more to make Charlotte happy than because I was hungry.

The door at the end of the hallway swung open and I jumped to my feet, nearly spilling my cup of tea. I set it on the tray, spilling most of it, before hurrying to talk with Dr. Verner.

"Does he need to go to the hospital? Is he going to be okay?" I asked, the words coming out faster than I had intended. "What's wrong with him?"

Dr. Verner straightened the stethoscope around his shoulders. "He's stable for now, but I want him to stay in bed and wear the heart monitor for a while." He motioned to the tea and crackers. "Please, have a seat."

I anxiously hurried over to my spot and sat down, hands in my lap eagerly awaiting the doctor's news. He didn't look tired, which I took as a good sign, but the last time a doctor told me to "take a seat," my whole world had spiraled out of control. "So?"

Dr. Verner's face was serious and he took a deep breath before giving me the news. "Your father had a heart attack."

I was glad I wasn't holding the tea because I would have dropped it. Charlotte gasped and grabbed my hand. I was glad she did, because I needed someone to hold on to.

"But he's so healthy!" I exclaimed. It didn't make any sense to me. "He doesn't have high cholesterol, he's not a smoker, and he just passed his physical a few months ago..."

"This wasn't caused by his lifestyle. Apart from running a stress test, there would have been no way to know about this," Dr. Verner explained. "From the tests I ran, it appears to be an arrhythmia, which means that his heart's electrical system isn't firing properly."

"Arrhythmia," I repeated. The word was bitter in my mouth.

He nodded. "Today, the electrical system in his heart malfunctioned. Instead of sending the normal beat pattern, it sent gibberish, which made his heart spasm. Luckily, it reverted back into a sustainable rhythm before too much damage occurred."

I took a deep breath, focusing on the fact that my father was okay. "What happens now?" I asked, almost afraid of what the doctor might tell me.

"First, I'd like him to rest while I monitor his condition," Dr. Verner replied. He tugged at one of the ends of his stethoscope. "There are some tests I'd like to run once he's feeling a little bit better, but he needs to relax and recover for a few days. Once I've had a chance to run those tests, we'll be able to look into treatment options."

"Like a pacemaker?" It was the first thing I thought of when Dr. Verner had mentioned electrical problems of the heart.

"Yes, a pacemaker might be a viable option."Dr. Verner smiled, warmth coming into his eyes. "I'll know more once I get the results."

"But, he'll be okay?" My voice cracked as I asked the question. Dr. Verner patted my knee gently.

"Yes, it looks like he will be," he assured me. "But, I will need to keep a close eye on him just to make sure."

I nodded, relief flooding my chest and letting me breathe again. *He was going to be okay.* Maybe not right away, and maybe he would need a pacemaker, but those were both things I could deal with.

"You said he'll need to take some time off?" Charlotte asked, still holding my hand in hers.

Dr. Verner nodded. "Yes. No work for at least the next three days. I want that heart monitor on him at all times. It's connected to my phone, so I'll have an alert the moment it does anything strange and I'll be within five minutes at all times. It also has the ability to shock him if necessary."

"Wait, you said no work?" I repeated, trying to ignore the part of his sentence that mentioned shock. "But that's the whole reason we're here. Are you sure?"

The doctor nodded. "Yes, I'm sure. He needs to rest. If you bring him work that he can do in bed and without getting his heart-rate up, I'll allow it." He gave me a stern look. "But no crawling around under furniture. He needs as little stress on his heart as possible."

I nodded, but grudgingly. This was going to make this week a lot more difficult.

"Now, if you'll excuse me, I need to send some of the findings off to a cardiologist to get his opinion on them." Dr. Verner stood, and I rose with him to shake his hand. "If you have any more questions, please let me know and I'll be happy to answer them."

I knew I should have a million questions, but there was only one that I could think of.

"Can I go see him?"

Dr. Verner smiled. "Of course. He's sleeping right now, but you're welcome to go in."

"Thank you, doctor," I replied, shaking his hand. I grinned at Charlotte and then took off for the door at the quietest sprint I could manage.

I paused for a moment with my hand on the doorknob. My whole body was shaking. I was afraid that I would see him hooked up to a bajillion machines like Mom had been. Slowly, I held my breath and opened the door.

Inside, Dad was fast asleep in a massive four-poster bed. For the first time in my life, he looked small. Human. The man who was always my super hero suddenly looked like an ordinary person. I stifled a sob and took a step further inside. There were some monitors and wires, but I was glad that he looked like he was sleeping normally. He was even wearing the pajamas I had gotten him for Christmas two years ago.

"Hi, Daddy," I whispered, kneeling at his side. I took his hand in mine, glad to feel it warm and full of life. He looked so peaceful, that if I hadn't just experienced the day, I never would have guessed that anything was wrong. His cheeks were pink again and his chest moved in a comfortable, easy rise and fall.

I kissed his hand, holding it to my cheek. I could feel the steady pulse of his heart through his wrist. "Don't leave me, Daddy. I don't know what I'd do if I lost you, too."

He just kept sleeping, and I finally let the tears I had been holding back all day stream silently down my face.

CHAPTER 9

I sat at the kitchen table with my computer, tablet, and several maps of the house scattered around me as I worked. A glass of lemonade sat half-full beside me, but I had mostly forgotten about it. I had to come up with a new plan on how to appraise everything in the house on the same timescale, but with my father laid up in bed. It was going to take some doing, but I think I had figured out a way to get it all done.

The kitchen light flickered on overhead, making me blink as the light blinded me. The sun must have set at least an hour ago without me noticing the change.

"Thank you," I said, trying to focus on the person joining me in the kitchen. "I didn't realize how dark it had gotten."

Mr. Belrose stood at the light switch. He was wearing a dark blue dress shirt and black dress pants that seemed like they might be a bit much for the tropical heat, even with the air conditioner on in the house. I was almost too warm in my linen pants and a tank top. I had abandoned the light, conservative sweater I wore to cover my arms hours ago.

"How are you doing?" he asked, taking a step further

into the kitchen and then pausing as if he didn't want to scare me. His eyes were tired and the scar across his cheek and eyebrow looked deeper and darker than they had this morning. I thought of his smile and just how long ago that sunrise had been. It felt like weeks instead of just a day.

I opened my mouth, ready to say the platitudes that everyone says, but then I looked at the table. He had been there today. I didn't have to lie and say "good."

"I'm not sure, to be honest," I answered truthfully. " I'm working on it, but I'm not sure. It's been kind of a crazy day."

He nodded, his gray eyes full of understanding and shadows.

"I want you to know, though, that we'll still complete the appraisal on time," I informed him. I picked up a piece of paper and frowned at it. "Well, pretty close to on time. It might take me a day or two extra, but I'll have it done by the time of the auction even if I have to work twenty-four hours a day to do it."

"Good."

A polite, but awkward silence hung in the air between us as he hovered in the doorway. He looked at me, his gray eyes taking in every detail. I knew I must look like a mess. I could see the tangles of my red hair from the corners of my eyes and I certainly felt like a disaster.

"Have you eaten anything today?" He finally asked, taking another step into the kitchen.

"Um..." I tried to remember, but I honestly couldn't recall the last bite of food I had put in my mouth. I wasn't about to tell him that though. "I'm sure I have..."

My stomach grumbled loudly, betraying me.

"I'll make you something then," he said, the corner of his mouth twitching up as he went to the fridge.

"You really don't have to go to any trouble, Mr. Belrose."

I watched in horror as the billionaire opened the fridge and began piling ingredients onto the counter. I was sure he had much better things to do than make some random employee dinner.

"It's no trouble. I was going to make some for myself anyway," he replied, pulling out a pan.

"Thank you." I bit my lip for a second. "And thank you for all your help today with my dad. I really appreciate it, Mr. Belrose."

"It was no trouble at all. I'm just glad I was there." He stopped and looked at me, his blue eyes going to mine and holding me captive. "Please, call me Bastian. If you're going to have me save family members and then sit in my kitchen in the dark, we might as well be on a first name basis."

"Okay... Bastian." I smiled. Saying his first name felt strange, but wonderful. I knew I would probably end up calling him Mr. Belrose out of habit, since he was still my employer, but I liked it. It felt right in my mouth.

"Do you like turkey or ham better?" he asked, looking up again from his cooking.

"Turkey," I responded. I watched him choose a knife and pull out a cutting board, wondering what kind of billionaire prepared his own food, let alone the food for others. "Shouldn't Lucia be doing this?"

He stopped and looked up. "Why?"

I shrugged. "Because you're a billionaire and it's her job?"

He set the knife down for a moment. "Lucia isn't my chef. She's the housekeeper who happens to enjoy cooking. She's at home with her family." He picked the knife back up and began chopping some sort of vegetable. "Why would I make her stay for me when that's not her job?"

"Oh... I didn't realize she was the housekeeper and not

your chef." I felt rather silly, and I tried to hide it by stacking up my papers into a neat pile. He threw some bacon into a pan and I could hear it sizzle as he continued to chop. "You don't have a chef?"

"When I'm in New York, I do. Here, I enjoy making my own food." He stopped chopping and grinned. "Though, I do enjoy the leftovers Lucia leaves for me. She makes the most amazing jerk chicken."

"I can believe it," I said, remembering how good the french toast was this morning. My stomach rumbled again. The bacon smelled wonderful and I was suddenly very hungry. "Do you want some help? It feels a little strange to have a billionaire making me dinner."

Bastian moved the pan holding the bacon, causing the air to fill with sizzles and pops. He then turned and gave me a playful glare. "That's twice now that you've mentioned my net worth. It honestly doesn't affect my cooking ability. I promise. This will be good."

"Sorry." I blushed and played with a loose strand of hair. "I guess I've just never talked to someone who makes my year's salary in a week."

"You're doing it again," he informed me, raising his eyebrows in warning. "And besides, it's more like your year's salary in a day, not a week."

I opened my mouth to protest until I realized he was joking with me. I giggled and he grinned at me.

"Fair enough." I sat back in my chair, watching him work. He moved around the kitchen with a calm serenity that I envied. When I cooked, I looked like someone on speed or with their hair on fire. "Where'd you learn to cook? Is that a class you have to take at Billionaire University?"

He laughed, a sound I hadn't heard yet. He had a great laugh. An infectious happy laugh that made my day instantly brighter. He swished the pan with the bacon in it again, making sure everything was cooking evenly before going to mix something in a bowl. I had no idea what he was making, but it sure smelled wonderful.

"No, I learned it from my mom." He tasted whatever was in the bowl and then added more spice. "She was a gourmet chef and she did her best to teach me."

My brain caught on the use of past tense. She *was* a gourmet chef.

"What about your dad?" I asked, trying to steer clear of the dead mother.

"He was a electrician." Bastion tasted the mixture again and set it to the side, content with whatever was in it. "But he loved my mom's cooking and wasn't half bad in the kitchen himself."

Again, parent in the past tense. *Both of his parents must be gone then*, I thought to myself. For a moment, I wondered what today must have been like for him. While I had nearly lost my father, he had already lost both his parents.

I didn't know quite what to say, but luckily he had finished and was coming around to the table with his creation in hand. He looked incredibly pleased with himself and it made me smile.

"Voila," he said, presenting the most amazing sandwich I had ever seen. Thick french bread layered with turkey, bacon, avocados, cheese, lettuce, tomatoes, and some sort of creamy sauce awaited me.

He sat down in the seat across from me, but waited for me to take the first bite. I carefully picked up the beautiful sandwich and tried it.

It was the best sandwich I had ever tasted in my entire life. The vegetables were just the right level of crispy compared to the bread and meat and the sauce was some sort of ranch dressing that brought out every other flavor. It was like taking a little bite of heaven in sandwich form.

"This is amazing," I gasped, stuffing another bite into my mouth. He grinned, obviously pleased with himself as I thoroughly enjoyed his culinary creation.

"What are you working on?" Bastian asked once I started to slow down my bites. He motioned to the paperwork still scattered across the table.

"Plan B," I explained. "With Dad out of commission, I had to come up with a new plan."

"Go on," he replied, smiling at me. He took another bite, but seemed genuinely interested in having a conversation. "Tell me more."

"Okay." I smiled, feeling flattered. I was actually quite grateful for any excuse to get to talk to him. His gray eyes were warm again in the yellow light of the kitchen. They weren't quite as bright as this morning, but the longer he sat, the less shadows seemed to haunt his face. "I'll take pictures of everything tomorrow. We needed the photos for the auction catalog, but this way Dad can appraise some things through photograph and keep up on all the paper-work, leaving me time to do the rest."

"Appraisal by photograph?" Bastian raised his perfectly groomed eyebrows. "You mean I didn't need to fly you both out here?"

"No, you still did." I blushed as I realized he was teasing me again. "A lot of this needs to actually be looked at, but some things, like that picture you saw me working on this morning, already have certificates of authenticity. From there it's just verifying the certificate and assigning a price."

He looked thoughtful for a moment. "So how much was that painting worth this morning? You were rather intent on it."

I took another bite and swallowed before answering. "It's actually worth more than the Degas."

He stopped chewing and looked at me in surprise before shaking his head in disbelief. "No."

"Yes," I insisted with a grin. "It's an authentic Berthe Morisot original. A similar painting was valued at just over fifty thousand dollars and actually sold at auction for just over one-hundred thousand."

"But, the Degas? It's a *Degas*." He set his sandwich down and watched me.

"The Degas is just a sketch on paper. It's worth around twenty-five thousand, so it's still worth quite a bit." I smiled. I loved talking about this stuff. I loved the nuances of the art world and how even though a piece might have a famous name attached, another painting could still be better. "Even though the Degas name is more well known, the Morisot is a painting whereas the Degas is just a sketch."

He nodded slowly, his eyes never leaving my face. I loved having his complete attention. When he looked at me, I felt special and wanted. "Is that why you ignored my advice?"

"To start on the Degas?" I shook my head. "No. I didn't know what the Degas was worth until this afternoon, but I did have a plan. I have a system and I wasn't about to let you interrupt me."

"Even though I'm a billionaire," he teased. "With a cooking degree from Billionaire University?"

"Yes," I said with a giggle before going serious again. "Everything has value. You just have to give things a chance to show you their worth. Just because something initially looks better doesn't actually mean that it is."

Something in his face relaxed and he leaned back in his seat, studying me. I hoped I wasn't blushing again, especially since I just went all philosophical on him.

"You've impressed me three times now, just today," he said after a moment. "Four if you count trying to stop a robbery last night."

"What? Three?" I racked my brain for when I could have possibly impressed him for the first time. It certainly hadn't been while I was ignoring the Degas.

"This, the fake Roux, and that you managed to keep very calm during your father's episode," he answered.

I gave a short laugh. "I think you might be remembering someone else. I was the exact opposite of calm."

"I don't know." He shrugged and leaned forward, eyes intent on me. When he looked at me like that, it made my stomach do happy flip flops and I wasn't quite sure why. "She was about your height, dark red hair, and the most amazing, beautiful green eyes."

I couldn't stop the blush that flared around my chest and up my neck and into my cheeks at the compliment. I looked at him, thinking he might be teasing me again, but he was completely serious.

"Thank you." I smiled and shrugged, trying not to read too much into flattering words. "It sounds like it could be me, but I still think you might have me confused with someone who wasn't panicking."

He smiled, light shining in his eyes. "What did you think of the sandwich?"

I looked down at my empty plate. It had been absolutely fantastic and now that it was gone, I was considering licking my plate to get at the crumbs.

"What sandwich?" I asked, trying to look innocent. "Someone must have taken it."

"Well, that is a shame," he agreed. "I'll just have to make you another."

"You really don't have to do that," I said quickly, reaching out and grabbing his wrist. He pulled away as if I had shocked him. "I mean, I'm sure you have more important things to do with your time than make me a sandwich."

"Does it look like I'm doing anything else?" he asked tersely.

"No," I admitted, shaking my head.

"Then, this is what I'm doing with my time." He stood from the table and collected my plate before going back to the kitchen.

I bit my lip for a moment, hoping he didn't find me ungrateful. I just didn't think I was worthy. "Thank you."

He threw more bacon into the frying pan before turning around. "Did you find any other treasures hidden away on my walls?" he asked, changing the topic back to art.

"A couple." I watched his steady hands as he chopped more lettuce, mesmerized by his sure and quick strokes. "I found another beautiful little Morisot in the hallway. I think there are several more of her works scattered throughout the house."

He paused, looking up at me. "I'm afraid I don't know much about her."

"She's one of my favorite artists," I explained. "She's considered one of the best female impressionists. Her work sells remarkably well."

"Then I'm glad she is on my walls, then." He flashed me another quick smile that had my heart speeding up again.

"Did you not pick the paintings?" I asked, curious as to why he didn't know what he had in his own house. I picked up my lemonade and finally started drinking it, suddenly thirsty.

"Me? No." He shook his head and made a face. "I bought this house a few years ago at auction. I wanted a beach house on the island, and the owners had passed away and the estate was being sold. It's time to sell it now while the market is good. What you are cataloging is what was in the house originally. I didn't pick any of it."

I nearly choked on the last of my drink. I set the glass down and stared at him. "This was all here? This place is practically an art museum!"

He grinned and adjusted the sandwich on my plate before coming back over. "I don't know much about art, but I know a good business deal when I see one."

I went to reach for the plate and in the process knocked over the empty glass. It rolled off the table but thankfully bounced on the floor instead of breaking. Bastian set the plate on the table and knelt beside me to pick it up.

He handed it back to me, our fingers touched for the briefest of moments, while our eyes connected. I gazed into eyes filled with the gray dawn and bursting with want and hope and so much more with every second I looked. He was close enough that I could smell the clean scent of his shampoo and my fingers ached to run through his hair.

"Hey, Bastian, Leo's on the line and he's..." Charlotte's called out, entering the room and breaking the spell. She had her phone to her ear but her hand over the mouth piece. "Oh, hey, Ava."

She glanced around at the tableau in front of her, with Bastian kneeling before me in the kitchen, our hands on the glass together, and what I knew must be a frightful flush on my cheeks. I could only imagine what she thought. "Am I interrupting?"

Bastian quickly rose to his feet and set the empty glass on the table. "Of course not."

Charlotte glanced back and forth between the two of us, one eyebrow arching higher than the other. I looked down at my plate, wishing I knew how to control my blushing.

Charlotte took an inhale to say something and then followed my gaze to my plate and instead burst out with, "You made Rough-Day Sandwiches? Did you make me one?"

"No. You said you were on a diet," he said with a shrug. That explained why she hadn't had any of the french toast this morning. She looked up at Bastian but before she could say anything he held up his hand. "See? I listen. No gluten, no Rough-Day Sandwich."

Charlotte stared at my sandwich like a starving person. I could hear her mouth watering from my seat at the table and felt the urge to scoot the sandwich closer to me before she could steal it and run off.

"Sometimes, Bastian," she said, turning to face him and crossing her arms. "Sometimes, you suck."

Bastian grinned at her. "You said Leo's on the phone?"

"Yeah. Main line, so it's business," she said, rolling her eyes at him. I wondered if they were secretly a couple since they were obviously close. The idea that Bastian might be with someone stung in places I wasn't expecting.

"Excuse me then, Ava," Bastian said, catching my eye. Looking into Bastian's eyes was like looking into deep water. There was so much there that I couldn't look away. I hoped that he and Charlotte weren't an item. That would ruin all the wonderful fantasies my brain was now starting to concoct around him. He carefully slipped past Charlotte and back into the main house, my eyes following him the entire way.

Charlotte watched him leave and then promptly looked at me.

"He likes you," she said, matter-of-factly.

"What?" I tried to laugh, but there was a thrill in the pit

of my stomach. I wanted him to like me. "What makes you say that?"

"He made you a Rough-Day Sandwich," she stated, as if that made everything terribly obvious.

"I don't know if you noticed, Charlotte, but I kind of did have a rough day," I replied with a shrug.

Charlotte laughed, grinning at me and shaking her head. "He doesn't just make them for anyone. You have to be special to merit a Rough-Day Sandwich."

"Maybe he just felt bad for me," I suggested. She stared at my plate like a ravenous animal. I smiled. "Would you like some? This is my second and I won't be able to eat it all anyway."

"He made you TWO?" she exclaimed. She shook her head incredulous, but it quickly shifted into an eager nod. "Yes, yes, I want some."

She hurried over to the kitchen and brought me a knife to cut the sandwich in half. I grinned as I cut into it, her excitement at the food contagious. She reminded me of one of my best friends from high school, so bubbly and easy to get along with that it was impossible not be her friend. I couldn't help but like her, even if she was with Bastian.

Charlotte could barely wait for the knife to finish cutting before grabbing her piece. She took a huge bite and sank into a kitchen chair with ecstasy written all over her face. "Oh my god," she groaned. "He must really like you. He made his special sauce."

I snickered slightly at her use of "special sauce," but she just rolled her eyes and took another bite.

"Why are they called Rough-Day Sandwiches?" I asked, taking another bite.

Charlotte swallowed, pausing long enough between bites to explain. "When we were younger, Bastian would make them for me whenever I had a rough day. They make a rough day better-- thus Rough-Day Sandwiches."

"When you were younger?" I asked, feeling a cold pang in my stomach. If she had known him since childhood, there was no way I could compete. "Did you know each other as kids?"

She nodded. "We basically grew up together. We had the same foster family. We may have different last names, but he's family. He's as much my brother as anyone can be."

"Oh." My heart stopped falling. He was her foster brother. Which also explained the use of past tense when referring to his parents. They must have died when he was much younger. "So is Kindling Romance a family business then?"

Charlotte laughed as if I had said something wonderfully clever and funny. "Oh, no. It's all Bastian. He's the one who convinced his two friends they actually had a legit idea. When he gets a notion in his head, the rest of us just come along for the ride."

I nodded. He seemed like the kind of person who would take charge and lead a business. But really, I was just glad to know that Charlotte considered him her brother. They weren't a couple. Butterflies happily danced around in my stomach at the thought of those gray eyes looking at me again, and knowing that they were actually looking at me.

"That was so good." Charlotte smacked her lips and licked the crumbs off her fingers. "Totally worth breaking the diet." She leaned forward and whispered, "Don't tell him you shared with me."

"Too late," Bastian whispered loudly from behind her.

"Damn it!" Charlotte jumped and then glared at him. "You know I can't pass up a Rough-Day Sandwich. That's like asking the ocean not to be wet."

Bastian just shook his head slowly at her. It was easy to see their brother-sister relationship now that I knew what it was.

"What did Leo want?" Charlotte asked, brushing crumbs off her blouse.

Bastian sighed, the shadows creeping into his eyes and losing the warmth of his smile. "The new app is a mess. I'm going to need you to cancel my morning appointments and schedule a conference call."

"Will do, Boss," Charlotte chirped, pulling out her phone.

"I'm sorry, but I have to go deal with this," Bastian said, turning toward me. I could see real regret in his face.

"No worries. I have plenty I need to do myself." I knew my face mirrored his regret, but I smiled and waved my hand at the papers on the table. "Thank you for dinner, though. I really appreciate it. It was wonderful."

And I didn't just mean the food.

Bastian smiled, the sun coming out from behind the shadows of his eyes. Seeing him smile, especially at me, gave me happy tingles in all the right places.

Charlotte cleared her throat, reminding me that it wasn't just Bastian and me anymore. I hoped I hadn't been smiling at him with my stupid happy smile for too long.

"Charlotte, go get the lawyers on the phone. We've got a busy night," Bastian said to his assistant before looking at me. His eyes met mine and I could see his smile lightening them. "Goodnight, Ava."

I liked the way he said my name. "Goodnight, Bastian."

He grinned, and then turned to hurry up to his office to work.

"Yes, good night, Ava," Charlotte mimicked her brother's farewell. I stuck my tongue out at her and she laughed before hurrying to follow him. She ducked her head back into the kitchen at the last second and whispered, "Thanks for the sandwich!" before disappearing up the stairs.

I shook my head and chuckled. It was an interesting dynamic between those two. It made me wonder what it would be like to work with a sibling. As an only child, I could only imagine, but since I worked with my father, my aunt and uncle, and my two cousins, I figured it was probably similar. Working with family was wonderful and exasperating at the same time.

I turned back to my paperwork, but the words just looked jumbled and unappealing. I couldn't concentrate, instead wanting to close my eyes and just remember what it felt like to have Bastian smile at me. I knew I couldn't just sit there basking in his imaginary glow, so I got up to put the dishes away. It was the least I could do since he cooked.

The kitchen was remarkably clean. Other than the frying pan and the vegetables neatly arranged on the cutting board, everything else was already neatly put away. I put the veggies on a plate and found some plastic wrap before placing it in the fridge next to his sauce. I hand-washed the frying pan and cutting board, leaving them out to air dry.

Glancing around the kitchen, I realized that Bastian really must know what he was doing. Everything was spotless and perfect, despite making a rather complex sandwich.

I smiled, thinking of him in the kitchen and the fact that he had made me a Rough-Day Sandwich. I was glad that Charlotte had told me just what they meant, as it made the act even sweeter. He may not know much about art, but he did know how to make a person feel better with food.

CHAPTER 10

I stood at my father's window, looking out at the gleaming ocean and wishing I was out there. *No, I chastised myself, I wasn't looking at the beach. I was looking at Bastian.*

I could see him just coming in off the water, walking across the beach with water dripping from his wetsuit in the morning light. I wished I could have seen that smile light up his face again as he greeted the dawn, but I had work to do. I sighed and he looked up, directly at the window as if he had heard me. I looked away, knowing that it was just coincidence.

"Are you listening to me?" Dad asked, cocking his head to the side. He was propped up in the massive four poster bed with more pillows than I think we had in our entire house.

"Yes, of course I am," I responded, pulling away from the window. Bastian was inside now anyway. "You want me to report in every hour. I know how to do this."

Dad frowned. I knew he wanted out of bed and to get to

work. This was going to be harder on him than it would be on me. He wasn't the kind of person who could sit still for more than five minutes, let alone lounge in bed when there was work to be done.

"Don't worry, Daddy." I came over and kissed his head. "I'm going to go get some breakfast, and then I'll get everything ready. You'll only have to be bored for a few hours before I inundate you with work."

"*Paper*work," he corrected me, but at least he smiled.

I grinned at him, turning to open the door. "I'll see you soon."

"Hurry back," he called out after me as I headed down the hallway.

I went to the kitchen and found a pot of fresh coffee. There was no french toast this time, but I found hard boiled eggs in the fridge and some cereal. It was a quick and easy meal before heading into the foyer where I had all my gear set up.

The light was perfect in here with the high ceilings and open windows. I picked up my camera and fired a test shot at one of pictures hanging on the wall just as Charlotte descended the stairs.

"I like that one," she said, pointing to the picture I was aiming my camera at. It was a calm, pastoral scene with calm blue skies, green trees, and rolling golden fields.

"Me too," I agreed, smiling at her.

"How much is it worth?" She came and stood next to me, looking at the painting.

"Only a couple hundred dollars," I replied, taking another practice shot and adjusting the settings slightly on my camera.

Charlotte looked over at me surprised. It was a large

painting, and in the same impressionist style as many of the other paintings in the house. "Why?"

"It's a replica of an Armaund Guillaumin painting," I explained. "It's a fairly famous painting."

"It's a forgery?" She sounded shocked.

I shook my head. "No, just a replica. It's pretty common for artists to recreate a famous piece of art and sell it. It's not a forgery as long as they don't try and pass it off as the original." I looked back up at the painting. "The artists did a fantastic job, but since it's just a replica, it isn't worth very much."

"Oh," Charlotte said, looking back at it with a keen eye. "It's still beautiful, though."

"Yes, yes it is," I agreed. "Things don't have to be worth much to still be beautiful."

She nodded and smiled at me. "How's your dad?"

"Grumpy," I answered and she laughed. "He hates being stuck in bed. Throw in that he's now going to be responsible for all the paperwork while there's amazing antique furniture down here-- let's just say he's a bit of a grouch."

Charlotte nodded. "And what about you? How are you doing?"

I looked around at the foyer and the massive amount of work I had to get done. "Stressed," I answered honestly. "But this-" I held up the camera and took another picture. "will keep my mind off of Dad, so it's all good."

Charlotte played with her phone, flipping it between her fingers as she watched me work. "You two seem close," she commented.

I nodded, taking another picture. "We are. It's been just him and me since my mom died, and then we work together at the family business. It means we spend a lot of time together."

"I'm sorry," she said quickly. I turned and frowned, lowering my camera.

"For what?"

"Your mom." Charlotte bit the inside of her cheek and shrugged.

"Oh... Thank you," I stammered, feeling awkward. "It was five years ago. Cancer."

The words came out flat. I had learned to just say it quickly, giving out when and how as simply as possible. People always wanted to know, and if I just told them, they would usually stop asking and not make me dredge up the bad memories.

"I'm sorry," Charlotte repeated, blushing slightly.

"Not your fault," I told her, raising my camera back up. I pointed to a small marble figurine of a woman with flowing robes. "Would you mind holding up that statue? I need a size reference."

"Sure." She smiled, happy that we weren't on the subject of my dead mom anymore. Since she was a foster kid, she probably knew all too well how it felt. She held up the statue and smiled like a model.

"Perfect," I told her with a grin, snapping another picture. "You're a natural."

"It's my fallback career," she replied with a laugh. She paused for a moment, looked up, and chewed the inside of her cheek again. "Can I ask you a personal question?"

I lowered the camera and peered at her. I had no idea where this was going. "Um, sure?"

"Are you seeing anyone?" Charlotte turned bright red. "I know that this is a weird question, but I might have someone who would be interested."

I swallowed hard, wanting to be delicate. She couldn't

possibly mean Bastian, but that just left Marcus or Elijah, neither of whom I was remotely interested in.

"I recently broke up with my boyfriend," I finally answered, making sure to accent the 'boyfriend' just in case. "It was kind of brutal, so I'm really not interested in a relationship right now. Thanks for holding that."

"No problem. I'm sorry about the breakup. Guys suck." Charlotte frowned and set down the statue. She chewed on her cheek for another moment. "Wanna tell me how terrible he was? It'll make you feel better. And I'm dying to talk to someone who answers relationship questions in sentences longer than 'yeah, she's hot.'"

She had the male answer down pat. I laughed. It had been awhile since I had some good girl time. Watching her light up at the chance, I had a feeling she felt the same. Working with Bastian all day wouldn't leave much time for friends, and Elijah didn't seem like much of a talker.

"Yeah." I pointed to another statue. "You mind being a model for a little longer?

"Gets me out of real work." She grinned and picked it up, holding it up for me to photograph. "So, brutal breakup?"

I snapped her picture. "I walked in on him banging the hot waitress he swore he wasn't interested in. That was kind of a deal breaker for me."

"Ouch." Charlotte grimaced and I laughed as I caught it on camera. That one was not going in the catalog. "Were you two serious?"

I sighed, feeling the sting of heartbreak again. As much as I wanted it all to be over, the betrayal still hurt. "He was talking about proposing."

"Damn, girl."

"It gets worse." I gave her a half smile. "We work together, so I have to see him all the time. The first week after I caught him, I couldn't even be in the same room. Talk about awkward."

"That sucks," Charlotte agreed. I nodded and pointed to another figurine. She quickly set hers down to pick it up and pose again. "What does he do? Does he do appraisals too?"

"No, he's an auctioneer," I said, shaking my head. "Since my aunt does the auction side of the business, he's technically her employee, but it's a small office."

"He's sounds awful."

I shrugged, lowering the camera. "I didn't even see it coming. He was talking about getting married and helping with the business more..." It had been months, but just thinking about it made my chest ache. "He swore he didn't find her attractive, and then I found out their little rendezvous had been going on for months."

Charlotte set the statue down with a thunk and hurried over to hug me.

"Sounds like a total jerk," she said, squeezing me tight. "I hope you at least slapped him or something."

"I threw a lamp at his head. Does that count?"

Charlotte grinned, releasing me. "I knew I liked you." She pointed to another statue. "This one next?"

I nodded. "Yeah, that's perfect."

She picked it up and stood in the light, holding it perfectly for the camera. "How long ago did you break up?"

"A little over two months," I replied, snapping her picture. "He's been trying to get me back since then."

"Seriously?" Charlotte's smile dropped with disbelief.

"Yeah," I shook my head. "He won't leave me alone. Emails, text messages, flowers at work. He keeps trying to remind me how awesome he is and how terribly lucky I was to even be with him. Like I should just get over the fact that he was sleeping around because he's God's gift to women. Chad's an idiot."

"With a name like Chad, can you blame him?" Charlotte grinned at me. This was nice. I liked having someone feminine who wasn't related to me to talk to. I had friends back home, but telling them how badly I had misjudged Chad was embarrassing. They were all his friends too. He was the hometown hero and I was the nerdy girl he had picked up. Without him, I wasn't special. It was nice to have someone firmly on my side of the breakup.

I was thoroughly enjoying hanging out with Charlotte. Unfortunately, her phone chirped. She set down the statue, checked it and then put it back in her pocket with a frown. "Just a reminder that I have work to do. What are you doing for dinner tonight?"

"I have no idea," I replied. "I haven't thought that far in advance yet."

"It's my night off tonight. Want to have a girl's night?" Hope shone on her face. Charlotte needed a friend as much as I did.

"I would love to have a girl's night." It was just the change of scenery I needed. Dad would be fine on his own tonight, especially with the doctor just minutes away. It was better than sitting and fretting all night.

"Excellent!" Charlotte beamed and picked up another statue. "I'll come get you at seven and we'll go to the local hotspot. They make the best daiquiris."

I snapped another picture as she posed for me. "What about you? You have a special someone?"

She blushed a deep red and shook her head. "Nope."

"Uh huh."

She rolled her eyes. "There's someone I wouldn't mind

dating, but I think he just sees me as an extension of Bastian." I frowned and she immediately held up her hands. "No, it's okay. I'm so busy right now that I don't have time to see anyone anyway."

I was about to say something uplifting, but Charlotte's phone started to ring. She set down the statue and mouthed a sorry before answering. "This is Charlotte Page, how may I help you?"

I moved to a painting, trying my best not to listen to her phone conversation, but her voice echoed through the big foyer.

"Oh, hi Leo... yes... okay, I can do that... Give me just one second." Charlotte touched my arm, and pointed to her phone with an apologetic face.

"Go, go," I whispered. "Thank you for helping me. I'll see you at seven."

Charlotte grinned and then hurried up the stairs, talking into the phone with Leo.

I smiled after her, feeling lighter than I had in weeks. I had only been here for a couple of days but I already felt comfortable here. I even had a friend. It felt good. Without worrying about seeing Chad all the time, having to remind him that he betrayed me and that no, we weren't getting back together, I felt like me again.

I held up the camera to take another picture, shifting slightly to adjust for the light. I looked up to check my light source, only to see Bastian's walking back into his study. My cheeks turned hot enough to start a wildfire and I hoped that he hadn't been listening to Charlotte and my conversation.

It was embarrassing admitting that I had been so stupid with Chad. I wanted Bastian to think I was more than what I was at home. When he looked at me with those beautiful eyes, I didn't want him to see that I was someone else's left-overs. If I wasn't good enough for Chad, then there was no way I would be good enough for someone like Bastian. That made him the last person in the world that I wanted to know about Chad.

CHAPTER 11

*D*espite the myriad of rooms in the mansion, I sat in the first room I had started the appraisal. I liked this one, as it had the most comfortable couch I had found and the Morisot painting. After running around the house taking hundreds of photographs and reporting to Dad, I had taken the room over as my office. Now that daylight was fading, I had retreated to the couch to upload all the images to get them ready for my father to organize and edit.

I stood up to stretch as my ancient laptop processed another batch, wandering over to the Morisot picture. The natural light was fading, but the picture was still vibrant. I stared into it, absorbing each brush stroke and imagining myself sitting at a dock along the Seine.

"And I find you looking at that picture again," a voice said from behind me. I spun startled to see Bastian leaning against the door frame. He was still wearing a full button-up dress shirt and slacks, but at least the top button on the shirt was undone. His eyes, blue-gray and fathomless were fixed on me.

I smiled, glancing back at the painting. "There's something about it that makes me think of Paris."

He nodded thoughtfully before walking over and pointing to the painting further down the wall. "That one reminds me more of Paris. Yours makes me think of Cannes."

"You've been to France?" I asked, looking at the other painting. It was a cityscape and I had to agree that it fit more with the image of the city of Paris than a boat did.

"Several times this year already," he said, moving to stand beside me. "It's a growing market for our website."

"Oh." If I dropped my hand to my side, I would brush his with mine, so I held my hands carefully in my lap instead.

He turned his head to look at me, his gray eyes sharp and keen. "What about you? When was the last time you were in France?"

I shrugged, wrapping my arms around my middle like there was an empty pit in my soul. "I've never been."

"No?" His eyes widened slightly. "But your specialty is French artwork. I thought I saw something in your resume about it."

"I was accepted into an internship at the Louvre, but my mom got sick, so I didn't go." I shifted my weight, and hugged myself a little tighter.

"I'm sorry," he said quietly, sounding very much like Charlotte. "Was she in appraisals as well?"

"No, my mom was an artist. Her impressionist work was as good as the masters. She taught me how to see every brush stroke as important and to look for all the details in a piece." I smiled fondly, diving into a memory. "We used to sit and talk in the mornings, and then during her chemo treatments, about going to Paris together. We had museums and tours all figured out. All the art we could take in."

"And you didn't go?" Bastian's voice was low and soft.

"She died before we ever got a chance." I shook my head, freeing myself from the memory. "I got a different internship and then things have just been so busy that I haven't found the time."

I thought of adding, "or the funds," but I doubted a billionaire would understand that part of my problem.

Bastian studied me for a moment, his gray eyes going over me like a painting, taking in every nuance of my face. I looked up at him, enjoying having his company all to myself for a moment. It reminded me of our sunrise out on the beach.

My heart skipped a beat as I realized how close he was. If I just leaned forward by only an inch or two, I would be nearly kissing him. His warmth radiated off him and I could smell the faintest hint of his aftershave and it was difficult not to inhale hard for more.

He glanced back at the painting for a moment before smiling back at me. "You'd like Paris. It's full of beautiful things. You'd fit in there."

I blushed at the accidental compliment, biting my bottom lip in a bashful smile as I fiddled with a strand of hair. The thought of kissing him slipped into my mind again, and I nearly did before remembering who he was. I couldn't just kiss a billionaire because he said something nice to me.

"I looked up her work," he said, turning to look at the painting again.

"Who?" I stammered, my brain spinning and sliding on the smell of his cologne. I took a step back in surprise and promptly lost my balance.

He caught me, wrapping me up in one of his arms before I even realized I was in danger of falling. His arm was steel muscle and I couldn't stop thinking about what it would be like to have it wrapped around me in an entirely different room. I pressed my thighs together, struggling to keep the image of his arms on either side of me, his chest bare and strong above me, his hair falling into his eyes with exertion...

"You okay?" He hadn't let go of me yet, but I also hadn't fully regained the use of my legs yet either.

"Yeah," I grinned, knowing I was blushing like a fool. "Just stepped back funny. I'm okay."

He waited just an extra moment before releasing me. I didn't want him to let me go. I was considering falling again, just to have him touch me, but I didn't want to appear weak or too obvious.

"Berthe Morisot," he replied, looking back at the painting. "One of the *'les trois grandes dames'* of impressionism. I like this one, but there's something about her landscapes that appeal to me more."

"Really?" I asked, surprised that he had even remembered her name. "Do you have a favorite?"

"'A Corner of the Rose Garden,'" he answered. A full smile filled my face. It was one of my favorites as well. It had always reminded me of mornings in my mother's garden when I was little.

"I can't believe you actually looked her up," I said, tucking the strand of hair behind my ear.

"What?" He grinned. "A billionaire can't use Google?"

I laughed. "I don't know, is there a gold plated version?"

"Platinum." He put on a straight face, but his eyes twinkled as he teased me. "Gold is for mere millionaires."

I giggled and he grinned. His smile had the same warmth as it did at sunrise and the beauty of it made my heart flutter. When he smiled, the world lit up.

I wanted to ask him so many questions. I wanted to know why he was in foster care with Charlotte, and how he had found the way to turn a dating company into a billion dollar empire from that background. Where did he go to school? Did he have any hobbies other than paddle-boarding? What was his favorite color? I wanted to know everything about him.

"Hey, you ready, Ava?" Charlotte called, stomping into the doorway. She stopped as she saw the two of us standing remarkably close and looking at one another. "Damn, I need to work on my timing."

"Are you two going out?" Bastian asked, a frown crossing his handsome features. It tugged at the scar on his cheek and eyebrow, making him look more serious than necessary. I liked the smile so much better.

"Yes," Charlotte replied, coming to my other side. "Just to Surf Shack for some girl time."

"Charlotte," he began, the scar darkening, "I-"

"Think it's a great idea," Charlotte finished for him. "Thank you, Bastian, for your opinion. We'll be fine."

Bastian's lips tightened and he glared at her. Charlotte rolled her eyes at him and sighed.

"Do you want Elijah to come with us?" she asked, pointedly raising her eyebrows at him.

"Yes." He nodded and the frown faded slightly. "It would make me feel better."

"You hear that, Elijah?" Charlotte yelled out toward the hall. I winced slightly at the increase in volume so close to my ear. "You get to come to girl's night!"

Elijah's head popped into the doorway. "I'm not drinking one of those frou-frou drinks again with you, Charlotte."

What had felt like a comfy, cozy, and possibly romantic location two seconds ago suddenly felt very public. I knew

Elijah followed Bastian around everywhere, but the fact that he had been just outside the doorway listening to us flirt was a little daunting.

"Aw, you're no fun, Elijah." Charlotte grinned wickedly at the bodyguard. "I was going to get you the one with whipped cream and the flower on the glass. I know how much you loved it last time."

Elijah didn't say anything back and the room went silent for a beat.

"I guess we should be going then," I said finally, feeling awkward. I wanted the moment before Charlotte arrived back. I wanted it to be just me and Bastian, giggling over art and flirting. I wondered for a moment if I canceled with Charlotte, if Bastian would stay and look at the painting with me.

"I should be getting back to work," Bastian said, as if hearing my thoughts. I tried not to look disappointed. "You two have fun. And be careful."

"Don't be such a worrywart," Charlotte chastised, sticking out her tongue at him. He glared at her as only a protective older brother could before walking over to Elijah. He looked back, his eyes meeting mine for a moment before he focused on Elijah. Bastian said something to the big man that only the two of them could hear but that had Charlotte rolling her eyes.

"You should have seen how protective he was on my first date," she said, looping her arm through mine and guiding me toward the door. "I'm surprised he isn't calling in more bodyguards since it's the two of us. Perhaps an armored car."

"I heard that," Bastian said loudly, still talking to Elijah. I giggled and he glanced over, his brow dark above his beautiful eyes. He looked quickly away and back to Elijah.

"I thought the island was a safe place," I said, frowning slightly. If Bastian was making this big a deal out of going out, maybe it wasn't the best idea.

"It is," Charlotte assured me. "The island is so safe that the police boast a less than two minute response time anywhere on the island. Not that they even need to respond half the time, There's enough private security on this island to win a small war. He's just over-protective. Though, he usually doesn't insist Elijah come when it's just me..."

She pulled me past the two men and out into the hall before turning back to face her brother. "You have our itinerary all planned out? We're going to miss happy hour if you don't hurry your secret service plans. I want my girl night even if you would rather Ava stay all safe and cozy here."

"I worry because I care," he informed her, but didn't correct her to say he wanted her safe too. His eyes briefly flashed up to me and I suddenly felt a little warm. He cared for me too.

"I know." She grinned up at him and pulled on my arm. "We'll see you later. Come on Elijah- we'll even let you ride in the car with us."

"Bye, Charlotte," Bastian called out as Elijah shook his head and followed us. Bastian looked right at me and his voice softened. "Good bye, Ava."

I looked back, losing myself in his eyes for a second. "Good bye, Bastian." He smiled at how I said his name and it made me blush.

Charlotte looked back and forth between the two of us, noting the sappy smiles and rolled her eyes. She pulled harder on my arm. "I'll have her back by midnight, Prince Charming!" she called.

I blushed even harder, but followed her down the stairs and out to our waiting pumpkin.

CHAPTER 12

Waiting outside in the giant driveway was a very expensive-looking, electric blue sports car. Charlotte jumped in the front seat and immediately stalled it.

"Would you like me to drive?" Elijah asked, managing to keep a straight face as he stood at the door.

"I hate this car." Charlotte made an exasperated sound and got out of the driver's seat. "Yes, you can drive."

I covered my mouth with my hand so she wouldn't see my smirk as the two of us got into the leather-encased backseat. Elijah waited to start the car until we were both buckled, but when he turned the ignition key, it purred like a content kitten. I didn't know that cars could actually sound like music and it drove smoother than any car I had ever been in.

"What kind of car is this anyway?" I asked, feeling the leather seat. It was like satin against my skin.

"Lamborghini," Charlotte replied, crossing her legs. I hadn't noticed her killer heels until right then, but she swung them around like weapons. I was terrified one would catch on the leather and rip it.

"And you hate it?" I asked, blanching a little. I had never even seen a real life Lamborghini, let alone gotten inside of one.

"It has the touchiest clutch in the world," she explained. Elijah made a snorting noise that she ignored. "I know how to drive a manual. Give me a good, old-fashioned, American-made truck and I can drive that sucker anywhere. This," she said, glaring at the very expensive car, "has nothing on my truck at home."

I smiled, imagining her in an old beater of a truck driving around a billion dollar estate. It fit Charlotte to a tee.

"So you and Bastian were looking at art?" Charlotte asked. Her tone was innocent, but I suspected she wanted more details than just *"looking at art."* "You two seemed awfully interested in that painting."

"Yes," I replied, just as innocently. "That painting is worth a lot more than he thought. We were simply discussing it."

"Oh, that's good." Her foot started bouncing in the air, and she chewed on her lip until she was unable to control her need for more gossip. "So, I think Bastian likes you," Charlotte blurted out. I immediately turned a deep, dark shade of crimson.

"Oh, come on, Charlotte-- me?" I laughed, but deep down I wanted it to be true. "I think you've had too much to drink and we're not even at the bar yet."

"What?" She grinned. "You don't think he's cute?"

I blushed even harder and she laughed.

"You *do* think he's cute!"

I rolled my eyes at her and pulled my hair back and out of my face, trying to relieve some of the heat. "What about you and whats-his-name? The one who doesn't know you exist?"

"Oh, no," she replied, holding out her hand as if that would stop my words. "We are not talking about me and Leo."

"Oh, Leo is it?" I teased, holding out the name for emphasis. "Bastian's business partner?"

"Damn it," she cursed quietly, narrowing her eyes and glaring at me. From up front, Elijah laughed. "Shut up, Elijah," Charlotte growled, kicking the front seat. It just made Elijah laugh harder and me worry about the leather with her shoes.

"We're here," Elijah said, pulling into the parking lot and stopping. It was a small dirt lot with an open air bar on one end with a restaurant and some small shops adjoining it. A dolphin statue stood in front of the restaurant, squirting water up into the sky and looking playful. It had all the charm of a small town bar and I already liked it.

Charlotte grabbed my arm and dragged me into the bar. It was nice and comfortable, but definitely full of more locals than tourists. Luckily, Charlotte headed to the back where it was open to the ocean, choosing a seat that was obviously her favorite.

The sun had set and twilight was twinkling across the warm waters of the Caribbean as the lights in the bar flickered to life. A server came up and grinned at Charlotte.

"We'll take two of the dinner specials and two drink specials," Charlotte told him. He didn't even write it down before heading off to the back. I looked over at her uncertain. I wasn't a picky eater, but Charlotte didn't know that about me yet.

"Trust me," Charlotte said, full of self confidence. "You'll love it. The restaurant next door is run by Lucia's sister who, if you can believe it, is actually an even better cook than Lucia."

"I'm not sure that's possible," I replied, which just made Charlotte grin wider.

"Plus, the drink special is this rum thing that they only make here. It's amazing and they have a two drink maximum, but you'll want more," Charlotte continued.

I decided to just go with it. I would have a lot more fun if I just let things happen instead of trying to control everything. I was just beginning to learn that I didn't even have as much control over the things I thought I did, anyway. This wasn't an appraisal. I could be spontaneous and have fun.

I relaxed back into my chair, looking out at the night falling across the water. It was beautiful. Looking in the other direction, I could see Elijah sitting at the bar drinking a soda and flirting with the bartender. He nodded when he saw me. I smiled back. He took his job seriously, but even he was going to have a good time.

"So, Leo, huh?" I asked, tucking my hand under my chin and watching Charlotte struggle not to turn bright red.

"I was really hoping you'd forget," she mumbled. "I need a drink."

"Tell me about him." I smiled, doing my best to charm her. She stared at me for a moment and then gave up her inner struggle.

"He's tall, dark, and handsome," she started, a cautious grin creeping on to her face as she thought about him. Her mouth twisted slightly. "And Bastian's business partner, so strictly off limits. Besides that, he thinks I'm just Bastian's minion. I'm not even sure he knows I'm female."

"Ouch," I replied. "At least you would look cute in those blue overalls."

Charlotte giggled as she shrugged. "Such is the life of a personal assistant. Now, you on the other hand..."

"No, no, no." I shook my head vehemently from side to side. "No."

"What?" She asked, her eyes going wide and innocent. "You're telling me you don't want to know that his favorite color is yellow or that he likes his eggs scrambled and orange juice without pulp?"

"No!" But I couldn't help it. I filed that information away and hoped I could use it at a later date. I couldn't let Charlotte know that, though, so I shook my head more fiercely, feeling my hair whip around my shoulders. Besides, he was a billionaire. He could date super models. He probably did date super models. Super models probably asked *him* out. Me? I got dumped for a big-chested blonde. He wouldn't want me. I wasn't anywhere near billionaire material.

"Charlotte, right now he's my employer. Even if I did think he was hot, and I'm not saying I do, I can't. Do you know what my dad would do if he ever found out I even thought of *flirting* with a client?"

"So you want to do more than just flirt, huh? What if he wasn't your client?" she pressed. I could see where her thoughts were going, and I couldn't stop the blush that seeped out from my spine and crawled up to my ears. The things I would do to him... The way those gray eyes would light up, and how he would smile at me...

I did my best to glare at Charlotte. I didn't trust myself to actually say anything. He was a billionaire and I wasn't even sure I was good enough to even think of dating.

"Fine, fine." She waved her hand through the air like she was giving up, but then leaned forward, a wicked gleam in her eyes. "He also likes two sugars and no cream in his coffee."

"Charlotte!"

"Just saying," she said with a all-too-knowing shrug. "It could be useful information."

I shook my head, exasperated. The worst part was that I wanted to know everything she told me. I wanted to know more. But he was my billionaire employer and I was fairly certain she was crazy. He could have anyone. Why would he want me?

"Do you try and set your brother up with every girl you meet?" I asked her, glancing around the bar and hoping our drinks came soon. I needed something stiff.

"Nope," Charlotte responded with a grin. "Just the ones that make him smile." She leaned forward conspiratorially. "I even caught him humming last night after he made you those sandwiches. He never hums unless he's really happy."

Unfounded hope surged in my chest and pressed against my ribs to the point of pain. I wanted to believe her. I wanted him to like me like I liked him.

"That could be anything," I said dismissively. As much as I wanted it to be true, I knew there were a million reasons for him to be smiling that didn't include me. "He could have just gotten a good weather report for his paddle-boarding the next day. Or his new paddle-board shipped from Billion-aire Paddle-boarders Emporium."

"Right..." Charlotte rolled her eyes at me like I was thick. "Sandwiches with a girl he won't stop staring at and the humming is all in my head. Seriously? Billionaire Paddle-boarders Emporium?"

She looked at me, begging me with her eyes to believe her. I wanted to. I wanted to believe that the billionaire had a crush on me.

"You really think he likes me?" I felt like a sixth grader. All I needed now was to pass her a note to give to him that read, *Do you like me? Yes or No?* I shrugged, trying to play it off. "Besides, he's said all of three words to me. And two of them were during my dad's heart attack."

Charlotte smiled and leaned back confidently in her chair. "My brother is a tough nut to crack. He has trouble trusting people. After his parents died, he didn't have anyone until he found me. And even then, it was him protecting me from the world. No one was there to protect him anymore."

I stared at the table in front of me, trying to figure out the riddle that was Sebastian Belrose. I had a girl with all the clues sitting in front of me, but I didn't dare ask. I wanted to find out his secrets from him.

Charlotte leaned forward and I looked up. "He's a great judge of character, but he's slow to trust. The fact that he made you that particular sandwich is actually a pretty big step for him. Honest. He likes you."

I opened my mouth, wanting her to explain how a sandwich was a big step. I wanted to believe her, but at the same time, I had been burned so badly in my last relationship that it was hard for me to believe that a sandwich meant something. Two years of love and devotion hadn't meant a damn thing, so I couldn't help but wonder what a sandwich did.

It was just then that the waiter arrived with our food and drinks. On the plate before me was some sort of pastry that smelled absolutely fantastic. I poked it with my fork, releasing steam and even more mouth-watering aromas.

"What is this?" I asked Charlotte, taking a careful bite. It was absolutely divine. The crust was light and fluffy while the inside was a curry-flavored beef that melted in my mouth. "It's so good!"

Charlotte grinned and stuffed a big bite into her mouth.

So much for her diet. "It's a Jamaican Patty," she explained through her mouthful of food. "They make them even better here than the ones in Jamaica."

I swallowed my bite and took a sip of the drink. Charlotte had been right to order for me. A combination of orange juice, rum, and a combination of fruit juices I couldn't decipher hit my mouth. It was strong, but I barely could taste it over the fruit juice. I could see why there was a two-drink maximum on them. It would be far too easy to drink them all night and never realize how much alcohol was in the glass.

"Amazing, right?" Charlotte asked, licking her lips. Somehow, the petite girl had managed to stuff almost the entire patty into her mouth.

"Mm hmm," I responded, not wanting to talk. All I wanted to do was shovel more food into my mouth, with possible breaks for more drink.

"So, anyway," Charlotte continued after a moment of chewing. "Bastian."

"Do I really want to know this?" I asked, pausing to take a sip of my drink.

"The last time he got close to someone, she ripped his heart out and stomped on it with cleats. He had fallen hard for her, but she was just stringing him along." She shrugged. "It was before he got rich, but he's the kind of guy that's good to have around so she led him on a leash. The two of them had very different goals. He wanted a family and she wanted fun."

"He wants a family?" My stomach did a little happy dance. I wanted a family. I had always wanted a family. Maybe a little bit of travel before having kids, but I wanted the white picket fence and everything that came with it. I wanted it, but my heart was still too fresh from being stomped on to believe I would ever get it.

"Yes, and from the stupid happy look on your face, you do too, so that's good." Charlotte took a big sip of her drink. "Anyway, the girl was sleeping around on him. Everyone saw it coming but him. It was a big part of how Kindling Dating was started."

"I thought you said he just did the logistics?" I stared down at my empty plate and wished I had more. That had been absolutely fantastic.

"Leo and Gabriel had the original idea, but he was the one who turned it into reality," Charlotte explained. I liked that she used her hands to talk. It made her easy to read. "He wanted to make sure that people found the people they were looking for instead of just randomly hoping to run into someone compatible."

"Does he use the service himself? I mean, if that was his goal..."

"Honestly, he's too busy," Charlotte replied. "We both are. And, since he deals with the inner workings of it all, he's rather jaded on the whole thing. It's lost a lot of it's magic for him."

"I could see how that could happen," I replied, licking my fingers. "He would see all the failures and why people didn't work out. It probably helps him make the whole thing work better."

"It does, but at a price," Charlotte admitted. "Honestly, I can't tell you how wonderful it is to see him look at a female and smile."

I rather liked him smiling at me, too. I took a sip of my drink, feeling a happy burn deep down in the pit of my stomach. "Enough about Bastian for now. Tell me about this

Leo person." I waggled my eyebrows at her, ready to find out more about her secret crush.

Charlotte's face paled and her eyes went wide as she looked into the bar behind me.

"Are you okay?" I set my drink down, thinking I had made a serious error. I wanted her to be my friend. "You don't have to talk about him if you don't want to."

"No, no..." she whispered, shaking her head but staring past me. "He's here."

"What?" I turned to see an attractive man in nice khaki's and a polo shirt walking up to the bar and greeting Elijah. He was tall, but well built with untamed hair and big eyes. He was definitely a looker.

"Oh, he's cute," I murmured appreciatively.

"He's mine," Charlotte growled. As soon as she said the words, her eyes went wider and she clapped two hands over her mouth.

"Relax, tiger." I giggled, a little loopy from the alcohol in my drink. "I'm still gun shy and he's not my type."

Charlotte dropped her hands. "Oh, god. He's coming this way..."

I giggled again. For being a spitfire billionaire's assistant who seemed like she could handle anything, a cute guy walking in her direction sure had her vexed.

"Hello ladies," said the man, coming up to our table. Charlotte looked like she might throw up. "May I join you? I don't want to intrude, but it's a busy night at the bar."

I looked around to see that every table had a patron. Considering how good my drink was, I wasn't surprised.

"You're not intruding at all," I replied smoothly. Charlotte's eyes were about ready to pop out of their sockets. "Please join us."

I heard a metallic ping and Charlotte's lips thinned. I

tried not to giggle, but I realized she had meant to kick me and had kicked the table instead. Served her right.

"Are you okay, Charlotte?" Leo asked, pulling out a chair and siting down.

"Fine," she replied, her voice just a little too squeaky as she glared daggers in my direction. "I just bit my tongue."

"I'm Ava, by the way," I said, holding out my hand across the table and smiling. "You must be Leo."

He stood to shake my hand, like a gentleman, and I immediately liked him even more. "Ava Fairchild? The woman who is running the appraisal at the mansion?"

"That's me." I smiled as he sat back down. "I'm glad to finally meet you, Leo. Charlotte has only nice things to say about you."

The kick from Charlotte connected this time, her heel digging into my shin. I managed to keep a grim smile as I glared at her. Those heels were truly wicked. She glared right back as we faced off in a silent battle of eyes.

"Have you eaten?" I asked, tearing my eyes away from Charlotte. "The special here is amazing."

"I have actually, but thank you," he replied politely, apparently oblivious to the kicks Charlotte was sending me under the table.

"What are you doing here?" Charlotte's voice came out squeaky and incredibly high. I was surprised Leo heard her at all. If he didn't know that she had the world's biggest crush on him, then he had to be the most oblivious man on the planet.

"I was in the neighborhood," he replied nonchalantly. "And since I was coming out for the auction anyway, I thought I might come a few days early."

"You flew out to a remote Caribbean island two weeks

early because it was in the neighborhood? I want your job." Damn, those drinks were stronger than I realized.

Leo looked over at me in surprise.

"Sorry." I held up my empty drink. "Watch out, these things are strong."

"I think I actually need another," Charlotte said quickly. She raised her hand and caught the waiter's attention, signaling for another round.

Leo glanced back and forth between the two of us, obviously evaluating the sanity of staying with us. I couldn't blame him. We both looked a little crazy.

"That and with the new app launch, I figured it would be one less conference call with Bastian," he explained, making the trip sound a little more logical. "Gabe is ready to murder both of us because we keep messing up the video feeds."

Charlotte laughed, but it came out far too loud and forced. I could barely believe how nervous she was. The waiter set down two drinks, one in front of me and the other in front of Charlotte. She immediately sucked down half of hers in one anxious gulp. It didn't help that her phone started to ring.

"Here, Leo. Have mine. I haven't even finished my first one yet." I pushed my new drink over to Leo as Charlotte held the phone up to her ear and hissed into it. Her embarrassed expression turned to worry.

"Ava, it's for you," she said, holding the phone out to me.

"Excuse me," I replied, taking the phone and standing up. I went to the corner next to the water where the sounds of the bar were just a little quieter, but I still had to press my finger into my ear to hear. "This is Ava."

"Miss Fairchild? This is Dr. Verner."

It was as if I were dunked in ice water. All the warm

tipsiness of the alcohol was gone and suddenly all the colors in the room were too bright and yet had no color.

"Is my dad okay?" I whispered.

"He's having another episode." Dr. Verner's voice was calm, and that was good. If he had sounded even the littlest bit stressed, I would have screamed. "I doubt we'll even have to shock his system, but I wanted to keep you apprised of the situation."

"Episode..." I gasped, trying to comprehend what was going on. It was hard to breathe.

"I'm fine, Ava," my dad shouted from the background. "The doctor is just being cautious, sweetie. Don't worry about me!"

"Should I be there?" I asked. Panic rolled in my stomach, threatening to bring everything back up. Dinner didn't taste so good anymore.

"He's doing fine at the moment," Dr. Verner assured me. "I can speak with you in the morning."

I looked over at Charlotte and Leo sitting at the table. They looked so blissful, with Charlotte turning a fantastic shade of crimson and purple as she attempted to speak with Leo. She looked happy, though. I knew I would be the most miserable company if I stayed.

"I'll be there in just a little bit, " I promised. I would worry and fret if I stayed. Better for me to go home where at least I could see the cause of my worry. "Thank you, doctor."

I hung up the phone, staring at it for a moment and holding onto the railing overlooking the ocean. My knuckles went white and I had to force my lungs to inhale. This couldn't be happening. Not again.

I walked back to the table in a daze. Charlotte looked up, her face full of concern. "What's wrong?"

"That was Dr. Verner," I whispered. I didn't want to say

the words aloud. If I didn't say them, maybe they wouldn't be true. Maybe my dad would just be sitting at home playing on his tablet and be totally fine. "He's at the house with Dad."

Charlotte's knees banged against the table as she stood up. "Holy crap, Ava..."

"He's fine," I assured her quickly. "But I'm going to head back home. If I stay, I'll just be a giant ball of worry that sucks the fun out of everything."

Charlotte didn't pause. "I'll come with you."

I smiled at her, knowing that she really was my friend. She was willing to give up a night with her crush to come hang out with her freaked out friend and her dad.

"No, please don't let me ruin your night as well," I pleaded. "Dr. Verner says he's fine, but I'm just a worrier. Please stay."

Charlotte frowned. I could see the conflicting desires in her eyes as she weighed her options. She wanted to do both but I could see her leaning towards me and I couldn't allow that.

"Leo, will you please make sure my friend stays and has a nice time tonight?" I asked, turning to appeal to Leo. "It's her evening off and I don't want it ruined on my account."

Leo nodded. "I'll make sure she has a wonderful time and gets home safely. You go be with your father."

"Thank you," I said, picking up my things from the table. "It was really nice to meet you."

"At least let me walk you out," Charlotte begged. I nodded, heading toward the exit while Leo held the table for her return. Seeing our motion, Elijah put some money on the bar counter and met us at the door.

Standing outside the bar in the warm night air, I felt

better. I was glad I wasn't staying, but I was disappointed to miss out on the rest of our girl's night.

"Are you sure?" Charlotte asked again. "I don't want you to be alone."

"I won't be alone," I promised. "I'll be with Dr. Verner and my dad. You stay." I took her hands in mine and smiled. "I really, *really* appreciate the offer, but I want you to stay here. Stay with Leo."

Charlotte bit her lip. "You're really sure?"

"Yes." I grinned at her. "Drink too much and kiss that man. Please."

Charlotte giggled, lightening my heart a little.

"How much do I owe you for dinner, Charlotte?" I asked, reaching for my purse. She stopped me halfway through the motion.

"Nothing. My treat."

I hugged her. I had known her for three days and I loved her to pieces already. I hoped she had the time of her life with Leo and finally got to make something of her crush. I couldn't wait to hear all about it in the morning.

I turned to look for Elijah, and saw him standing further down the porch talking to another man. If two men could look anything more like hunting lions, I would have eaten my shoe. I was very glad that at least one of them was on my side as Elijah strode back over.

"I'll take you home, Ava," Elijah said. "Murdoch will watch Charlotte until I get back."

I looked over at the other big man. He had to be Leo's bodyguard. The man looked just as competent as Elijah and possibly more deadly. Bastian wouldn't be able to complain about that.

"Okay, let's get going," I replied. I gave Charlotte another hug. "Thank you again. I'm so sorry to ruin girl's night."

"Not your fault," she replied, hugging me back. "It just means we'll have to do it again. Give your dad a hug from me and keep me updated." She held up her phone. "I'll be there in two seconds if you need me. Okay?"

"Thank you," I said, meaning it from the very tips of my toes.

Elijah put his hand on my shoulder and guided me to the waiting Lamborghini. Charlotte waited to go back inside until the car rolled out of the lot. I sincerely hoped that she had the time of her life with Leo. It would make such a wonderful story for something like love to come out of my leaving early. I was still incredibly touched that she was willing to leave with me, though. She was a real friend.

Elijah handled the car with ease and even sped just a little. Not enough to get in trouble or pulled over, but just enough that it made the ride home that much faster. Even with that, I was still a nervous mess when he pulled up to the front of the house to drop me off.

"Take care, Ava," he said, waiting for me to exit the car so he could go back to Charlotte.

"Thanks, Elijah," I replied and then quickly turned and ran into the house to find my dad.

CHAPTER 13

*L*ight fluttered on my face and woke me from an unpleasant dream. In my dream, Dad and Bastian were sitting on the beach, but Chad kept chasing me away from them. No matter how much I ran, he never let me get to them. Then the flying pineapples came, and I was just glad I had woken up.

I stretched my arms up over my head, but they caught on the arm rest of the couch. I sat up slowly, my back groaning and complaining as I shifted my weight and figured out where I was.

I was on the couch in the room with the Morisot painting. I didn't remember falling asleep, but my computer was tucked up neatly on a coffee table with the rest of my gadgets and supplies and there was a light blue blanket draped over me.

I scrubbed my face with my hands, feeling dirty and exhausted. I still had on the same clothes from the bar the night before. The last thing I remembered was sitting down on the couch to try and get some work done while Dad rested. I had thought I was too ramped up on worry to sleep, but apparently I had been wrong.

I looked down at the blanket and knew I hadn't brought it to the room. Someone else must have come by and seen me passed out on the couch and covered me up. I smiled. It was probably Charlotte. She'd be that sweet.

I stretched again, feeling the bones in my spine attempting to realign themselves. For being such an expensive couch, it wasn't that comfortable and I had slept poorly. I stood up and shook my legs out before hurrying down the hallway to my father's room.

I slowly opened the door and peeked inside. My dad was asleep in the giant bed, still attached to the monitors while Dr. Verner snored gently in a big reclining chair beside him. The monitor beeped softly and steadily. No charges had been given.

I closed the door and sagged against it. Last night, Dr. Verner had said my father needed to go to the mainland hospital today. Bastian had already granted Dr. Verner access to his private jet to do so. I wished I was going with them, but dad had insisted I stay. I had to finish the job. He promised he'd be fine and Dr. Verner promised hourly updates. I was hesitant on both their promises, but I said I would stay.

If I didn't finish the job, Fairchild Auctions and Appraisals would be finished, and that really would kill my dad. I didn't really have much of a choice.

The front door rattled and I heard a curse before the door slammed. I walked quickly down the hall to see who was making such a ruckus. Charlotte stumbled in, looking hungover and absolutely miserable.

It took me a moment to hurry down the staircase to where Charlotte sagged in the main entrance. Her dress was lopsided and her long brown hair was pulled back, but terribly messy.

"How'd it go?" I asked cautiously, moving slow so I didn't startle her.

"It didn't," she mumbled. She closed her eyes and sighed.

"What happened?" I took her hand and started leading her toward the kitchen. She looked like she needed a cup of coffee and a hot bath.

"After you left, I was so nervous, I chugged my drink," she explained. Her voice caught. "I puked all over him about thirty minutes later."

"Oh no!" I exclaimed, feeling absolutely awful for her. That was not at all what I had hoped would happen.

She looked up at me, the morning light glinting off her pallid skin. "How is it that I can handle Bastian's incredibly complex scheduling needs and telling investors to go suck it, but the minute I see Leo, I turn into a mush-brain?" She paused and then sobbed. "And now I'm hung over, too."

"Let's get you some coffee," I coaxed, pulling her toward the kitchen. She collapsed at the wooden table and cradled her head in her hands as I looked around the kitchen for coffee.

It only took me a moment to find it, as everything was neatly organized. I could see Bastian's hand in the kitchen. It made sense to me now that the kitchen felt homey while the rest of the house didn't. This was where Bastian spent his time, and thus he had redecorated it to suit his tastes. I certainly liked his tastes better than the stuffy, overdone opulence of the rest of the house. There was such a thing as too much luxury.

I opened up the fridge and pantry, finding eggs and a

coconut while the coffee brewed. I was going to make poor Charlotte something that would make her feel better.

"Thank you for the blanket last night," I told her as I started the stove. "I can't believe I fell asleep on the couch."

"What are you talking about?" Charlotte half raised her head from her beneath her arms to look at me, but her gaze was unfocused. "Leo brought me home and I passed out in the guest house. I'm surprised I'm even moving right now."

"Leo brought you home?" Bastian repeated, striding into the kitchen. He was wearing a full suit again, this time in a beautiful gray charcoal that made the blue in his eyes pop. His hair was still wet from his morning swim and it made butterflies fill my stomach. "That explains why you didn't answer your phone this morning and why Elijah was such a grouch this morning."

"Hangry," I supplied, and Bastian nodded. Considering the way Elijah had wolfed down his sandwich the other morning, I could only imagine how grumpy the bodyguard would be without one. Especially after being out all night.

"Yeah, Leo brought me home, but only after I puked on him," Charlotte groaned, putting her head back down. He sat down at the table next to her and wrapped his arm around her shoulder. His face was creased with concern and brotherly love. It completely melted my heart and made me like him that much more because he so obviously cared for his little sister. Despite the initially cold exterior, he had a warm and caring heart.

I realized that he must have been the one to put the blanket over me last night, and I nearly turned into a puddle on the floor. Dad and Dr. Verner hadn't left the room all night, and Charlotte had been out puking on Leo. He was the only one who had been home.

To distract myself from turning into complete mush, I

turned to start cooking up the eggs. I remembered that Bastian liked his scrambled and I stirred the yolks before I could stop myself. I hoped he was hungry, because scrambled eggs were one of the few things I actually knew how to cook well.

"Would you like some eggs, Bastian?" I asked, thrilling at his name. It was silly and I knew it. I was crushing hard, but I couldn't help it. At least I hadn't made out with my pillow, imagining it was him. *Yet.*

He held up two fingers. "Two please. I didn't get my sandwich this morning, either." I added a couple more eggs into the pan, letting them melt into the butter while I added my seasonings. Then, it was just to keep stirring them until they were done.

I picked up the unopened coconut. "Do either of you know where a nail is?" I asked after a moment of searching. "The milk will make you feel better, Charlotte. It's one of the best re-hydrating liquids around."

Charlotte groaned, burying her head further into her arms. Bastian gave her shoulders a gentle squeeze before he stood up. "Here, I'll do it."

He came around the center island, holding out his hand for the coconut. My own hand shook a little as I gave it to him, and I froze as he reached behind me, his hand going just past me, close enough to touch my hip but not quite. I could smell his shampoo, fresh and clean and I could barely stand it.

He pulled back, a wine corkscrew in his hand. I wondered if he knew just what his presence was doing to me, and he grinned. He knew. Those eyes seemed to always know. With practiced ease, he "uncorked" the coconut and poured the milk into a glass, setting the rest of the coconut on the counter for later.

Bastian set the glass of coconut milk in front of Charlotte. She raised her head just enough to look at it sideways, turning a little bit green in the process.

"Drink up," Bastian said cheerfully. "You have work to do today."

Charlotte pouted, but dutifully took a sip before putting her head back into her arms. Bastian winked at me, and I giggled as I finished cooking the eggs. He wasn't going to actually make her work, but he wasn't going to tell her that.

The silence as we waited for the eggs was comfortable, as if mornings like this were how things were supposed to be. I let out a happy sigh and just let myself enjoy it for a moment. If I closed my eyes, I wasn't working, or worrying about Dad, or rushing to meet a deadline. I was just making breakfast for people I cared about. I was where I was supposed to be.

The eggs finished and I scooped them onto the plates, leaving some in the pan. I had made far too many, but I figured I would just bring some up to Dad or eat them myself later. Bastian was sitting next to Charlotte, so I put my plate across from her and sat down to eat.

Charlotte peeked one eye up over her forearm and glared at the plate. "I hate food."

"Eat it," Bastian coaxed. "It will make you feel better."

With a pained expression, she took a tiny bite of egg and then put her head back on the table. Bastian and I made eye contact and I couldn't help but giggle. Poor Charlotte. She was absolutely miserable.

"Smells good down here," Dr. Verner announced, entering the kitchen. His dress shirt, this time a light green, was wrinkled, but he looked remarkably awake for having slept in a chair all night. His short brown hair stuck up at odd angles, but had damp spots from where he had obviously tried to smooth it down.

Just seeing him made me think of my father. Worry hit me like a physical punch in the stomach. "How is he?"

"Still sleeping," Dr. Verner answered, going to the coffee pot and getting himself a cup. "Our flight is scheduled for noon and I'd like him to rest as much as possible until then. We have a busy day once we get to the hospital."

I swallowed hard against the growing tightness in my chest. I felt like a terrible daughter for not going with them. Seeing my face, Bastian reached across the table and squeezed my hand. The butterflies that lived in my stomach didn't know whether to continue being worried about Dad, or if they should jump and dance because Bastian touched me.

"Thank you, Dr. Verner. I appreciate you taking care of him," I whispered. I looked up and into Bastian's gray eyes. "And Bastian, I don't know how we'll ever repay you."

"No need," he assured me, giving my hand a gentle squeeze before letting go.

"What about me?" Charlotte asked, her words muffled as her head was still wrapped in her arms.

"Thank you for being such a good friend, Charlotte," I told her, patting her elbow. She made a noise that sounded happy. It made me smile and shake my head.

"Would you like some eggs, Dr. Verner?" I asked, looking at Charlotte's rapidly cooling plate. "I made too many and it doesn't look like Charlotte's going to eat hers."

"I'd love some. And she should eat them." Dr. Verner sat down in the empty chair beside me. "The cysteine in the eggs breaks down acetaldehyde, the yucky headache-causing chemical that's left over when the liver breaks down whatever you had last night."

Charlotte looked up. "Give me the eggs, Ava. Give me all the eggs."

I laughed and pushed her plate toward her before getting up to put the extra eggs on a plate for Dr. Verner. He attacked them like a starving man, leaving Charlotte holding her fork above her own plate and staring at it like she was preparing for battle.

"These are wonderful," Dr. Verner congratulated me, snarfing down the eggs.

"Agreed," Bastian added. I was glad to see his plate was empty. "Best eggs I've had in a long time."

I blushed slightly at the compliment. I took a bite myself and decided that they were pretty good. Maybe not my best batch ever, but pretty close. Charlotte's phone started to ring, vibrating and skittering along the wooden table. She grabbed it and just slid it over to Bastian stuffing a bite of eggs into her mouth before she could think about it.

Bastian rolled his eyes, but answered the phone. "This is Bastian. Hi Leo... yeah, she's alive. Your favorite shirt, huh?" He stood up and covered the phone with his hand. "Please excuse me."

The room felt empty despite being full of people when he left. Dr. Verner stood and put his empty plate in the sink before coming back over to me and putting his hand on my shoulder. "I'm going to go get everything ready for our flight. If you need anything, let me know."

"Thank you, doctor," I replied, pushing the eggs around on my plate. I knew I needed to eat, but I just wasn't hungry anymore. He patted my shoulder gently before heading out the door and leaving me with Charlotte.

Her head was back on the table and she wasn't moving. I poked her arm and she started to snore. I shook my head and made sure her hair was pulled back out of her face before taking her plate to the sink. At least she had managed to keep the two bites of eggs down.

I sat down at the table again, knowing I needed to finish my breakfast and get a cup of coffee in me so I could get going. I had a long day ahead of me, and if Charlotte could at least get her eggs down, so could I.

CHAPTER 14

The house was eerily quiet as I tiptoed down the empty hall. I could still see as moonlight flooded the windows with her mystic light, but it still felt dark and lonesome. I paused by the room that had been my fathers and stopped to peek inside. There was nothing of his left and the bed was made back into magazine perfection.

I already missed my dad. I had gone with him to the airport and said my goodbyes, but I felt like the worst daughter in the world. My father was going to the hospital because his heart didn't work properly, yet I was staying in the Caribbean at a mansion. It didn't feel right, yet I knew it was how things had to be. I had to finish this project, or we would never be able to pay his medical bills and we would lose the business.

I sighed, going to the window. The waves lapped at the moonlit shore in regular intervals, reminding me of a creature breathing. I thought about going outside, but a glass of wine sounded better. I had left a bottle down in the kitchen from dinner, and now it was calling my name.

The kitchen was dark. Everyone was in bed except for

me. I couldn't sleep, but my brain refused to concentrate on work. I had worked since returning from the airport until Charlotte forced me to eat something. She was the one who had given me the wine. I had worked after dinner, but now that it was long past bed time, I couldn't work anymore.

My brain was just too full.

My phone chirped with an email update as I poured a large glass of the dark red liquid. While I didn't use my data or phone plan, the mansion had wifi. Dr. Verner sent me his hourly email updates, though now they were from my dad's hospital nurse and just read, *Fast asleep* or *snoring softly*. I would have to thank his nurse as one message had read: *I came in to check his vitals and and he called me Jackie. Jackie is a lucky lady.* At least I knew good people were taking care of him.

I swirled the wine around in the glass, watching it trickle back down with slow, long legs. I couldn't sit still, even in the warm kitchen, so I decided to explore the mansion on my own.

The wood floors were cool on my bare feet. The house felt different at night, like the paintings were waiting for me to turn my back so they could come alive. It wasn't creepy so much as I felt like I didn't belong. It didn't help that so many of them were overly lavish and displayed in garish frames that accentuated their worth rather than their beauty.

I walked up the stairs to the second floor, and banged my hip against a gilded table. I sighed and gazed down the second floor hallway at gilded frames and overly ornate furniture. Everything in this house was designed to proclaim wealth, but from what I had seen of Bastian and Charlotte, neither cared about flaunting their money. They should be living in something full of bamboo furniture and open windows. There was too much finery and not enough warmth for them here.

I turned and found myself standing in front of Bastian's study doors.

I was curious. What did it look like inside? Was it opulent and rich like the walls of the mansion, or warm and homey like the kitchen? I felt like if I could see how he decorated his living space, I would have some insight into him. I knew so little about him, but I wanted to know more with a desperation that surprised me.

I set my empty wine glass on an overly ornate hallway table and listened for any noise in the study. If I heard him inside, I could just knock and perhaps he would let me in. I rather liked the idea of being invited in.

Without thinking, I tried the door handle. It swung open on silent hinges and I stared after it with an open mouth. Standing in the hallway, I heard a loud thud come from inside, as if something heavy had been dropped.

I swallowed hard and justified going inside. What if he had fallen like my dad?

Just past the doors, I could hear the shower running and Bastian cursing at his shampoo bottle. I nearly giggled before catching myself. The wine was making me bold and careless, but it was still funny to hear him swear at the bottle.

The idea of Bastian wet and soapy, and totally naked, made my insides flutter and the space between my legs tighten. A naughty part of me wanted to go and take a peek, just a glimpse, but I pushed it down. I was already someplace I shouldn't be. No need to push it, no matter how much I wanted to see his muscles dripping with soap.

I knew I should leave, but I took a moment and looked around the office. It was a large room, as all the rooms in the mansion were, but it didn't feel overwhelming. Every light was on and the walls were painted a warm butter yellow that made it almost feel like daytime. A large, heavy wooden desk sat in the corner with a computer and a comfortable-looking leather chair. Nothing was antique or gilded in the entire room. Every piece of furniture was expensive only because it was well-made. He had chosen things that utilized function over form.

A big leather couch sat under the wide open window. The curtains billowed in the breeze off the ocean, and I could imagine laying on that couch and reading for hours. Looking closer, I realized that the blanket from this morning was draped on the arm. It had been him.

Smiling, I looked at the pictures on his wall. There was no artwork and for the most part, the walls were bare, but above his desk was a cork board filled with smiling people. Most of them were of him and Charlotte in various places around the world. The Great Wall of China, The Eiffel Tower, the Pyramids, Stonehenge, The Taj Mahal and dozens of others. He smiled in all of them.

In the center was a long picture with a row of men in dark suits all smiling and laughing with a beautiful bride at the end of the line. Looking closer, I recognized the woman as Emma Saunders, the wife of oil baron Jack Saunders. Faces popped out at me from Forbes magazine's most wealthy as I looked down the line. That must have been a crazy wedding.

Other than one small picture of him, Charlotte and a kind looking couple, there were no pictures of family or childhood. Every picture was college aged or above. I even spotted several of him with Leo and another man that must be Gabriel, but nothing that hinted at his life before starting his company.

Moving away from the wall, I saw one last picture. It was on his desk in a simple golden frame that couldn't have cost more than a couple of dollars. It was a picture of him and Charlotte, sitting on a boat. The sun was in his face but he was smiling just like he had the other morning, looking like he might burst into laughter at any moment. I reached out a finger to stroke his face, wishing I could see him like that.

"What the hell are you doing in here?" An angry growl came from behind me. I spun to see Bastian standing in the doorway to the bathroom. He was dripping wet with just a precarious towel wrapped around his waist. He was even more glorious than I had imagined.

That's when I realized the water had stopped.

He stepped forward and into the light of the room. Scars ravaged his body. Long gashes ran across his arms and chest before wrapping around his back to disappear beneath the towel. The scar on his cheek was just part of a larger series of scars covering his body. I could see now why he wore long sleeves and pants all the time.

Rage burned red in his gray-blue eyes. I couldn't look away from his body, not because of the scars, but because of the way his muscles tightened and flexed and how the towel hid almost nothing. Pecs to die for, six pack abs and a strong V that pointed to his towel all had me drooling.

"I... I... heard a thud... and..." I stammered, unable to take my eyes from the towel. The knot was loose and was about to fall apart at any moment.

I took a step back, running into his heavy desk. It hurt enough that I looked up from his towel and into his extremely angry face. He radiated a rage that I didn't know was possible in a human being. He had seemed so calm and in control that I barely recognized him. All thoughts of the towel disappeared at his rage.

"Get out." His voice was thick with fury and his eyes flashed lightning. "GET OUT!"

I ran.

I didn't stop in the hallway. I didn't stop on the stairs. Even in the foyer, I could hear him cursing. The whole house vibrated with his anger and I ran out to the beach to try and escape it.

Tears stung at my eyes as my feet hit the sand. *What had I done?* Why didn't I just leave things well enough alone? He had one request of me, not to go in the study, and I had blatantly disregarded it. I was the worst kind of person and he had every right to be furious with me. Hell, I was furious with me.

I ran along the cold, wet sand, letting the full moon light my path. I followed the curve of the cove, up the hill to another beach until I finally came to a rock outcropping that I couldn't get past, at least not in bare feet. There I collapsed into one of the larger rocks, my calves aching and twitching like rubber bands. I gasped for breath, and not just from the running. Falling to my knees, I sobbed into the sand.

It was too much. All of it was just too much. All the aches, the worry, the tension, the hopeless dreams came tumbling down on me. Between my father, Chad's betrayal, the lack of direction in my life, and now the rage in Bastian's eyes, I just lost it. It was all just too much to bare.

I sat and cried into the night. It felt good to finally let it all out. I cried until I couldn't breathe and then I just gasped at the air like a fish out of water. Giant sobs racked my body, shuddering cries that ached down through my toes. But it was what I needed.

I wasn't sure how long I cried, but after a while, the tears dried and I stared out at the ocean. I was finally empty. I had held in my emotions for so long that they had overwhelmed me and now I didn't know what to do.

I heard footsteps behind me, but I didn't turn around. I knew who they belonged to. The steps paused and then came closer.

Bastian sat cautiously beside me, close enough that I could feel his presence but far enough away to give me distance. He stared out at the moonlit water for a moment before offering me a hanky. It was just a simple white cotton square of fabric, but it smelled like him. It was more than I deserved.

Holding on to his hanky, I held my breath for as long as I could before finally releasing it. My lungs ached and my cheeks were still wet.

"I'm sorry," I said quietly. I didn't look over at him. "I didn't mean to pry."

He let out a long slow breath.

"I let my temper get the best of me," he replied after a long moment.

"I shouldn't have been in there." I shook my head, looking only at the white hanky in my hands. "I always seem to be walking into rooms that I shouldn't."

A breeze rolled over us from off the ocean. I shivered, not just because the breeze was cool for the Caribbean, but from emotional exhaustion as well.

"Come here," Bastian commanded, his arms wrapping around me, holding me close to his heart and warming me up. I leaned my head against his shoulder, and he pressed his cheek into the top of my head. He was so warm and strong that I clung to him like a child. I felt completely safe with him holding me, like the world could crumble into a million pieces, but with him holding me, I would be safe.

"I liked the pictures above your desk," I said quietly after a moment. I figured there was no reason to hide what I had done now. I wanted to ask him about the scars, but given that he was now wearing pants and a long-sleeved t-shirt, they obviously were something he didn't want people knowing about.

I felt his lips curl into a smile above my hair. "I like them, too."

"I recognized Leo in some of them. Is the man in the others Gabriel?" I felt my muscles finally relaxing. "The three of you look close."

I felt him nod and he began to stroke my hair. "Yes, all the pictures on my wall are of my family." He shifted his weight, getting more comfortable. "After my parent's car accident, I didn't have anyone. My parents didn't even have wills made up. I went into the foster system. I had a decent family, but they weren't mine. Charlotte was the closest thing to family I had until Gabe moved in next door. I spent more time at Gabe's house than I did at my foster's. Then we met Leo our freshmen year of college."

"What school did you go to?" I asked. He smelled so good, especially this close. Clean yet masculine. "Billionaire Harvard or Billionaire Yale?"

"Neither. I went to a state school I had a partial scholarship, but I still had to work full time to pay it off." He shifted his back against the rock, finding a more comfortable position. "I wasn't a billionaire then."

"You said you met Leo in college? Is that where you guys came up with your business?" I asked, snuggling deeper into his arms. He was so warm that I never wanted to leave.

"Just after graduation is when we came up with the idea. We all had degrees in business but no ideas on how to use them." He shrugged. "So we made our own. Charlotte helped."

I thought of Charlotte trying to be in the same room as Leo to start a business. I wondered if she had even been able to get three words out. "You know Charlotte's crazy about Leo, right?"

"I know." He chuckled, the warm sound vibrating through his chest and into mine. "He's actually crazy about her, too. Why do you think he flew out so early? They've been circling each other like scared cats for years now."

"And then she puked on him. Poor Charlotte," I said softly into his chest.

"I have a feeling they'll end up all right in the end," he assured me. "You can't find anyone more loyal than Leo."

I shivered again as the cool breeze came off the water. It was well past midnight, and I was exhausted. Bastian pulled me in closer, rubbing his palms against my bare arms to warm me up. I was glad he didn't ask me to go in. I liked it better out here in his arms.

"How's your dad doing?" he asked. I knew he suspected it was part of why I was so upset.

"He's fine," I replied. "They're running tests. I started looking up what each one does, but I stopped when each one scared me more."

He hugged me tighter. "I'm sorry."

"I just can't imagine life without him." My breath caught. "I mean, I know I'll have to eventually, but I always imagined it when I'm old and my own children are grown."

I suddenly remembered that he had already lost his parents. He had already lived this nightmare and here I was complaining when I still had my dad. He didn't have anyone. "I'm sorry," I stammered, trying to pull back. "I didn't mean..."

"No, you're right," he said softly, keeping me pressed up against him. "We're supposed to lose them when they're old and sick, not when they're young and vibrant. If anything, I understand more than anyone why you don't want to lose him."

"Thank you," I said softly, returning to my nook within his arms. "Thank you for taking care of us. I promise I'll repay you." I stopped and thought about how I would ever afford such a thing. "You don't have to pay us for this appraisal."

"No," he said firmly. "You will get paid."

"But..."

"I have Dr. Verner on retainer," he explained. "I've already paid for his services."

"But..." I still felt like we were taking advantage.

"And as you are so fond of pointing out, I am a billionaire after all," he reminded me. He moved so that he could look me in the face, his gray eyes bright and the moonlight frosting the tips of his hair. The corners of my mouth twitched upwards. "There, I knew there was a smile in there."

I smiled a little bigger. He was serious. And so wonderful that I wanted to cry again.

"Now, tell me about the painting you were looking at yesterday," he commanded, pulling me back to his chest. "Tell me about your Paris plans."

I knew he was just trying to take my mind of my worries and I loved him for it. I felt warm and gooey inside because he had remembered our conversion. Like it had mattered to him. Chad had never asked me about it, and my Dad had heard it all so many times that he had long ago stopped asking. I relaxed into him, pressing my cheek against his chest and feeling the rise and fall of his lungs, and then I began to tell him my dreams.

CHAPTER 15

Water splashed at my feet, waking me from the most amazing dream. I had dreamt that I had fallen asleep in Bastian's arms, telling him all my dreams. It had been wonderful.

And then I realized it wasn't a dream. I was out on the beach, wrapped up in Bastian's arms with our back against a big rock and the ocean rolling towards us. I shifted slightly, feeling the grit of the sand beneath my calves. The water was cool and made me shiver a little, but Bastian was warm beside me.

"Morning, sleepy-head," he said softly. His voice was gravelly, as if he too had talked too much before falling asleep. I loved the idea of sleeping with him, the both of us wandering the world of dreams together.

Pre-dawn light filled the sky with gray promise. Soon the pinks and golds of sunrise would peek up over the horizon and banish the remaining stars from the sky. I couldn't remember when I had fallen asleep, but I knew I hadn't slept for very long. The two of us had talked for hours, and my sore, overused throat attested to not enough rest.

"You're going to miss your paddle-board session," I murmured, looking up at the sky. Pink was now the dominant color.

"This makes it worth missing," he whispered, nuzzling my hair and breathing in the scent of my shampoo.

I took in a deep contented breath. Bastian was warm and strong behind me and the waves were soothing. This was a perfect moment.

I turned to smile at Bastian, wanting to share in the morning's perfection. He was so beautiful that I couldn't help but stare. His eyes matched the sky behind him, a gray with just enough blue to make it soft. Even the scar along his cheek was softened in the morning light.

"Do you always go out at the dawn?" I asked, memorizing his face.

"I like seeing the world come up new." He nodded, his eyes going to the horizon and waiting there for something to happen. "The light washes everything and gives a fresh start. It's the end of the dark." He dropped his eyes back from the horizon to look at me. "It's the one time of day that I feel like anything is possible."

I smiled, reaching up to touch his cheek. He had a light stubble, but I didn't mind. I wondered how he didn't see how much he made possible every day. He had accomplished so much. He had come from a bad situation and made the impossible happen. It made my heart ache that he still felt he needed the sunrise to banish the dark.

My fingers touched the scar running down his face, grazing the raised skin. He froze and I tried to pull away, but instead he captured my hand in his and pressed my palm to his cheek.

"You haven't asked about them," he said quietly, his gray eyes serious and full of shadow.

I looked down, trying to avoid his eyes and instead seeing the lines of past pain hiding under his shirt collar. "I didn't want to be rude," I mumbled. I figured they were something in his past that he didn't want to talk about, especially not to some random girl.

"Ask," he commanded. I looked up, unsure if he meant it. The sky was turning a pale violet behind him, but his eyes were clear and he still had my palm pressed to his cheek.

I swallowed hard. "How did you get them? What happened?"

"The car accident that killed my parents-- I was in the backseat." His eyes never wavered from mine, though they did take on a distance. "None of us were wearing our seat belts and we all flew through the windshield."

His words were even but his voice wasn't, as if he had rehearsed its telling a million times but this was the first time he had ever actually said it aloud. He released my hand, shifting his body so that he could pull his shirt off. Jagged lines marred his smooth skin, highlighting just where the broken glass of the windshield had ripped his small body to pieces.

I stared for a moment, trying to take in the pain. The scars were old now, but they held an ache that would never go away. They were a constant reminder of what had happened. Of his loss. I tentatively touched one, right above his heart. He didn't shy away and I looked up.

His jaw was tight, in fact every muscle in his body was tight. Vulnerability shone in his eyes as he gazed back at me. He was trusting me not to hurt him.

The first glimmer of sunlight burst over the horizon, casting him in a warm golden glow. His skin, scars and perfection, lit up in the most beautiful shades of the sunrise.

My fingers traced the darkened skin of a scar up his

chest, up to his cheek. Our eyes met and I knew my world was about to spin out of control in the most amazing way. My chest tightened with anticipation and breathing no longer seemed important.

His hand was on the back of my neck with his fingers tangling in my hair. He pulled me toward him, pausing just a breath away. Our lips hovered apart for an infinity, sharing a breath in the moment, knowing that we could never go back to the way we were after this.

I closed the last centimeter, pressing my lips into his. His lips were so soft against mine that I forgot entirely what I was doing.

He pulled back, a smile crossing his handsome face before pulling me into him. It was a no-holds-barred, rock-my-world kiss that left me unable to do anything but kiss him back. Our tongues tangled and merged, as the tide surged against us.

Our lips parted, our foreheads still pressed together as we panted for air. His heart pounded against my shaking palm, his heartbeat flowing through my fingertips and mingling with my own frantic pulse. He was steady while I trembled, still recovering from his kiss.

The sun finished escaping her watery bed, shining brightly and filling the sky with color and heat. Waves lapped at our feet as he pulled me further into his lap to kiss me again I wanted to kiss him for eternity with just the sun and the waves as the world.

"You are so beautiful," he murmured reverently, taking a strand of hair and tucking it carefully behind my ear.

"So are you," I replied, blushing. I wished my words were better, but they were still true. His chest was hot and smooth against my bare arms as he pulled me into yet another mind-shattering kiss.

"Charlotte is going to wonder where we are," I said with a giggle as the sun continued her climb.

"Let her worry for a moment," Bastian whispered, his lips going to my throat. I moaned softly as he nipped the delicate flesh. I was turning into a puddle of want in his lap and I wanted so much more than just kisses on my throat.

I then let out the biggest yawn in the history of mankind.

Bastian chuckled. "And now I've kept you out all night."

"Worth it," I informed him with a smile. I would have gladly spent a year awake for his kiss. For this moment, I would have done anything.

His face split into that heart-shatteringly beautiful smile. It was even better than the first one. Happiness made his eyes shine in the morning light, sparkling with gray and blue hues of joy. I nearly died a little.

"Let's get you home," he said softly, disentangling his body from mine. I loved the way he said home. As if it were ours. As if we belonged together there.

He rose smoothly to his feet and then helped me to mine. He picked up his fallen shirt and shook the sand out of it before draping it over my shoulders and leaving his own bare. The sun glistened on the scars, but I could only see beauty in them. He was a survivor.

Walking hand in hand, we made our way back along the shore to the giant mansion. The beach was fairly flat, but now that we were moving and not sitting, exhaustion was stealing over me. I grew more tired with every step, my feet turning to lead as what was left of my energy was quickly drained. I couldn't believe how far I had ran last night, and now I was regretting it. I could see the house looming over the cove, but I was so tired I wasn't sure I would make it that far. I stumbled, my feet catching on the sand and exhaustion, but Bastian caught me.

In an easy motion, he saved me from falling and instead swept me off my feet and into his arms. I tried to protest, but I was so tired that I was having a hard time finding the words. He just murmured softly, silencing my objections and carrying me the rest of the way and up into the house.

He paused before the stairs for just a moment and I tried to get out of his arms. "You don't have to carry me..."

He tightened his arms, pinning me in place against him. "Maybe I want to," he informed me as he shifted my weight and began to climb. He made it feel easy. He wasn't even breathing hard at the top.

I snuggled into his chest, closing my eyes and inhaling the scent of his skin. He smelled of sea salt and a masculine musk that I was quickly falling in love with.

I whimpered when he set me on my bed, disappointed at the loss of his chest against my cheek.

I opened my mouth to ask him to stay, to crawl into bed with me. I wanted more of his touch, but no words came out. The bed was just too soft and my eyelids just too heavy.

He kissed my forehead just as I lost the battle to stay awake, sending me off to dreamland on a kiss.

"Sleep, Ava," he whispered as I stole into dreams involving him. "I'll be here when you wake."

I woke to an empty room. The space was too big for just one person.

At first I thought the whole thing must have been a dream. In what world did a billionaire kiss me on the beach at sunrise and then carry me home? I had to have dreamt it, because things like that didn't happen to me. I was ordinary and that was extraordinary. But then I moved and felt the sand in the bed and I knew it was real.

I glanced at the clock to discover that it was nearly lunch time. I couldn't blame Bastian for not being here. As much fun as I was asleep, I knew he had a business to run and things to do. He couldn't just sit in my room watching me sleep all day. And actually, the idea of him doing just that was rather creepy.

I got up and stretched my arms out over my head. It felt good to be alive today. I ran to the bathroom and quickly freshened up before picking up my phone. All the email updates were good and I let out a relieved breath. I picked up the house phone and dialed my dad's cell phone.

"Mr. Fairchild's phone," a sweet female voice answered. I

frowned, and did a double take. Where was dad?

"Um, I'm Ava Fairchild and I'm looking for my dad..." Panic starting to bubble in my chest. *Why was someone else answering his phone?*

"Oh, good! He made me promise to carry his phone and answer it in case you called." The voice was warm and friendly. "My name's Audrey and I'm one of the nurses here. He's in having a test done but he's doing great. He wanted you not to worry and that he can't complain about anything here except for the food."

I chuckled. That sounded just like a message Dad would leave. "What kind of test?" I asked. I was sure Dr. Verner would have told me if something had happened that necessitated something drastic.

"Nothing serious," the nurse promised. "I can't give that information out over the phone, but your dad really wanted you to know he's just fine. Jackie is here if you'd like to speak with her about it. I believe she's out in the waiting room. Cell reception is terrible out there, so he asked me to keep his phone."

"No, that's all right." I shook my head, realizing that she couldn't see me through the phone. If Jackie was there, then he was fine. Besides, Jackie would talk my ear off about her bowling game instead of telling me about my Dad and my stomach was rumbling. I liked her a lot, but the woman loved to talk. "Will you have him call me this evening?"

"Of course," the nurse promised. "He actually wanted me to tell you he'd be calling you if you didn't."

I laughed and thanked her before hanging up the phone. I was so glad dad was doing all right. I was glad Jackie was there taking care of him. It made me feel less guilty knowing that someone who loved him was with him. I trusted Jackie enough to entrust my father into her care.

I ran a brush through my hair one last time, smiling into the mirror and deciding that I looked very pretty this morning. It probably had something to do with how happy I felt. Kissing a gorgeous man on the beach had that effect on me. I winked at the mirror and hurried down the stairs to the kitchen to stop the rumbling in my stomach.

I could hear Charlotte's sweetly pitched voice contrasting with Bastian's deeper tones long before I entered the kitchen. I walked in to see him at the stove cooking something while Charlotte sat at the table with her laptop reading off numbers and figures.

"Good morning, sleepy-head," Bastian greeted me, talking over Charlotte's readings. I beamed at him. "Want some food?"

I nodded and sat at the table next to Charlotte so I could watch him. He moved so smoothly in the kitchen that it was like watching someone dance.

"Rough night?" Charlotte asked, glancing back and forth between the two of us with one eyebrow raised.

"It started out that way," I said, unable to stop the grin forming on my face. "But it's been a great morning."

"Oooooookay..." Charlotte shook her head at both of us, and then went back to her computer. Now that I was there, she just mumbled quietly as she input information.

It wasn't long before Bastian brought over three plates of big, beautiful sandwiches with artfully arranged potato chips on the side. Since I didn't see a bag, I had a feeling they were homemade.

Bastian's arm grazed mine as he set the plate down in front of Charlotte, sending a surge of electric desire straight through me. It was like the hours between our kiss and this minute had never passed. All I could think about was kissing him again.

I looked up at him and immediately blushed and looked away. Just looking at his face reminded me of kissing him. And now I wanted to do so, so much more than just kiss him. My fingers ached to touch his skin again and to tangle in his hair.

Charlotte watched me closely for a moment, before swallowing her bite of grilled cheese and looking over at Bastian. "I don't know what put you in such a good mood that you made your Famous Grilled Cheese," she said, taking another bite and turning to look pointedly at me. "But thank you."

I blushed and giggled nervously, trying not to look up at Bastian. "I didn't do anything..."

"I don't want to know," Charlotte quickly amended, holding up her hand. She looked back and forth at the not-so-secret gazes between Bastian and me. "So seriously, I do not want to know what the two of you were out doing all night."

"Who says we were out all night?" Bastian asked, smiling. I had to struggle not to giggle like a school girl at anything he said. It didn't help that my stomach was full of happy butterflies or that I suddenly was finding everything very amusing. I was drunk on happiness just by being around him.

"I don't want to know." Charlotte shot him a dirty look. "I don't want to know so much that I'm going to take this delicious sandwich to the other room. You two can sit in here making googly eyes without me. I'd like to keep my lunch down."

She picked up her plate, but left smiling.

"You think she suspects anything?" Bastian asked, taking the last bite of his sandwich.

I giggled, and took another bite of my sandwich. It was

definitely the best grilled cheese sandwich I had ever eaten. Three kinds of cheese and the bread was toasted to perfection. I knew that grilled cheese wasn't usually a gourmet event, but Bastian made it one.

"Okay, sister in the room," Charlotte announced, walking back into the kitchen with one hand covering her eyes as if she were afraid she might see us doing something naughty. As tempted as I was to take Bastian on the kitchen table, she had no reason to cover her eyes.

"I'm seriously just eating a sandwich," I told her. "And now that sounds dirty."

Charlotte snorted and dropped her hand. "I'm sorry to interrupt your *sandwich,*" she said the word slowly and deliberately. "But Leo's here for the conference call."

Charlotte managed to only blush a little, but her cheeks still told the full story about how she felt about Leo. Bastian sighed and stood up, putting his plate in the sink before standing beside me.

"Dinner?" he asked. His eyes sparkled and I wondered just what he had planned. I hoped it involved him shirtless.

"Yes, please," I answered, a little too breathless. He grinned as if he could read the dirty thoughts in my mind. I wanted to kiss him again so badly it was driving me crazy.

Bastian grinned and walked past me to the door, skimming his hand along my shoulders as he passed. The deepest parts of me tightened at his wonderful touch, my skin aflame from his fingers. If he did this to me all day, I would go insane for sure.

Charlotte waited until he passed her to leave before giving me two big thumbs up. I laughed as she then followed him out. As much as she joked, I was glad she liked the two of us together. I knew I didn't need it, but I was glad to have her approval.

CHAPTER 17

"Hi, Daddy," I said, picking up the phone and grinning from ear to ear as I set down my work. I glanced at my watch and saw it was much later than I thought. I had worked all afternoon and into the evening without realizing it.

"Hi, kiddo," he replied, sounding relaxed and happy. "How's work coming?"

"Slow but steady," I told him. "I'll get it all done in time. How are you?"

"As good as can be expected. The food here is terrible," he complained. I could hear the TV on in the background. "They won't let me have any salt."

I smiled, thinking of him pouting while watching Jeopardy in bed. "At least I'll get the appraisal done on time," I promised. "That should make you feel better."

"Don't work too hard," he cautioned. "You should have some fun while you're out there. You need a little distraction."

I thought of how Bastian kept finding excuses throughout the day to walk through whichever room I happened to be working in, even if Charlotte or Leo happened to be with him. It made it very difficult to concentrate, knowing he was there, watching me with his blue-gray eyes. I had at least managed to sneak in one short kiss before Charlotte nearly walked in on us.

"What about you, Dad? What was the test for today?" I asked, changing the subject. I didn't want to talk to my father about Bastian or the way he kissed.

"Dr. Verner assures me that he's getting good data," Dad explained. "It looks like I'm going to need a pacemaker, but I'll let him explain it to you when you get here."

"A pacemaker?" I felt a jolt of panic again. Pacemakers meant that something was wrong. I shook my head. I already knew something was wrong, but it was still difficult to let the reality set in.

"Yes, and don't worry, Ava." Dad turned down the TV in the background. "He says once it's in, I'll be right as rain. It's a very simple procedure. I even get to go home the next day. No more scares. I'll be back to usual."

"I wish I could be there for you, Dad," I pouted. I wanted to run out the door and hop on the first plane home. "I feel so guilty. You're sick and I'm here, and..."

"No," Dad interrupted me. "No, Ava. Do not feel guilty about this."

I played with a strand of hair, twirling it between my fingers. "Can I feel a little guilty about it? I mean, it's your heart."

"Ava," Dad warned, his voice going deep. That tone used to scare me when I was a child and it hadn't lost much to the years.

"Please?" I begged. "It feels like such a big deal."

"Fine, you may feel a little guilty." He sighed, giving into me. "You can make it up to me at Christmas and make me an extra batch of those cookies I like."

"Done," I promised, my heart feeling a little bit lighter. It wasn't a real solution to my guilt, but at least Dad sounded like himself again. "I'm glad you're feeling better, Dad. I don't know what I'd do without you."

"You'd do just fine," he assured me. "You're strong. Like me. Besides, you aren't getting rid of me that easily. Dr. Verner says with this new pacemaker, you'll be struggling to keep up with me."

I smiled, knowing that my dad was going to prove Dr. Verner right even if it killed him.

"Everything's going to be just fine, okay?" Dad's voice was soft. I heard a voice in the background that I assumed was a nurse. "Hey, honey- the nurse is here to check my vitals. Can I call you in the morning?"

"Yeah, I'll be waiting for it," I answered. "I"m glad you're doing good, Dad."

"Better than good," he promised. "I love you, Ava. More than words."

I smiled. It was something we had said for as long as I could remember. My mother used to say, "I love you more than words can say," but as a child, I couldn't repeat the phrase properly. It had morphed into, "I love you more than words," and stuck. I knew Dad was feeling better if he used that expression.

"I love you too, Daddy," I replied. "More than words."

I hung up the phone with my heart feeling heavy and light at the same time. So many emotions were rushing around my head that I didn't know what to feel. At least until my stomach rumbled. Then I decided I felt hungry.

I head down to the kitchen, hoping to see Bastian or Charlotte on my way, but the house was deserted. The kitchen was dark and empty. I knew Bastian was busy with work today and an idea came to me. He probably hadn't stopped working long enough to realize it was dinner time.

I pulled out a platter from one of the many shelves and began piling it high with cheeses, crackers, cut fruit, leftovers from Lucia, and whatever else I found in the fridge that looked good. Once I had enough to feed four people, I snagged a bottle of wine and four glasses from the pantry and headed upstairs.

It took some balance, and I decided that I had a future in waitressing if I ever needed one, but I managed to get all of it upstairs and in front of the doors to Bastian's study. I set the tray down on the hall table long enough to knock on the big doors before picking it up.

I heard the turn of a lock and the door opened to reveal Bastian. He smiled as soon as he saw me and then grinned as he saw the food.

"I brought provisions," I announced.

He held open the doors to let me in to his sanctuary. "Come on in."

I carefully maneuvered past him, trying to keep my attention on the very full tray of food and not on how close he was. I nearly dropped the platter and the glasses were slipping by the time I set them down on the table by the couch.

"Where are Charlotte and Leo?" I asked, looking around. Bastian was the only one in his room, though every light was on.

"They left," he explained, sounding tired. He ran a hand through his hair, mussing it's already tussled locks further. "The app's a mess, so they took the helicopter to the mainland to meet with Gabe and the programmers directly."

"I'm sorry, Bastian," I said quietly. My heart thrilled a

little at his name. And that we were now alone in the mansion. In his room. "I guess I didn't need to bring up so much food, then."

He looked at the food and then at me. The gleam in his eyes left no doubt that he wanted me more than the food. "More for me, then."

My heart fluttered and I felt my face heat. I could still taste his kiss on my lips from this morning. All day, he was all I had thought about. He was all my body had craved. I ached for his touch again. I wanted more than just a kiss. I looked over at the bathroom door and remembered the way the water had run down his chest, the muscles and the soft skin. I wanted so much more than a kiss.

"Thank you for bringing this all up," Bastian said, drawing me back from my memories of his naked body. He was wearing long dress pants and a light blue, button up dress shirt. I thought he looked better with just the towel, but I wasn't going to complain.

"You are very welcome," I replied, picking up the bottle of wine and reaching for the corkscrew. I, of course, put it in at an angle and was left struggling to try and remove it without sending wine everywhere. The cork was stuck and I was using all my strength and getting nowhere.

"Here, let me." Bastian reached for the bottle, taking both it and my hands in his. I trembled slightly, exhilarating at his touch. His hands were strong and warm, and sending electric currents of want straight through my spine.

In a smooth motion, he uncorked the wine as if it were the easiest thing in the world. "We should let it breathe for a few minutes," he said, setting it off to the side.

"Breathe," I repeated, more to remind myself to do so than to agree with him. He was so close to me now that I could smell his cologne. It was light and clean, yet incredibly masculine. It drew me in closer to him, making me want to rub myself all over him like a cat in heat. I couldn't think of anything but how much I wanted Bastian to do more than just stand here and breathe.

I looked up at him. Every fiber of my being wanted me to throw myself at him, to kiss every inch of his skin I could get my lips on. From the way he was looking at me, he felt the same. The sexual tension in the room was thick enough to cut with a knife. I couldn't stop thinking of our kiss. My hands on his chest. His taste. His fingers tangled in my hair...

The wind ruffled the curtains as it came in off the ocean, and as if on cue, our willpower to stay apart broke at the same time. Whatever was holding us back and keeping us acting like civil, rational adults was blown away on that wind.

A low growl rumbled in his chest as he slid his hand into my hair and put the other to my hip. He pulled me into him, pressing his body against mine as our lips collided. His lips were on mine, stealing my breath and making my knees wobble and go weak.

The kiss was hot and heavy, full of the first desperate rush of desire. There was need and want in this kiss that I couldn't fight against, didn't want to fight against. I could sense the same inner struggle for control waging in him as he kissed me senseless.

Every ounce of desire poured from his mouth into mine. His face was rough with stubble from the day, but it felt deliciously male and masculine beneath my lips. I rocked my body into his, wanting more and a low groan rumbled in his chest and his hands tightened. It was more than just wanting. This was a desperate craving that I couldn't resist.

My body reacted instantly. All the flirting and secret glances, the fluttering eyelashes and hidden smiles, they were all teasing me for this moment. Now that I had him, with no one to walk in or interrupt us, I wasn't willing to stop at just a kiss. Not when he kissed like this.

His kiss put all sorts of naughty ideas, desires and wants, hurtling through my veins like a drug. I couldn't get enough and I wanted more. More than just this kiss. I pressed my chest against his, trying to soothe the ache growing at the tips of my breasts. I need more.

Reaching for his shirt buttons, I slowly undid each one as he undid my soul with kisses. He kissed me slow and long, learning the corners and curves of my lips and mouth. His tongue caressed mine, tempting me to just rip off the shirt and have my way with him. Instead, I went slow, letting him tease and excite me with his expert kisses.

With the buttons undone, I pushed the light fabric from his shoulders. He paused in his kissing to help shrug off the dress shirt, raising his arms for a moment to remove the white undershirt beneath.

I had seen him shirtless this morning. I knew he was a big man, but to see him now, muscles rippling and waiting for my touch, I trembled. Scars twisted along his smooth skin as he moved, but I found them strangely beautiful. He was pure testosterone and sinew beneath them, and they added an element of darkness to him that I couldn't resist. I wanted to kiss every one of them and run my fingers along every inch of his skin.

"You're beautiful," I whispered, not even meaning to say anything aloud. I bit my lip and he blushed slightly. The pink on his cheeks looked out of place on his strong features, but wonderfully human and real. It made my heart speed up even more.

He leaned forward, pulling me into yet another amazing kiss. I melted into him, pressing my palms into his muscled pecs and feeling pure strength. His fingers pulled at the hem of my shirt, pulling it up and over my head. The cool breeze from the window hit my skin, making me shiver with the unexpected sensation.

Ducking his head, he kissed the lace along the edge of my bra, sending heat straight down to my legs. My lips kissed his jaw, the corded muscles of his neck, his shoulders-- any patch of perfect skin I could reach. I couldn't resist taking a bite of his muscled shoulder. I couldn't control myself.

"Do it again," he dared me, nipping at my own shoulder and making me shiver.

Looking behind him at the couch, I pushed his shoulders gently to sit. He willingly obliged, looking me up and down before I straddled his lap. The bulge in his pants pressed upward against the ache of warmth between my legs, teasing me with what was next.

"Oh, Ava..." he groaned, tilting his hips up for more. Desire rippled through me at the need in his voice. I couldn't think straight, let alone breathe when he sounded that raw with want.

He pushed one white bra strap from my shoulder, leaning forward to nibble on the exposed flesh while pushing the other side off as well. I gasped as he reached his arms around me, undoing the bra clasp with only a little bit of difficulty. Torture was the only word to describe the wait as he pulled the lacy bra away, his eyes going dark with desire as he saw my bare skin.

He lowered his head, slowly placing one very excited nipple into his mouth. His teeth and tongue worked it into a hard ball of desire. While his mouth worked on one, he didn't neglect the other. He rolled the sensitive peak between his thumb and forefinger, pulling and teasing it until I couldn't tell which side felt better.

My head fell back and I arched into him, driving my hips against the hard swelling of man beneath me. I had never come off of just this, but what he was doing was threatening to get me there.

"You are so perfect," Bastian murmured, his eyes dilating with want as he watched me writhe. I wasn't sure if he had meant to say the words aloud, but there they were. I looked at his blue-gray eyes and was surprised at the honesty and reverence in them. *He thought I was perfect.*

No one had ever looked at me like that. No one had ever told me I was perfect. Hot, occasionally, or pretty. But never perfect. But when he looked at me, I knew he meant it. His simple words sent me reeling, and I buried my head in his shoulder, trying to keep myself steady. *Perfect.*

"Ava?" Bastian stroked my hair, and I sat back up. Our eyes connected.

"Yes," I whispered. *Yes. Anything he could ask of me, the answer was yes.* I nodded and kissed him, undulating my hips to tell him that, yes, I wanted everything. I wanted him.

He smiled against the kiss, understanding me without speaking another word. In a smooth motion, he twisted and flipped our positions so that I was now laying on the couch with him straddling me. I loved being under him. He kissed down my throat, pausing to nibble on my collarbone before gently nipping at one breast. He didn't stop there. Leaving a trail of kisses, he kept working south until coming to my pants.

He tugged at my pants and I raised my hips up to let him take them off. He pulled them down and tossed them on the ground, licking his lips as he looked me over. For the first time in a long time, I felt sexy. Wanted. The way he looked at me drove me wild- like he was barely containing the beast inside of him from coming out and gobbling me up right there.

Slowly, so slowly it was close to torture, he pulled the lace around my hips down and off. One finger traced the curve of my stomach from my belly button to my hip bone, circling it before going central again and stopping directly at the sensitive apex of my legs. I trembled, waiting for whatever was coming next. Just having his finger on me was driving me insane with desire, making me ache and heat.

He used his finger as a guide and kissed me right where the ache was growing unbearable. I gasped, my hips arched upward into his mouth with the sudden explosion of pleasure. He chuckled, pushing my legs wider with his broad shoulders to give him better access to do it again.

I fought him for a moment, my own self-consciousness and nerves finally making an appearance. He simply raised his head and shook it slowly, smiling evilly. He wasn't going to take no for an answer. Placing his palms on my inner thighs, he pushed gently. I resisted for a moment, but stopped as soon as he bent his head and went to work.

He hummed into me, using his teeth and tongue to pull out pleasure I had never imagined to be possible. His fingers found their way to join his lips and tongue, teasing and beckoning me toward a golden edge of wonder. My knees started to shake and my breath was coming in fast, uncontrollable pants. I found myself bucking and arching against him faster than I ever had in my life.

"Come for me, Ava," he whispered, his breath only adding to my lust. My name on his lips was my undoing. I came apart, vibrating and shaking with overwhelming sensation. I tangled my fingers in his gold touched hair as my bones turned to jelly and I skittered over the edge into glorious oblivion. Never had anyone gotten me there so quickly or so thoroughly.

Breathless and dizzy, I opened my eyes to find him watching me with a content smile on his face. No, not content. Pleased. Like a cat in the milk.

He stood slowly, desire painting his face with broad strokes. I could see just how hard he was now, his erection struggling beneath his dress pants for escape. I loved that he was turned on by me, that he was excited by my pleasure.

I sat up quickly, feeling lightheaded for a moment but absolutely fabulous, and struggled with his belt. He nimbly undid it, letting me tug on his pants. His boxers fell away with his pants and it was hard not to stare.

Sheer desire threatened to overwhelm me at his perfect masculine form. I want to touch him, want to take him into me, and I want him all for myself.

I stood and pressed my palms against his skin, kissing him with everything that I had. His erection was a living thing against my lower stomach, searching for something I was all too willing to give him. His tongue danced with mine, daring me to take more. I arched my back, pressing my hips into him, feeling his hard, hot length respond against my skin.

I looked up to see his eyes darken with lust. My stomach fluttered, more with want than nerves.

"Bastian, I need you..." I whispered, reaching up to touch his cheek. The day's worth of stubble was rough, but tantalizing under my fingers. His erection throbbed against my hip. I was surprised I was able to get the words out, considering how much brain power I was using not to just take him right then and there.

He pulled me into a kiss, tangling his fingers in my hair and pressing his obvious desire against my body before letting me go. The loss of his touch was enough to make me cry out as he stepped away and hurried over to his desk. At least I got a nice view of his ass as he bent to open one of the desk drawers.

Grinning like an idiot, I lay down on the couch and listened for the crinkle of a wrapper. My heart was beating out of my chest, thumping with sheer want and need. He was about to be mine. All the wonderful, sinful things I had thought of throughout the day were about to be mine. I had never wanted anyone this badly, never been this turned on. The ache in my core was nearly destroying me as I waited the last few seconds for him to return.

The corners of his mouth twitched upward as he came back around and found me ready and willing. I loved the way he looked at me. It was like he couldn't stop staring and smiling. I knew I certainly couldn't looking at him.

Slowly, he put his strong arms on either side of my head. He was hard and thick and hovering just between my legs. I arched my hips, trying to take him in, but he just pulled back further, teasing me with how close he was.

"Bastian…" I whimpered, wrapping my legs around his and trying again. He kept me just on the edge of getting what I wanted. "Please…"

I was going insane. Literally insane with want. Desire was melting my brain and the only cure was to have him inside of me.

He smiled, inching forward, but the same need that was driving me mad was written all over his face as well. His arms trembled and I knew it wasn't from holding himself above me. It was taking everything he had to make me wait.

With a slow, smooth stroke, he gasped and gave me what we both wanted. I curled my fingers into the couch, needing to hold onto something as he took my body. He thrust deeper, claiming me for himself and making me cry out for more.

I rotated my hips, taking him deeper yet. My name crossed his lips in a ragged breath that drove me wild. For every thrust, I matched him, meeting his movements in a dance that was growing faster and more insistent with every beat. A low flutter in the pit of my stomach started to stir, heating me from my toes up.

I needed every inch of him. I needed to be filled with him to the brim and then to overflow.

Bastian's breaths came in fast pants, his face lined with concentration. He pulled my hands into his and raised them over my head, levering into me with such heat and power that I forgot how to breathe. The pleasure coiled and undulated through me, tightening in my belly and in the tips of my breasts until I couldn't separate out the points of pleasure anymore.

His arms shook against me as he struggled for control. He was trying to hold back, but that was the last thing I wanted. I wanted him to lose control, to free himself in me. I arched harder, pressing my hips up to meet his in a rhythm I knew we couldn't sustain for long. I wanted what came next more than anything in the world, except to maybe stay right here on the cusp of heaven with him forever.

Fisting one hand in my hair and holding my wrists above my head with the other, Bastian buried his face in the crook of my neck and shuddered as he whispered my name. My body clenched around his, not wanting to let him escape and pulling me along with him as he came. I lost myself to his pleasure, spinning and shaking with him into heaven.

After a few moments, face still pressed to my skin, I felt him slow and finally take a breath. It was shaky and ragged, as I knew my own breathing to be. I had never experienced anything like that before. Never anything that intense or powerful. No one had ever gotten me to climax with them, but Bastian had taken me there as naturally as breathing.

He raised his head, a wolfish grin spreading across his face. My heart clenched, loving the way he looked at me, so satisfied and full of ownership. I loved the way he wanted me. Desired me. Claimed me as his.

I grinned back, gasping for air and covered in sweat. He nibbled on my shoulder, tasting the salt of my sweat.

"You completely undo me," he whispered. I made a pleased noise and stretched out my neck to give him more skin to work with. It felt wonderful. "How do you do that?"

"Do what?" I asked as he nuzzled my collarbone.

"Turn me on so completely that I can't control myself," he replied. He kissed my throat right where my pulse was beating out his name. "I wanted to make that last, but I couldn't stop as soon as I started. I can't control myself with you."

"It was perfect," I told him, and meaning it. He pulled back and looked at me. His eyes were vibrant blue around his pupils that then lightened into gray. They were the most beautiful thing I had ever seen. It was difficult not to just stare into them and forget everything. "Perfect."

His face melted into a smile just before he leaned forward and kissed me. His five-o'clock shadow was rough on my lips, but I wouldn't have stopped kissing him even if he had been made of sandpaper. I loved the way he tasted far too much to stop.

He pulled back just as his stomach grumbled against mine. His brow came together as he looked down at the offending noise and I couldn't help but giggle.

"Good thing I brought you some food," I told him.

"Yes," he said slowly, looking me up and down with a

wolfish, hungry grin. The way he was gazing at me had me forgetting about food entirely. I was heating again with just the intensity of his gaze. "That means I don't have to take a break to run downstairs."

I knew now I would never be able to get enough of him. Instead of quelling my need for him, this had only whetted my appetite. Now, my body knew just how amazing he could make me feel and I would never want to stop. I licked my lips, ready for more. Ready for a whole night of more.

And judging from the way he was looking at me, so was he.

CHAPTER 18

I was surrounded by masculine strength and I didn't want to move. *This is the way to wake up*, I thought, snuggling a little bit deeper into Bastian's arms. I was fairly certain I had died and gone to heaven. Or at least, my version of heaven included my back pressed firmly against Bastian's front in all our naked glory.

"Good morning, sleepy-head," Bastian whispered, his breath tickling the small hairs on my neck.

I rolled over and opened my eyes, finding myself positive I was in heaven. A blue-gray heaven that shone with affection for me. "Definitely a good morning."

He smiled, lighting up the room. "It's almost dawn. Would you like to join me out on the water today?"

I bit my lip. I wanted to so badly, but I didn't want to ruin his morning ritual either. "I don't know how to paddleboard," I reminded him gently.

"I'll teach you," he promised, kissing the tip of my nose. I chewed my lip for a moment, but his smile never wavered. He wanted to teach me and, truth be told, I would have learned how to hang-glide on paper mache if he wanted.

"Okay."

He lit up even more and I loved it. "Get your swimsuit and I'll meet you at the beach with a board," he promised, leaping out of bed. He was so beautiful, scars and all. I could watch him all day.

I followed him out of bed, moving much more slowly. Every muscle in my body had the most wonderful aches. Last night had been amazing. The best sex of my life amazing.

I went to the door, looking back just in time to see his wonderfully perfect ass disappear into a pair of board shorts. I grinned, excited to spend the morning with him and scampered back to my room as quickly as I could.

I put on my own swimsuit, debating between the bikini or the full piece for a good thirty seconds before deciding on the bikini. If I lost my top, I wouldn't mind having him help me look. I put on a pair of board shorts, ran a brush though my tangled hair, put on some spray sunscreen, and used a little mouthwash. I don't think I had ever gotten ready that quickly.

Dawn was almost here by the time I hurried down the wooden porch steps to where Bastian waited for me. I loved that he was wearing men's board shorts instead of his full-body wetsuit. I loved his scars as they were a part of him, but I loved that he wasn't ashamed of them with me.

I put my palm on his bare chest, loving the rush of adrenaline I got at just touching him before spiking it with a quick kiss. He grinned.

"You ready?"

"As much as I can be," I replied with a shrug.

"Raise your hand up," he commanded. I complied and he placed one of three paddles he had out in my outstretched palm. "Perfect fit. Now, come with me."

I followed obediently as he handed me a long surfboard and together we entered the water.

"Have you ever been surfing?" he asked, as we waded out to where the waves no longer mixed with the sand.

"Once," I answered. "But I never actually stood up."

"This is easier," he promised. "Now hop on your board and we'll swim out a little further."

I climbed up onto the board, feeling unsteady even as I lay on my stomach with the long paddle tucked underneath me. Together we paddled out to where I wouldn't be able to touch before sitting up on the boards. I knew the water was deeper here, but I could still see every grain of sand through the crystal clear blue ocean. A small school of silver fish flitted across the sand before disappearing from my sight.

Bastian floated next to me, sitting on his own board as he looked at the horizon. The sun was coming up gold and setting the sky aflame. I gasped. It was magical to be out here, floating with my feet in the water as the sun came up. Just as the last inches of the giant ball of light left the horizon, he leaned over and kissed me.

I closed my eyes, feeling his warm tongue and tasting the salt of the ocean while the sun heated my skin. *No, this is heaven*, I decided, losing the rest of my thoughts to his gentle lips and tongue.

I sighed with contentment when he pulled away. His kisses were magical. He grinned at me. "You ready?"

I nodded. "Yup."

"First, we'll go to our knees," he explained. "Find the sweet spot, where the balance is best."

"That's what she said," I quipped. Bastian burst out laughing, stopping in his demonstration and nearly falling into the water.

"Just get up on your knees," he told me, splashing water at me with his hands.

I stuck out my tongue at him. "Again, that's what she said."

This time he used his paddle to splash me, drenching me instantly. I wiped the water from my eyes and slowly wobbled my way up to my knees. The board dipped and swayed with the rolling ocean waves, but it actually took less balance than I thought it would.

"Excellent," Bastian praised me. I glanced up at him, proud of myself and wobbled. He smiled. "If you fall off the board, ditch the paddle. You can always get the paddle back once your back up. Go ahead and get it ready."

I nodded, and picked up my paddle. "Ready."

"Good," he said, moving around on his own board. "Go ahead and choke up on the paddle. It'll make it easier."

I moved my hands down the shaft of the paddle and then confidently put the blade into the water. The board moved forward and I grinned. I went a little faster, dipping the paddle in deeper and using a stronger stroke. I could see how Bastian had such a wonderful body. It wasn't terribly aerobic exercise, but it required a lot of stability and strength.

"This is fun," I yelled, looking back at him. He grinned and caught up easily.

"Are you ready to stand up?" he asked, practically steering circles around me. I nodded.

"Okay, feet on the sweet spot, and stay low..." he instructed. I did exactly as he told me, wobbling but finding my balance. "Now, stand up slowly and go to a staggered stance- one foot in front of the other."

I grinned as I found my way to fully standing. I was up. I wasn't moving yet, but I was up.

"Keep your arms straight and use your core to paddle," he instructed, making a down and back motion. I nearly fell off as the sun glinted off the muscles in his arms and back as he demonstrated. I definitely wasn't paying attention to his technique. "The closer you stay to your board, the straighter the line you'll travel on."

"Uh huh," I replied, trying it out. It was even more of a workout than kneeling. I didn't think I was that out of shape, but this was working my core in ways that I knew would have me sore by dinnertime. This was way better than crunches at the gym. *Company's better than at the gym, too,* I thought.

"Ava, look over there," Bastian called out, pointing his paddle to off to the side. I raised my gaze from the water to see a pod of dolphins, at least four or five of them, leaping through the water.

"Dolphins!" I squeaked with excitement, jumping up and down with glee. Which meant I promptly fell face first into the water.

"You okay?" Bastian asked, saving my paddle for me as I climbed back onto my board.

"Dolphins!" I squealed again, grinning with sheer delight. Bastian laughed at my childlike enthusiasm as the pod swam closer. I wished I could touch them, but they changed direction and went off in search of food in deeper water.

When they left us, I stood up again, determined to get better before we had to go in. Bastian watched me carefully, praising me and giving me pointers as he zoomed around me, going backwards and forwards and showing off. He never fell in the water though.

Bastian groaned as his watch began to beep. "Time to go back."

I pouted, sticking out my lower lip at him.

"You'll have to explain to Charlotte and Leo why I'm late then," he replied. "And if Gabe's there, she'll be mean."

I pouted bigger, but I began paddling back in the direction of the mansion. I wished we didn't have to go in. I would have stayed out on the water forever with him. Out here, it was just the two of us, and possibly some dolphins. There were no worries or obligations. No phones or deadlines. I didn't want to go back to land and back to reality. Even the Caribbean mansion reality I was currently in.

Bastian paused as we approached the shore, slowing down his paddling and waiting for me to catch up. I could tell he was just as reluctant as I was to return.

"Thank you for sharing this with me, Ava," he said softly.

I smiled and tried to steer closer to him, but instead rammed my board into his instead of coming along side it. He jumped into the water and pulled me with him.

"Thank you," I told him once we surfaced. "This has been the best day ever."

He grinned. "And it's just starting." Then together, we brought our boards into shore to start the rest of our day.

CHAPTER 19

"Would you like to have a drink with me?"

I startled and banged my head on the bottom of the desk. I could see Bastian's feet in the doorway as I worked my way out from under the antique writing desk.

Bastian chuckled, coming over and holding out his hand to help me up. I rubbed the sore spot on my head, and he leaned over to kiss it.

"You really should be more careful under furniture," he teased. "You keep bumping your head."

I stuck out my tongue at him and he kissed my head again, mussing my hair in the process.

"So, drinks?" he asked, smiling gently.

"Are we actually going to go drink, or will it end up like last time I had alcohol with you?" I grinned at him, remembering our dinner last night. "Because I'm up for either."

Bastian's eyes twinkled and he wrapped his arm around my waist, pulling me into him. I loved the way his body felt, and I pressed closer. I rocked my hips against his and was rewarded with a passionate kiss.

"I was thinking drinks at a bar, but you are certainly tempting me to just raid the wine cellar," he murmured. "I wanted to take you out."

"You mean you are willing to be seen in public with me?" I asked, pulling back slightly.

He cocked his head to the side with a confused smile. "Why wouldn't I want to be seen in public with you? I want to show you off."

I smiled as a happy warmth filled me. He wanted to show me off. I felt like running around doing a little happy dance because Sebastian Belrose liked me. Really liked me. But that would mean getting out of his arms.

"I'd love to get drinks with you then," I told him proudly. He let me go, smiling broadly at my acceptance.

This would be great. I would put on a cute dress and some makeup, and maybe even curl my hair...

"Excellent," he said. "I'll go get the car."

"Wait, you mean right now?" I ran a hand through my hair. I had been working all day and it was just up in a ponytail. I had sweat-stains on my t-shirt and my shorts had a mustard spot on them from lunch. I was not ready to go out.

"Well, yes." Bastian looked at me like I might be a little slow. "Did you have other plans this evening?"

"Let me go change," I begged. "It'll take two seconds, I promise."

"I think you look great, but if you want to, go ahead." He shrugged. He of course looked amazing. He had on light linen pants and a long sleeve t-shirt that covered his scars but showed off his impressive frame. He looked like something straight out of a billionaire yacht club magazine.

I flashed him a quick grin and ran out the door to my room. I didn't have enough time to do much, so I just found my dress, a cute pair of heels, some mascara and a dot of perfume. It wasn't much, but it was better than mustard shorts.

I came out the front door to find Bastian sitting in a fancy European sports convertible. It looked even more expensive than the Lamborghini, or at least flashier. It was a car meant to show off the people inside of it. I was glad I hadn't done anything with my hair, because the open top would have destroyed it.

He turned at the sound of the door and raised his eyebrows as he hurried out of the car.

"You look amazing," he complimented as he opened my car door for me. I blushed. This was one of my favorite dresses and one that I actually felt pretty in. But, having Bastian tell me I looked good made it even better. "And you smell even better."

"Thanks," I said. I had forgotten what it was like to have someone other than Dad compliment me. It felt wonderful.

I wasn't used to getting in a car in a skirt, especially one that the breeze kept trying to pick up. It was a little tricky, but I thought I managed. It did make me wonder how superstars did it all the time. *There must be lessons,* I thought as I battled my skirt, trying to put one foot in and not lose my balance with the other. *Otherwise, there would be a lot more pictures of undies on the tabloids.*

"So, where are we going?" I asked, once in the car and carefully pulling the seat-belt tight across my lap. Bastian pulled his tight as well before starting the car. I barely felt the vibrations of the engine it was so smooth. He pulled out onto the main road, and I felt like we were floating rather than driving.

"Surf Shack," he answered. "I hope that's okay. I know you went there with Charlotte already, but-"

"No, it's perfect," I interrupted him. I had liked the feel

of the bar there. I had been a little afraid he was going to take me to some billionaire hangout where I would be completely out of place. The cute little bar by the ocean was something I could handle. "They have the best drinks."

He grinned and drove a little faster. The car responded to his touch like a lover, and would have made me jealous if it hadn't been a car. The warm tropical air whipped through my hair as evening descended on the island. It was hard to talk with the roof down, but it was comfortable just to be in the same car as Bastian. We didn't need to talk.

He pulled into the bar parking lot just as the streetlights started to turn on. The place looked just as busy as it had been the other night. Bastian parked, and hurried over to open my door before I even had a chance to undo my belt.

He held out his hand to help me out of the car. I loved it. Chivalry was not dead, and I found I rather liked it.

We managed to find an empty table in the back on the porch. It was the farthest we could be from the actual bar without falling into the ocean, but at least it was a table. It was perfect. Bastian caught the waiter's attention and we ordered drinks and some food. I ordered the special again, both the drink and the Jamaican Patty, and Bastian requested a whiskey and coke with his food.

"So you left Charlotte here alone with Leo drinking those," Bastian said as the waiter returned with our drinks and meal. Bastian raised his eyebrow at the very girly but delicious fruity drink with an umbrella in front of me. I pushed it toward him and he took a sip. His disgusted face told me what he thought of the fruity alcohol. "Poor guy's shirt never stood a chance."

I giggled quietly and sipped on my drink. "Poor Charlotte."

"She'll be fine," he assured me. "They'll figure it out eventually. They really are perfect for one another."

"How do they manage to get any work done?" I remembered the vivid shade of red she turned when he sat at our table. "She's so nervous around him."

"She's actually gotten better. You should have seen her when I was in college." He chuckled and smiled at the memory. "She was still in high school, so Leo was like a god to her. She couldn't even be in the same room with him for months without stuttering and blushing."

I could just imagine a cute little star-struck Charlotte in awe of the older, handsome, college boy. It was rather adorable.

"If you knew Leo, though, you'd know that he's just as love struck about her. He just hides it better." He smiled, remembering something. "The first time she met him, he was actually naked."

"Naked? Do tell," I asked, sipping on my drink. Bastian scooted his chair closer to mine so that our legs touched. It made it easier to hear him over the bar, but far more distracting.

"Gabe had this crush on this cute blonde cheerleader across the hall. He never stood a chance with her, but somehow, Leo found out that she had never gone streaking." He took a sip of his drink and grinned at me. "Have you ever gone streaking?"

"Once, but I want to hear your story first," I teased.

"Anyway, Leo wanted to help Gabe out, so he organized the whole dorm floor to go streaking down the Oval. He even made up posters to hang in the bathrooms to advertise it." He laughed. "Gabe was thrilled. Practically the entire hall went. We got out to there and everyone starts dropping their clothes. Of course, it's cold."

I laughed. "So you just looked normal, right?"

"Yup." Bastian grinned proudly at me and continued his story. "We all took off running. There's naked people everywhere. And then the cops showed up."

"Oh no!" I slurped at the last of my drink. I hadn't meant to drink it so fast, but it tasted so good I hadn't slowed down.

"Everyone panicked. Clothes were flying as people scrambled for cover and of course, Leo lost his pants and his shirt in the process. He ran the whole way back to the dorm, butt naked, thinking the cops were after him the whole way."

"Where was Charlotte?" I asked, wondering how she fit into this story.

"In my room waiting for me to get back. She was visiting me for the night, and I didn't want my little sister streaking with a bunch of college boys, so I told her I had class and that I'd be back in an hour," he explained. "Leo's keys were in his pants and his room was across the hall from mine. So when he saw my open door, he ran right in thinking he could borrow some clothes from me until he could get back in his room."

"And there was Charlotte..." I could just imagine Charlotte's face when Leo walked into her brother's dorm room butt naked and flushed from running in the cold. No wonder she couldn't stop blushing around him.

"It was rather traumatizing for both of them." Bastian laughed, shaking his head. "Gabe never let him live it down."

"Did Gabe end up getting the girl?" I asked. "I mean, that was the whole reason for going streaking, right?"

"She ended up dating one of the cops." Bastian's eyes twinkled as he sipped on his drink.

"Poor Leo! All that work and nakedness and Gabe didn't even get his girl." I started laughing and Bastian joined in.

I loved hearing Bastian laugh. It was rich and deep, with a joy that just made me want to join in with him. I could listen to him laugh all day. I could listen to his stories all day. I wanted to hear more, to find out more about the people in his life and everything I could in his world.

Bastian reached in his pocket and pulled out his phone. I could see the light going off as a call came in. He looked at it and then looked at me apologetically.

"It's Charlotte with an update on the app. Would you mind terribly if I took this?" His gray eyes held hope that I wouldn't be angry.

I smiled at him. "No, say hi for me. I'll go get us more drinks."

"Thanks." He smiled, relieved that I wasn't going to get angry. I understood that he was a billionaire and that required he take the odd phone call when we were out having fun. Business never stopped. Besides, I liked Charlotte.

I made my way over to the bar. It was busy, with three servers working. I found an empty space and wiggled my way in to get my order.

"Hey, hot stuff," a drunk voice said behind me. I didn't turn to acknowledge him. I was here with someone and I wasn't interested in dealing with anyone who called me "hot stuff."

I grabbed my drinks from the bartender and turned to leave, but blocking my way was Mr. "hot stuff." He had on a garish salmon t-shirt and lime-green plaid shorts that made my eyes hurt just looking at them.

"Excuse me," I said, trying to work my way around him

and not spill my two drinks. I just wanted to get back to Bastian, not deal with some drunk frat boy.

"Come on, baby, let me buy you a drink..." the man slurred, looking me up and down and grinning. His over-sized aviators fell off his head and he stumbled to pick them up. It gave me my opening to escape.

I held up my two drinks, as I moved. "Not interested."

"Denied!" yelled one of Salmon-shirt's buddies, pointing at Salmon-shirt. There were three of them at a pool table, all wearing different versions of the plaid short/garish t-shirt combo. They all began to laugh at Salmon-shirt, so I just I hurried away and back to Bastian.

"Anything important?" I asked as I sat down and slid him his drink.

He shook his head. "Just Charlotte checking in. Things are right on schedule."

"How is she?" I asked, hoping he would read into the question a little bit.

"Fine." He took a sip of his drink and leaned back. "And, no, there isn't anything interesting going on between her and Leo. She wanted me to tell you that."

I giggled and scooted my chair back to where our legs could touch again. "Tell me more about your adventures in streaking," I asked, batting my eyelashes at him.

"I actually think it's your turn," he replied, grinning from ear to ear. "I want to hear all about you being naked."

I blushed, but took a sip of my drink and started to tell him the story of how I went streaking that one time in college.

～

Several hours and some drinks later, Bastian and I stumbled out of the bar. It had become even more crowded as the night had gone on and we both had work in the morning. Even so, I was delightfully tipsy, and from the not-quite-straight way Bastian was walking, he wasn't much better. It felt wonderful.

I held onto his burly arm as we stepped out into the hot night air. It felt almost cooler out here without all the people crowding into the small space. Bastian patted his pocket for the keys and I giggled as he stumbled on a perfectly straight step.

"I can't drive," he announced. He looked at me and how I was hanging off of him and giggling uncontrollably. "And neither can you. I'll call Elijah."

"Where is he?" I asked, looking around. I hadn't seen him all night.

"I asked him to be discreet tonight," Bastian informed me with a wink. I giggled, feeling naughty.

Bastian pulled out his phone and hit a button. "Elijah. We need a ride." Someone said something on the other line and Bastian hung up. He glanced back at the bar door. "He'll be here in just a minute. I'm going to go use the bathroom for a second."

"You can use it for more than a second," I teased. "In fact, I'd recommend it."

Bastian chuckled and kissed me on the forehead. He looked so relaxed and calm. This had been a great evening. He grinned and headed back inside.

I stood out on the front porch, watching the insects buzz the lights. It was quiet out here, as the party was going on inside. The sounds of the bar were muffled through the heavy door as I made my way to the far end of the porch. The night air was thick and heavy. *I could get used to nights like this*, I thought, taking a deep breath in. *Especially with Bastian.*

"All alone now, aren't you, hot-stuff?"

I spun to see Salmon-shirt walking up the side steps of the front porch. The hairs on the back of my neck started to prickle.

"My date's just in the bathroom," I stated, looking at the door to the bar and suddenly finding it very far away. "He'll be back any minute."

"Sure he will," Salmon-shirt agreed. The stagger and red in his eyes said that he was definitely drunk. I swallowed hard as his three buddies came out from behind the bar and stood in the parking lot. One of them opened the door to a very expensive-looking car and pulled out a flask. As if they hadn't had enough to drink already.

"Please, I don't want any trouble," I said, trying to figure out if I could make a run for the bar doors. I didn't want to appear to obvious, but I no longer felt safe out here alone. Everything about these men screamed spoiled, rich brats. They were all Chads, but with an unlimited supply of money. If they wanted something, they could just take it.

"It's no trouble at all, hot-stuff," Salmon-shirt assured me. He strode toward me, putting himself quickly between me and the door to the bar faster than I had expected. I was trapped. "But you see, you embarrassed me in front of my friends."

One of his friends yelled out something that sounded vulgar. My heart started to pound and my palms went sweaty.

He licked his lips and raised his hand, trying to brush a strand of hair out of my face. There was no way in hell I was letting him touch me, even if it was just to brush some hair away. I smacked his hand away from me as hard as I could.

"Touch me again, and I'll put you down," I threatened. The forcefulness of my words caught me by surprise. It probably had to do with that he reminded me so much of Chad. That and the alcohol.

"Ooh," he giggled. "I like a little bit of fight in my girls."

He moved so quick I didn't have time to react. His hands went to my arms, pinning me to the wall and holding me there. I tried to struggle, but he was stronger than he looked. I kicked out with my legs, but I didn't have a good groin shot and he made sure to stay far enough away that my heels couldn't come directly down on his feet. Panic started to pump through me.

"You'll put me down, huh?" Salmon-shirt smirked. His friends laughed behind him, watching him and egging him on. "How about you go down?"

Suddenly, Bastian's hand was on the guys shoulder and the next thing I knew, Salmon-shirt was flying off the deck and into the parking lot. He landed with a thud in the dirt, looking up to see Bastian advancing on him.

Even from my position, Bastian looked terrifying. His big shoulders were outdone only by the massive snarl across his face. The scar running down his cheek caught the streetlamp light and made him look vicious and feral.

Salmon-shirt stood up, puffing his chest out and putting up his fists. Bastian waited for him to throw the first punch, dodging it easily before socking him squarely in the jaw.

Salmon-shirt went down like a sack of potatoes. His friends got very quiet.

"Get up," Bastian commanded. His voice was low like thunder and just as menacing.

Salmon-shirt shook his head, holding his hand to his jaw. He didn't look quite so drunk or so brave anymore. He looked like a spoiled, petulant child.

Bastian grabbed the back of his shirt and hauled him to his feet. "I said get up," Bastian snarled. Salmon-shirt was visibly quaking and turning a strange shade of pale green. Bastian tightened his grip on the salmon shirt. "Apologize to the lady."

"Sorry," Salmon-shirt whispered, looking anywhere but at me.

Bastian shook him like a rag doll and growled. "I think you can do better."

Salmon-shirt looked up at me, fear and honesty pouring out of his eyes. His voice cracked. "I'm very sorry, miss."

"Are you ever going to bother her or anyone like her again?" Bastian 's voice was so low and angry even I was frightened. Car tires squealed as Elijah peeled into the parking lot. Bastian lifted the man up higher, threatening to shake him again.

Salmon-shirt shook his head vehemently from side to side. "No, sir!"

"Good." Bastian dropped him. Salmon-shirt went to his knees, tears running down his face. Bastian turned to face his buddies and gave them a death glare that should have killed each of them three times over. They each took three steps back and cowered a little.

It was over by the time Elijah came running up, ready to defend me and Bastian to the death. The whole thing had taken less than thirty seconds.

"Take care of this," he instructed Elijah before running back to where I stood shaking like a leaf.

"Are you okay?" His voice lost all traces of the anger and violence that had been there just seconds ago. He took my chin in his fingers and looked me over, his eyes full of care and concern.

I nodded, not trusting my voice. I hadn't realized how

strong he was. There was a fierceness and violence to him that frightened me, but when he looked at me, all I could see was the sweetness and kindness I knew from him.

He wrapped his arm around my shoulder and escorted me down the stairs to the car Elijah had arrived in. The car was the same one as Charlotte and I had taken the last time I was at this bar. I decided that as much as I enjoyed the drinks here, I didn't want to come back. Both times I had left had been in disaster.

He opened the door and helped me in, hurrying around to get in as well. He buckled my seat belt for me before doing his own, taking my hands in his when he finished.

"You're shaking," he told me, squeezing my hands tighter. I watched the muscles in his arms twitch under his shirt from exertion.

Elijah opened the front door and started the car, driving us home. I hoped he sped, because I just wanted to get home. I wanted to curl up with Bastian and forget that moment of fear.

"I tried to fight them off." I wanted to explain. I needed to tell him that I hadn't just stood there and let it happen. "I tried, but he had me pinned...

"I know," he cut me off gently. "You're a fighter. I'm sorry I wasn't there. That shouldn't have happened to you." There was true regret in his voice. He blamed himself and I hated it.

"You had no way to prevent that," I insisted.

"Doesn't matter," he said quietly, keeping my hands folded securely within his. "I want you safe."

I pulled one of my hands free from his and touched his face. He looked at me with failure in his beautiful gray eyes. His scars gleamed in the moonlight. I was so grateful to him for rescuing me that I didn't want to see that regret in his eyes.

"Thank you," I whispered. "You saved me."

I leaned forward and kissed him. It started innocently enough, but the adrenaline and fear mixed with gratitude and attraction overwhelmed me. I found my tongue pushing to enter his mouth, wanting his in mine and my hands pressing into his broad chest for more.

He pulled back, grabbing my wrists and holding me in place.

"I don't want to hurt you," he groaned, fighting with his own desire. "I don't want to take advantage."

I pushed harder against him, imploring with him with my eyes not to stop. "Please," I begged, unable to fight my attraction for him. His chivalrous refusal not to take advantage only made it that much harder. I wanted him even more. "Please..."

His brow softened. He picked at a loose strand of hair by my cheek, carefully tucking it behind my ear. His eyes absorbed me, trying to decide if I really was asking.

"Please, Bastian..." I whispered one more time. The sound of his name was his undoing. He kissed me just as the car pulled to a stop in front of the house. It was a short kiss, but full of raw passion.

He had my seat-belt undone in an instant, picking me up in his arms and carrying me up the steps to the main entrance. Elijah opened the door, but that was the last I saw of him as Bastian carried me up the stairs and to his bedroom, kissing me the entire way.

I loved his bedroom. It was obviously Sebastian's private space, and I loved being surrounded by the things he had chosen. The room was painted to match the sand outside and every piece of furniture was practical yet beautiful. It was comfortable and welcoming with a tranquility that made sleep come easily in that room.

But not tonight. Tonight, the bed was anything but tranquil.

I kissed him, hard and fast as he entered the bedroom. He let my feet go to the floor as he took me in his arms, fisting his hand into my hair and making sure that I couldn't escape his lips. His kiss sent a bolt of hunger through me so strong, I wasn't sure I could survive it.

The all consuming thought of having him naked spurred my fingers to the hem of his shirt. He only paused long enough from his kisses to pull it over his head before greedily finding my mouth again. I arched into him, wanting bare skin to skin but tolerating having just my hands on him for the moment.

His skin was smooth and hot under my fingers. The ridges of old scars flowed into the strength and firmness of his muscles. Just touching him was a drug and I couldn't get enough. Neither could he.

With a growl, he turned and pressed my back into the wall by the door. With the wall to my back he had me pinned in the most delicious way. It wasn't frightening or intimidating, other than how turned on I was becoming. Every nerve wanted him to press harder, to take me in any way he wanted.

I needed him closer, so balancing on one foot, I wrapped my other around his waist, pressing my aching need into his groin. A deep rumble of lust echoed through his big chest as his hand went to my thigh and slid up under my dress.

The pads of his fingers were rough against the vulnerable flesh of my inner thigh. It made the fire burning in my core spark even higher. I pressed my dampening lacy panties against the hardening bulge in his pants, loving that he obviously wanted me as badly as I did him.

My fingers went to his pants, struggling with the buttons for a moment before loosening them. I tugged hard on his pants and underwear until they pooled at his ankles. The only thing keeping his erection from completing me was the thin lace of my panties.

Our eyes met. His pupils were huge with pure lust that had me panting and pressing against him harder. His fingers tightened on my thigh, and he rocked his hips into mine. His brows came together and he glanced toward his desk in the other room. The drawer with his condoms was so far away and he would have to let me go to get them.

I wanted him in me. Joined to me. No, not wanted. *Needed.* I needed him to soothe the ache between my thighs more than I needed to breathe.

"Don't stop," I gasped, grinding into him with desperate want. I put my hand on his cheek, peering into his eyes and making sure he knew I wanted this. "I'm on the pill. Just don't stop."

I didn't know it was possible to have my heart beat so fast at just a look. He growled, thrusting the thin lace of my panties to the side and thrusting his hard member deep into my throbbing, needful core.

He glided upward, filling me completely with one swift, powerful motion. I gasped, my mouth opening at the plea-sure of his entrance and the way his eyes widened in ecstasy. He groaned softly as he began to repeatedly bury himself deeper and deeper into me. I arched into him, crying out as he completed me again and again.

His strong hands cupped my ass and he used the wall as leverage to drive into me. It was easy to lift my other leg around his waist, pumping my legs with his hips for more.

He held me easily, rocking into me with powerful thrusts that rocked the axis of my entire world.

The fever pitch inside of me grew, and my thighs tightened and contracted around his waist. His teeth bit down gently on my shoulder, the sharp edge of pain shocking my system into overdrive. My core clenched, surprising me with the sudden blinding swirl of colors that filled my vision. Bastian didn't stop his carefully timed thrusts. I barely heard him groan with pleasure as my body contracted and convulsed around his.

"More..." I gasped as my body fell from the sudden high. I needed more of him. All of him. I was a drowning woman and he was air. I couldn't get enough of him.

A wordless, lustful, growl reverberated through his chest and he spun from the wall and tossed me onto the big bed. I bounced twice as he kicked his clothing away from him and stalked toward the bed.

He was all muscles and masculine power. Huge. Strong. And ready for more.

I slithered out of my panties, tossing them to the floor before reaching behind my neck to find the zipper to my dress. Bastian didn't wait for me to find the zipper, let alone let me undo it. His hands caught the back of my skirt, pulling me to him using my dress like a rope.

"Get on your hands and knees," he commanded. His voice was husky and primal with desire. I melted a little, quivering in the deep recesses of my core for more. I had the power to make his voice that rough with want, and the power to give him more.

My knees rested on the edge of the bed while my hands met in the middle. Bastian still held my skirt bunched in his hands like reigns as I wiggled my hips, inviting him back into my trembling heat. The tension in the skirt increased as he filled me to the hilt.

I cried out, falling forward and screaming with pleasure into the bed. The sensations and emotions rolling through me were primordial and animalistic, turning me on in such a primal way that I was about to explode. I loved it.

I could hear him panting behind me, his grip on my dress tightening as he took me. I clawed at the bedspread, desperate to stay on this plane of existence and not vibrate off into another without Bastian. I loved the small noises of effort and pleasure he made.

I leaned forward, needing to see his face. I wanted to watch him, to see his pleasure and not just feel it. I twisted back, seeing the flicker of controlled anger at losing my body flicker across his face.

"Lay down," I commanded, my voice surprisingly steady.

He didn't hesitate, but he moved with languid beauty that made my breath catch. He was so beautiful. And all mine.

I put one leg on either side of him, enjoying the way his eyes ran up and down my body and the cocky grin spreading across his face. His hands went to my hips, holding the dress up so he could watch as I slowly lowered myself onto him.

Using my hips, glutes, and thighs I started to dance. Up and down, circles and gyrations, I let my body find a way to let him touch every inch of my insides. Bastian whimpered and his eyes rolled back into his head as his fingers clamped harder on my hips.

He thrust upward, unable to control his own body's reaction to the pleasure I was causing. I paused, holding myself just out of his reach. I was in control.

Bastian swore, trying to raise his hips to find me. When I didn't give him what he wanted he struggled to stay still. Every muscle in his chest was taut and drawn as he used every ounce of his willpower to remain still and thus have me continue.

I began my slow dance once he settled. I loved the tightness in his jaw and the frown of concentration as he focused on the pleasurable sensations without following through on the natural inclination to join in.

The power of another release was growing in my center again. Leaving me to my own movements, it wouldn't take me long to climax again, doing exactly what felt best for me. I sped up and Bastian's eyes flicked open, realizing what was happening.

He shifted his grip on my hips so that his thumb came to rest directly on my pleasure center. Watching me with confident eyes, he began to move his thumb in small circles that matched the cadence of my dance on his manhood.

"Fuck..." Bastian groaned. "You're so beautiful, Ava..."

It was his eyes that did it. The truth shining there, the emotion and the raw desire in his beautiful gray eyes. It sent me spinning and skittering into unfathomable pleasure. Every muscle in my body tightened and stretched at the same time. I forgot to breathe. I forgot everything but Bastian and what he was doing to me.

I sagged against his chest, gasping and still trembling on the aftershocks of the most powerful orgasm of my life. Bastian's fingers found the zipper of my dress, pulling gently and then moving to pull the dress off. I sat back slightly to allow the fabric up and over my head before Bastian tossed it to the floor.

Bastian's fingers traced the line of white lace on the cup of my bra. My nipples hardened under the silky fabric, aching to be touched. I whimpered, ready to evaporate the bra with just the power of my mind. Bastian chuckled, wrapping his arms around me and then rolling so that he was on top.

He kissed me softly. It was gentle, but full of need and power. He was in control now. I was at his mercy, but looking into his face, I knew I was safe. He would only take me to wonderful places.

His hips began to pump and his hand tightened on my shoulder, putting me right where he wanted. I writhed under him, completely under his control and at his pleasure. I loved the way he felt and the fact that he was growing harder and going faster only proved that he found me the same.

With every inch he moved deeper, not just owning my body, but a piece of my soul. One I wanted to give him. I wanted him to have me completely, to be completely his.

I felt it then, an orgasm so big that it put my previous ones to shame. It was going to shatter my mind. It started at the tips of my toes and rippled up, through my calves, into my thighs and detonated in my core. I rippled around him, quaking and spasming in indescribable ecstasy.

Bastian's fingers tightened on my shoulder and his body stiffened in response to the pleasure racking through mine. Every muscle of my body was trying to draw him deeper, to take him further into me. He started to shake and his thrusts rocked the bed.

I wanted it all. I wanted him. His eyes met mine, asking and yet not asking at the same time.

"Take me, Bastian," I whispered, urging him with my hips. "I'm yours."

My name fell from his lips as he buried himself so deeply my breath caught. He claimed me completely. His eyes held me prisoner the same way he held my body prisoner. Fireworks were going off in his eyes. I watched galaxies explode and create in the depths of his eyes.

It was a beautiful eternity before he collapsed, hiding his head in my shoulder. His breath was hot and heavy on my skin and our bodies sticky with sweat, but I didn't want him to move. I never wanted to move from this spot, never wanted to have him leave me.

I was wanted here. Safe. Desired. No one had ever made me feel that way before. Not just the sexual part, which was off any chart I had ever had, but the protected and desired part.

I breathed him in. He smelled so good, I couldn't get enough of him into me.

He rose slightly, a crooked grin spreading across his handsome features. He touched my cheek, and I turned and kissed his palm before cradling my cheek into his fingers.

I had never felt like this before. It was a pleasure so deep that I wasn't sure how either one of us was going to survive without it.

He rolled to his side, tucking me into the nook of his shoulder. His arms encircled me, wrapping me in his warmth and protection. I was safe here. I would always be safe with him.

I closed my eyes, feeling sleep coming to finally claim me from the stresses of the day. Bastian's breaths were a soothing melody that was drawing me into calm serenity. I knew this couldn't last. He was a billionaire and I wasn't part of his world. But, even knowing that, a spot of warmth settled in behind my breastbone and didn't leave even as I drifted off.

CHAPTER 20

I entered the details for the last painting in the room into my tablet. I needed to turn on a light, but the light from the hallway was just enough for me to finish. The appraisal was going faster than I had anticipated, which was wonderful. It meant I could justify spending time with Bastian without feeling guilty about not working.

This was supposed to be a job. Except it was so much more than that now. This was a vacation, a job, and something else. A romance? A fling? I didn't know what to call what was going on between Bastian and me. I just knew that I was enjoying it.

I still felt a little guilty about my father, but being ahead on my work even helped with that as well. I had continued to receive updates from him, the nurses, and even Jackie. Everyone promised he was doing just fine and that I had nothing to worry about, but I still felt like I had abandoned my father to hook up in the Caribbean. I knew that wasn't true, but it still nagged at me. Working helped that feel better.

The small hairs on the back of my neck tingled, telling

me that someone was watching me. Turning slowly, I found Bastian leaning against the door frame. He filled the doorway, both in presence and body. His lean muscles were tight under a dress shirt with a tie and dark slacks that accented the wonderful curve of his ass.

"Are you spying on me?" I asked, grinning playfully.

He stepped forward, walking into the room and making my heart start to speed up. I loved the way he moved. "You get this little line, right here," he said, gently touching my forehead with one of his fingers. "It's quite charming."

I couldn't help but blush a little and smile. He stepped closer, putting his hands on my neck, preparing to draw me in for a kiss. His arms flexed, showing me his muscles. I loved those muscles.

"But, I do think I like it better when you smile," he said softly, soliciting another smile. "Yes, I definitely like it better when you smile. It's close, though."

"I like it best when you smile," I replied. I loved the way his hands felt on me. I pressed my palms against his chest, feeling the rock hard pecs underneath.

"Really?" he asked, raising his eyebrows. He smelled so damn good. I didn't know how anyone could smell so wonderful.

"Your whole face lights up," I whispered. My heart was fluttering. Every nerve in my body screamed for his touch. He leaned forward and pausing just above my lips. I held perfectly still, smiling as he hovered just millimeters from kissing me. "It's absolutely breathtaking."

It was hard to think of anything but his hands on me. The way his fingers caressed my skin and how he seemed able to elicit pleasure from just looking at me properly. I pressed my hips against his, asking but not taking.

"Though, there's another face that I think you like just as

much," I whispered, watching his lips. They were so perfect. Full, yet masculine.

"And which one is that?" he asked, his perfect mouth curving into a curious smile.

"This one," I replied, making the most ridiculous "O" face I possibly could before dissolving into a fit of giggles.

"I do not look like that," he said, his face stern and serious. It made me laugh even harder. He shrugged. "I guess I'll just have to prove it to you"

He released me and undid the top button of his shirt, loosening his tie in the process.

"Right here?" I asked, looking around the room. There was a small lounge chair and a writing table from the 18th century, but most of the room was dedicated to the art on the walls.

"Why not?" he purred, unbuttoning each button one at a time. I gasped a little when he slid the shirt from his shoulders. I loved how broad they were and how strong every inch of him was. The suit was nice, but naked was even better.

"I guess it *is* still your house," I whispered, my mouth watering at the sight of his body. He was all strong lines and sinew. Every inch of him radiated strength and desire.

"Damn straight," he agreed. His voice was low and hungry. His eyes shone with want.

Heat skittered through my belly, then directly south. The confidence in his voice only turned up the flame from slow burn to forest fire.

He dipped his head and let his lips slide along my throat, igniting yet more flames along the sensitive skin. Bastian paused at the delicate hollow of my throat, right where my pulse was beating out his name. He nipped at my collarbone, sending a tremor of sheer desire straight through my core.

I arched my hips, begging him for more. I needed more. I didn't care where we were anymore. I didn't care about the work or the 18th century furniture. All I knew was that I needed him. I needed him more than I had ever needed anyone.

That alone surprised me.

I had never craved Chad this way. I had never felt this alive with anyone. Bastian had the ability to turn me on with just a glance. The way he looked at me... I knew he wanted me as much as I wanted him.

As he nibbled on my shoulder, pausing only for a moment to draw my shirt up and over my head, I realized I was falling for him. And falling hard. It wasn't just the sex, though what he was currently doing to me was making it hard to think of anything else.

It was how he made me feel.

Safe. Wanted. Perfect.

I closed my eyes, reveling in his arms. I was falling for him. I was falling for the billionaire.

A billionaire.

"Something wrong?" Bastian asked, pulling back, his eyes dark with lust and want. I had frozen without meaning to. He was a billionaire. I couldn't be falling for him. I shouldn't be falling for him. It was like falling for a prince, and I was no Cinderella. There was no way I would ever fit in his billionaire world.

I shook my head, pushing the dark thoughts aside. "No, keep going," I murmured, arching my hips into his again. My body didn't want him to stop and was urging my mind to follow along.

"You taste so good," he murmured, running his tongue

along the ridge of my collarbone. Uncontrollable fires of need raged within me. I focused my attention on Bastian, ignoring the emotions rolling around inside of me.

Right now, Bastian wanted me. Here, on this island, in this room, he wanted me. I didn't know how long this feeling could last, but I knew I couldn't waste this moment. For today, I just wanted to think about how he made me feel. To enjoy this moment, even knowing that I wasn't worthy of it.

I didn't know why he would want me. Just that he did.

And for now, that was enough.

CHAPTER 21

*D*elete email.

I stared at my laptop screen. Whatever Chad and I had once had, it wasn't love. I could see that now. I had been in love, but looking back I didn't think he had been. He had wanted something from me, and I hadn't been able to give it to him.

I sighed and changed tabs to check my myFace.

No. Delete. Again.

I scrolled through my news feed, seeing pictures of friend's babies and puppies and the occasional funny cartoon. Dad had posted that I was coming home today with a smiley face. Jackie had liked it.

A news article on Kindling Romance scrolled up. The

picture showed all three of the handsome owners smiling for the camera in front of their New York office. I smiled back at Bastian and clicked on the article.

It was just an update on the launch of their new dating app. The news article claimed that it would change the dating game yet again, and I almost believed it. If Bastian was involved, he was certainly a game-changer.

I read to the end and saw a related article. *Who is Billionaire Sebastian Belrose?*

My mouse hovered over the link as I considered clicking it. I knew who Sebastian Belrose was. He was the wonderful man I had just finished paddle-boarding out on the ocean with. I had just spent the last week having the most amazing time with him. Sebastian Belrose protected me and treated me like I was special. I didn't need a clickbait article to tell me that.

I clicked on it anyway. I couldn't help myself.

The article was full of useless speculation. It seemed that very few people actually knew the real Sebastian Belrose. He had managed to keep the major secrets of his life out of the public, letting Gabe and Leo have the spotlight.

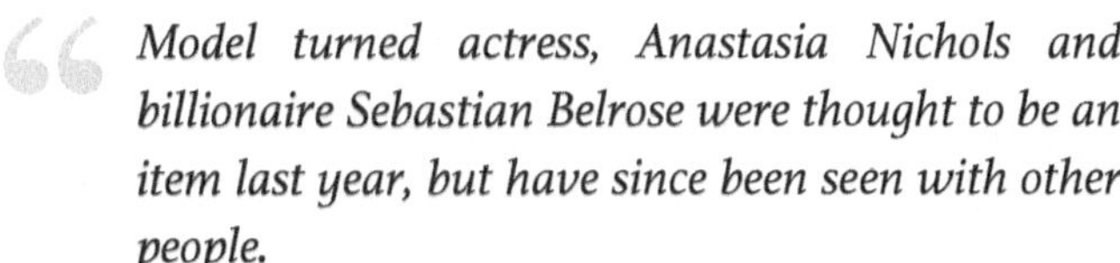

> *Model turned actress, Anastasia Nichols and billionaire Sebastian Belrose were thought to be an item last year, but have since been seen with other people.*

A picture of Bastian and the most beautiful woman I had ever seen filled my screen. The two of them were obviously on a date at some sort of fancy restaurant. She had on the most amazing, form-fitting, red dress and her hand was resting on his arm. The picture had him caught in mid-laugh from whatever clever thing the stunning woman had to say.

I looked up at my reflection in the wall mirror, noting how I appeared nothing like the supermodel in the photo.

My hair was a disaster as I hadn't brushed it yet after our morning paddle-board session. In fact, there was even a piece of seaweed still lodged in it from when I fell in the water. I hadn't showered yet, so I hadn't put on any makeup. My nose was sunburned and freckles had started to pop up on my cheeks.

I wasn't anything close to a model. Why would he even bother with me? I wasn't anything spectacular.

My computer binged as an email arrived. I clicked to check it, thinking it might be an important update from Dad, only to find it another message from Chad.

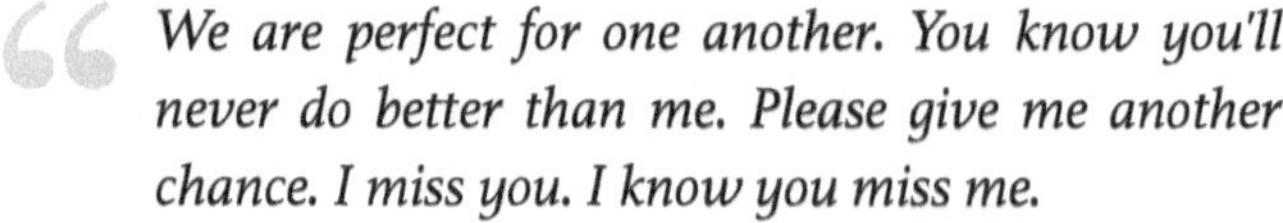

We are perfect for one another. You know you'll never do better than me. Please give me another chance. I miss you. I know you miss me.

I hesitated to delete it, reading it twice more before finally hitting the delete button. I flipped back to the article on Sebastian, looking at the perfect woman that was making him laugh. He was so handsome and the two of them made an amazing looking couple. They would have beautiful children. Besides, looking at their elegant surroundings, I would never fit in there.

Maybe Chad was right. Maybe he was the best I could have hoped for. I looked in the mirror again and saw another piece of seaweed.

Bastian deserved someone better than me. He deserved someone who could fit in his world and complement him. I would never be able to wear that red dress without being incredibly self conscious and having to adjust it every two seconds. The woman in the picture didn't appear to have that problem.

I sighed and closed the window. I needed a shower.

I FOLLOWED the smell of bacon into the kitchen. Bastian was busy mixing something in a bowl while bacon hissed and sputtered on the stove behind him. He had showered and shaved, but was wearing just a t-shirt and shorts. He smiled as he saw me come in.

"Ready for breakfast?" He held up the bowl. "I'm making waffles."

I went to the coffee pot, pouring another cup. This was the last day of this tranquil domestic scene. The last day I would have this coffee mug and the last time Bastian would make me waffles. I didn't want this dream to end.

"I can't wait," I told him, smiling and sipping at my coffee. He grinned and poured the first waffle into the waffle iron.

"You want to make the eggs?" he asked. "Yours are better than mine."

I smiled at the compliment and went to the fridge to pull out the eggs. I was going to miss this.

"You're awfully quiet," Bastian noted, checking his waffle before flipping the iron. "You okay?"

I pushed the butter around the skillet, watching it melt and change into something else.

"I leave in a few hours," I said finally, my heart aching at just saying the words. I didn't want to leave, but I had to get back to my life. I had to get back to Dad. He was getting a pacemaker and I needed to be there for him. I had responsibilities and I couldn't stay in the Caribbean playing happy honeymoon forever.

"I know." Bastian's voice held as much sadness as mine did.

"What happens next?" I asked. I cracked an egg, watching it sizzle in the butter before I mushed the yolk into a yellow mess. I turned around slowly to watch him.

"What do you mean?" Bastian removed his first waffle and put it on a plate. It was a perfect golden brown. He added more batter to the iron.

"What happens with us, Bastian?"

It was one of the few things we hadn't discussed this past week. We both had silently agreed to avoid it, finding other topics far more interesting. Our time together had been better than either one of us could remember, but we both knew that talking about it meant that it would come to an end. Except, even without discussing it, it was still ending.

"I don't know." He ran a hand through his hair, spiking the still damp golden-brown tresses up. "I don't want to lose you, though."

I turned around, focusing on stirring the eggs. I knew what had to be done. What had to be done to keep us both from making promises we couldn't keep.

"I think we should just end it."

"What?" Bastian's voice cracked slightly.

I turned the heat down on the eggs and turned around, biting my lip. This needed to be done. I was giving him his life back because I wouldn't fit in it. I never would have fit.

"I have to go back home," I said slowly. "You have to go back to New York. I can't work in NY. You can't work in my tiny town."

"We could find a way," he insisted. He set down the bowl of waffle batter.

I shook my head. "Bastian, you're a billionaire. I'm not. You drive luxury cars and I drive my cousin's hand-me-down car. You deserve someone better than me."

There. I said it. The truth was out now.

"No, I don't," he growled.

"Yes, you do," I insisted. I motioned to my sunburned nose and cheap clothes. "Look at me. I can't go to your fancy galas and dinner parties. I don't fit in that world."

Bastian's gray eyes narrowed. "You could."

"No," I said, shaking my head. "When I leave tonight. I leave."

"Ava..."

"It's been a wonderful trip, but that's all it was." I swallowed down the ache in my heart. I wanted to throw up, but this was how it had to be. He deserved someone worthy of him and his world and that person wasn't me. He would drop me just like Chad did, only harder. It was only a matter of time before he saw that I wasn't worthy of him. I couldn't take that pain. The knowledge that I didn't deserve him and he just hadn't realized it yet pounded in my head like cruel drum beats. I had to make them stop. "Let's not make this into something more than the two of us having a good time."

The waffles started to burn.

Hurt painted across his face in broad strokes. Shock and anger replaced it. His scar was livid against his pale cheek as he processed my callous words.

He ripped the waffle iron out of the wall and threw the entire thing in the sink. I jumped at the loud and angry motion. The iron clattered and hissed against the stainless steel sink, smoking and steaming as the ruined waffle ran out the sides.

He turned and stormed out of the kitchen, leaving the

mess of waffles in his wake. I held my wooden spatula in shock as I heard him thunder up the stairs. The slam of his study door made the mansion shake and I could hear the harsh turn of the lock even from the kitchen.

My eggs were burning.

I didn't care. Saying those words had hurt far more than I had expected. They were lies and I knew it, yet I had said them.

I pushed them to the side, sliding down to the floor and sobbing for the man I knew I couldn't have.

CHAPTER 22

One week. One glorious week.

I put my swimsuit carefully away in my suitcase. I couldn't believe how fast the week had gone. I needed to find my sandals and put them in next, but I was taking my time and moving as slowly as possible. I didn't want the week to end yet. I wasn't ready for it to end yet. I didn't want this dream to end.

The week had been a glorious blur of Bastian, paddle-boarding, art, and the most mind-blowing sex I had ever had. Up until this morning, it had been heaven.

I was going to miss Bastian, but I knew it was better for him for me to end it. It wasn't just the sex that made him so amazing, though it certainly didn't hurt. If I ever told him that he was sweet, he would most certainly deny it, but it was true. He was incredibly intelligent with a sharp sense of humor that had me laughing and smiling without realizing it. He deserved someone worthy of him. Someone better than me.

He was perfect. And wonderful. And everything I ever wanted.

And I had to leave him. For his own good. He deserved someone who could be his equal. Past experience had taught me that it wasn't me.

I had no reason to stay. The appraisal was done. I had completed it in time and was actually quite proud of my work. It had been hard, and there were a couple late nights, but between sending pictures to my father and working every moment that I wasn't with Bastian, I had gotten it all done. It was the biggest job I had ever done. It was time for me to go take care of Dad, now.

All good things must come to an end, I thought as I stuffed my last shirt into the bag. The auction would be next week, but that was my aunt's domain. My part of working for Sebastian Belrose was complete and I had nothing left to do. I was supposed to go home now. It was time for me to go back to my regular life where I belonged. As much as I wanted to belong here, I knew I didn't.

I closed my eyes and imagined what life would be like if I hadn't told him I was leaving.

I would be flying to New York all the time. Missing business. He would be flying to me all the time. We wouldn't have any time together. We would fight. I would embarrass him at social situations. He would find someone better. If I wasn't enough for a small fish like Chad, then Bastian would tire of me even sooner.

I would only end up hurting both of us. It was better this way.

The light in the room was fading quickly, making everything appear gray and drab. I looked out the window of my room. The sky was quickly darkening as the sunset approached. Bastian stood at the water's edge, staring off at the blackening horizon. I didn't want to leave, but I knew it was time. My dream job was over. Despite this morning, I needed to say goodbye. I had to see him one last time.

I did one last sweep of the room, making sure that everything was neatly packed away into my suitcase. Someone would come and take it to the car for me soon. I placed my bag on the bed and went down to say my goodbyes.

I had already said goodbye to Lucia at breakfast, and Charlotte had apologized over video chat for leaving and not coming back days ago. She was still stuck on the mainland working on the company app with Leo. I hoped things were going well for her and that she would finally get the courage to tell him she liked him. I hoped I would see her again, but I wasn't sure.

I stepped out onto the fine white sand. Bastian was wearing his full length shirt again, after an entire week of wearing short-sleeves or nothing. It looked strange now. Like he had on the wrong skin. The wind tugged at his hair, messing it's warm brown and golds into a tangles.

I stood beside him, watching the horizon grow dark as the sun set behind us. We were looking toward the dawn, both of us wishing the sun were coming up instead of going down. He moved his hand, then paused, as if unsure how I would react. In a quick movement, he took my hand in his, holding onto me tightly.

Our shadows stretched out far into the dark water until the stars started to twinkle, but still we stood. Finally, he turned, his gray eyes full of a sadness I shared and a pain I had caused. His hand held onto mine like I might turn to mist at any moment and disappear from his sight. I could still see the anger, deep in his dark eyes, but it was overshadowed by sadness and acceptance.

He was letting me leave because I had told him I needed to. He was giving me what I asked.

I hated thinking about it, but now it was time. We were

from separate worlds. We were both trapped by our businesses and our obligations to others.

Our worlds were just too different, our lives too separate. *A fish may love a bird, but where would they build their nest....* We both knew it. Better to end it here before we really hurt one another.

Shadows filled his face. The scars on his cheek and eyebrow darkened as the sun faded into obscurity. He touched my face, caressing my cheek with his fingers like he was memorizing me.

"I have to go," I said quietly, leaning into his touch and never wanting him to stop. My chest ached with an unexplainable pain. I hadn't expected this moment to hurt this much. "My plane will be leaving soon."

"I know," he replied, tucking a strand of hair behind my ear. His hand went to the back of my neck. He slowly lowered his face to mine, kissing me goodbye one last time. The kiss was soft and warm, lingering and full of memory. I closed my eyes and took in every detail. The way his five-o'clock shadow scratched my lips, how warm he was, the taste of his tongue, and the scent of his cologne. I wanted to remember every detail.

"I've never liked the dark, but with you, it's tolerable," he whispered, his voice cracking slightly. He caressed my cheek again, his fingers soft with regret. "In fact, I think I could get used to the dark if you were there with me. Possibly even enjoy it."

My throat constricted, and I couldn't speak. I didn't have the words to tell him how I felt. How I needed him. He didn't deserve to be stuck with me when he could have someone so much better. I wasn't good enough for anyone, let alone Bastian.

So, instead I kissed him, pouring every fiber of my being

into the kiss and hoping that he understood. I wanted to stay with him more than I wanted to breathe. He was a part of me now, and leaving was like losing a limb. *If it hurts this much now, imagine the heartache later,* I told myself.

Elijah cleared his throat. "It's time to go," he announced, as gently as he could from behind us.

"Goodbye, Bastian," I whispered, pressing my forehead into his. *Better to prevent the pain,* I reminded myself. *Better for both of us.*

"Goodbye, Ava," he whispered back. I kissed him one last time before summoning every ounce of strength I had to turn and walk away.

An ounce of prevention is worth a pound of cure. I could do this. I could leave him now and it wouldn't be as bad as it would be later. In a few days, this would just be a happy memory. We would be back to our normal lives within forty-eight hours.

This was a fling. A beach romance. An impossible love. It could never survive outside the sandy shores of the Caribbean. If we brought it back with us, it would die a cold and cruel death in the winter winds of reality. This was for the better. *This is for our own good.*

The walk to the car was longer than I could have imagined. Elijah padded softly behind me as I left the man who meant so much to me standing on a dark beach. I wanted to cry, but it hurt so much that I didn't even have tears for it yet.

"Have a safe trip home, Ava," Elijah said, opening the door to the car. "It was wonderful to have you here."

"Thank you, Elijah," I replied. He would know just how much Bastian meant to me. How much I meant to Bastian. "It was wonderful. Like a dream. I wish I didn't have to leave."

My voice cracked and the tears finally found their way to the surface. Elijah gave me a small, sad smile and then tapped on the roof to signal the driver. Marcus waited until I had fastened my seat-belt to start the engine.

The car purred to life as Marcus maneuvered out of the giant driveway and to the main road. I looked back, seeing the ocean glinting of the receding moon as we drove away. I could just make out Bastian's silhouette against the water. His head thrown back as if he were screaming at the water.

I turned away, not wanting to look anymore. It was time for me to go home.

CHAPTER 23

The flight to Florida was short. The private jet was just as huge as the one we had arrived on, but it felt too small now. I was confined by the plane. Confined to going back to my life. Alone.

I stayed awake, keeping myself busy with paperwork, but I kept having to redo it. I couldn't concentrate. Every time I had to write Sebastian Belrose's name as the owner of an item, my brain would freeze and I would picture his face. The way he smelled. The touch of his skin.

"Miss?" the flight attendant caught my attention, smiling politely. "We need to refuel. You're welcome to go into the airport and walk around for a few minutes."

I looked down at the blank form in my hands. All I had accomplished in the past thirty minutes was filling out Sebastian's name. Twice. In the wrong locations.

I sighed, folding the paper into fourths to throw in the trash. "Thank you, I think I will," I said, standing. "The fresh air might clear my head."

I carefully navigated the stairs out of the plane and onto the tarmac. It was a private airport, but it still smelled of asphalt and jet fuel. At least it was quiet. The humid air hit me like a punch in the face after the dry air of the plane. Ominous lightning flashed in the distance. I could smell it on the wind. It would probably rain later.

Moving felt good. I walked the length of the terminal, just stretching my legs and getting blood to flow again. I found a cute little coffee-shop and purchased an overpriced latte. But some caffeine and mocha sugar sounded like comfort food and I needed some comfort.

The barista finished my coffee and I continued to wander the terminals. The plane would be ready soon, but I wasn't. Florida was still closer to the Caribbean than Colorado was, which meant that right now, I was still closer to Bastian than I would be in several hours.

I stopped in front of a big window looking out on two private jets. Beyond them, the lights to whichever city was closest twinkled in the distance. It was pretty, but in a lonely way. The lights were people but far away.

"You look amazing with those lights behind you," said a voice I didn't want to hear. Every muscle in my body tensed as I turned, praying it wasn't Chad. I knew he was supposed to go to the Caribbean to prep for the auction, but what where the odds that he would have a layover at the same airport at the same time I was leaving?

The odds were not in my favor. It was him.

He stood in the private airport, looking for all intents and purposes like he belonged. He had on pressed khaki's, a pink polo shirt, and had even tied a sweater around his shoulders. He looked absolutely pretentious.

"What are you doing here, Chad?" I asked, coldly. I had to focus on not crushing my coffee cup into oblivion. Luckily, it was mostly empty, so even if I did lose my cool and squeezed, it wasn't the end of the world.

"We're refueling before heading to the island," Chad announced stepping forward. He oozed suave confidence. "I'm the lead auctioneer for the Belrose Estate. Gotta have the best."

I wanted to smack his cocky grin off his smug face. But I had enough fighting today to last me a lifetime. Instead I did my best to smile politely. I wanted to walk away, but he had me pinned between him and the window. The only way back to my plane was past him.

"You look like the island was good to you," he commented, his eyes doing a once over. I instantly felt dirty.

"It was. Excuse me, I need to get back to my plane," I replied, sidestepping him and walking away. I was already heart-sore and homesick. I didn't need another fight with Chad.

"Ava, please... please don't walk away from me," he begged. "I just want to talk to you for a moment." For a second, I thought he might actually be human and feel regret, so I paused and instantly regretted it.

He took my hand in his, holding it up to his cheek. He was certainly handsome, but he lacked Bastian's charms. Where Bastian's eyes told me everything I wanted to know, Chad's were flat and deceptive. I had once believed those eyes, but now I knew better.

"I love you." He said it like the words had meaning. Except I had heard him say those words every day before going off to bang Charity. They were just a leash to tie me to him.

"I don't want to hear this." I tried to pull my hand back, but he held on tight.

"Ava, I want you back. I've missed you so much." He fluttered his long lashes, doing his best to make me believe but failing. I had seen what it looked like when someone wanted me. Bastian had wanted me. Chad wanted something I had to offer, but it wasn't me.

"I don't believe you." I wanted to get away from him.

"All our friends say how good we are together," he tried again. "Please, just give me another chance."

I ripped my hand from his grasp, stumbling back in the process and spilling what was left of my coffee on the floor. He was a liar. All his friends said we were good together. I had lost my friends when he came into my life. I realized that now. He had distanced me from anyone who would say anything ill about him.

"It's too late, Chad," I snapped. He had broken something inside of me and I didn't want him touching me anymore. I wanted him to stop trying to make me forget the pain he had caused. I was never going back to him. "I'm seeing someone else."

I had no idea what possessed me to say such a thing, especially to Chad. While it was partially true, it was such a juvenile comeback and I knew it carried almost no weight. Chad obviously wasn't too keen on exclusivity.

Chad laughed. It made my teeth stand on end. I hated his laugh. "It's a small town, Ava. I know you're not seeing anyone."

"Who said it was in town?" I nearly clapped my hands over my mouth. I needed to stop talking. I needed to get back on my plane and run from Chad. He was nothing but bad news.

"Who then, Ava?" Chad's eyes widened and then narrowed. "The billionaire?" His laughter was cruel, contrasted with a beautiful face. "I don't believe you. I don't believe someone like that would even look once at you."

Indignant tears welled up in my eyes. The insult stung far more than it should have. I knew I should have just stayed quiet. I should have just gone back to the plane and drowned my heartache in some of the rum the stewardess kept offering me.

"Shows what you know," I hissed. I wanted to hit him. I needed to strike back at him somehow, so I said the first thing that popped into my mind. "I wouldn't go back to you if you were the last man on earth. I wouldn't go back to you to save the human species."

I turned and stalked away, knowing that I wouldn't be able to stop the blush now raging across my cheeks. The words sounded so stupid and immature now that I had said them, but I had needed to say something. Anything. He had hurt me and I had wanted to hurt him back, even if it was stupid.

"Ava!" Chad called, but I was running to my plane. I couldn't take any more of Chad and his backhanded insults.

"Miss?" The stewardess looked concerned. "Are you all right?"

"There is a man out there. Don't let him on the plane," I said. I considered telling her that he was a terrorist, but I wasn't that cruel. Or stupid. Besides, he had a job to do. Bastian wouldn't appreciate having his auction short an auctioneer because I decided to unleash Homeland Security on my ex. "It's my ex."

The stewardess nodded, knowingly and shut the door. I collapsed back into my oversized leather chair and stared out the window as I waited for the engines to start. I wanted to go home, but I wasn't sure where that was at the moment.

"I don't believe someone like that would even look once at you."

Chad's words echoed in my mind, slashing my thoughts to pieces. I tried to push them away, but it only meant they cut deeper.

Who did I think I was, anyway? Falling for a billionaire? I shook my head and sunk lower into the chair. What in the world did someone like Bastian see in me?

I didn't have an answer and that made it worse. It was easy to see why someone would want to be with Bastian. He was smart and sophisticated, and even without the money he was a catch, but me? I wasn't sure if I was a catch. That was why I had left him.

The fact that Chad had come even close to my reasoning was frightening.

I sighed and crossed my arms. It was all moot anyway. I wasn't going to see him again. Even if I could somehow take back the words from this morning, I had no way to see him again. Bastian was now back in his world of billionaire private locations and security. I couldn't breach that world if I tried.

The thought made my eyes burn with tears. I sniffled and grabbed a blanket, pulling it up over my head. I closed my eyes, willing myself to join with the darkness so I could sleep until I found my way home

SOMEONE TOUCHED me and I nearly jumped out of my seat to punch them.

"We've landed, miss."

It was just the flight attendant. I was glad I hadn't started swinging.

"Thank you," I mumbled, wiping drool off my chin. I hated the time change already, more just because it was a change.

With bleary eyes, I collected my things and hurried off the plane. A cold wind ripped at my light jacket as I stepped onto the dark tarmac and hurried away from the last bits of life with Bastian. It smelled like snow here. Snow and airplane fuel. I felt sick to my stomach. And cold. So very, very cold and alone.

Someone was waving to me at the end of the tarmac. They were big and hidden within a winter coat, but I knew that coat. I knew the worn elbows and faded blue denim of that coat like it was home. I dropped my bags and took off running. It was exactly who I needed to see. My Dad.

"Hey there, kiddo," he greeted me, wrapping his big arms around me as I nearly knocked him over with my hug. I held on to him like I did when I was child and he was still the strongest man alive. I had no idea what he was doing here, he needed a pacemaker after all, but for the moment, I didn't even care. I was still beyond glad to see him.

"What are you doing here, Dad?" I asked, not relaxing my hug an inch. The stiff fabric of his winter coat was scratchy against my cheek, but I didn't want to move. "You're supposed to be in the hospital."

"About that..." He pulled back and I relaxed my grip on him slightly. He tapped his chest and grinned. "Good as new."

"What?" I stared at him in disbelief, noticing that his cheeks had more pink in them than they had before and his eyes seemed brighter. He didn't look tired, even though it was late at night. It wasn't possible, though. I had only been separated from him for a week. Dr. Verner hadn't said anything. Jackie hadn't said anything. Dad hadn't said anything.

"They put the pacemaker in four days ago," he announced. He smiled wide.

"AND YOU DIDN'T TELL ME!?" I shouted, smacking him on the arm. His winter coat easily absorbed the blow.

No one had said anything. I should have been there. If I had known I would have flown home the instant he had the appointment. If I had known, I wouldn't have left his side the entire time.

"I didn't want you to worry," he replied, looking sheepish. "You had a job to do."

"What if something had happened?" I yelled at him. I was supposed to be there for him. It was him and me. And Jackie. I was okay with Jackie being there, too. But I certainly should have been there. It was surgery. "What if-"

"Honey, this is why I didn't tell you," he interrupted. "Jackie was there the whole time. If anything would have happened, you would have been the first to know."

"Dad..." My throat felt tight. What if I had lost him? I had looked up the risks. They were relatively minor and kept getting better every year. But that didn't take the fear of losing him away. It was the what-ifs that scared me more than the procedure.

"I didn't want you to worry and the doctor said it was practically a minor procedure," he said softly. "You have enough on your plate without me there, too."

"Daddy..." I sighed. I knew he thought he had done the right thing and there was nothing I could do to convince him otherwise. Besides, it was in the past. There was honestly nothing I *could* do about it now anyway."I don't know if I want to hug you or strangle you now."

"I'm going to vote for the hug," he told me, trying to get me to smile. A gust of snow blew behind him, reminding me that we were standing out in the middle of a tarmac in freezing temperatures.

I leaned forward and held him close again. I was so tired that I wasn't able to tell how angry I was. I was really just glad that he was okay.

"What are you doing out of the hospital and driving?" I asked, pulling back. "They put a pacemaker in you, Dad."

"I barely had to stay the night after they put it in. And that was just for monitoring. Easy peasy," he explained. He looked rather pleased with himself. "It's now considered a relatively minor surgery. I didn't even get knocked out for it."

"I don't care. No surgeries without me. Even if Jackie's there." I sighed and hugged him tighter. "I'm leaving Jackie with explicit instructions next time. Hell, I'm leaving Aunt Jenny with special instructions to let me know the next time you catch a cold."

"Do not get your aunt involved," he pleaded, making a desperate face. My aunt could be a real witch when she wanted to be. She was as stubborn as my dad, but more serious. "But Jackie, well, she's in the car. You can tell her now."

I frowned, looking over at the parking lot. I could see lights on my dad's truck and the petite form of a woman in the driver's seat.

"She won't let me drive on my own yet," he admitted, grinning bashfully. "Oh, and we're officially dating now."

I laughed. The woman practically did his laundry. He had been having a lovely romantic vacation of his own while I had enjoyed mine. I wondered if that was a part of why he hadn't told me about the surgery. If I had been home, he wouldn't have gotten near as much Jackie- alone time. Though, I sincerely hoped they were just playing Parcheesi. The man did just get a pacemaker.

"Good. It's about time. I'm glad you've had someone taking care of you since you refused to let me do it." I shivered. My coat was meant for traveling. Not for standing around in the snow.

"She was looking for an excuse to have me at her beck and call," Dad explained, trying to make the fact that he was dating someone sound logical and rational. Love was neither of those things.

I shook my head. "I have to go get my luggage."

"It's already here," Dad said, motioning to a man bringing it toward us. "The benefit of flying your own plane is that yours is the first bag off every time."

I chuckled, glad to see my dad in such good spirits. I didn't know if it was the pacemaker or Jackie, but either way, he seemed happier than he had in a long time.

"You look great by the way. All tan and, well, there's a sparkle to you," Dad said, insisting on dragging my suitcase behind him. I made sure he had the lighter one, but I didn't tell him that. "I want to know all about the rest of your trip. Did you get to spend much time with Mr. Belrose?"

I tightened at his name, my heart skipping a beat. Blue-gray eyes and a smile that lit up like the sun flashed through my mind. "Yeah, I did. He and I actually became... friends."

I hesitated at the last word, unsure of how to define him. I certainly wasn't ready to tell my father that we had been anything more than companions, but I wasn't sure what to even call him in my own head. It didn't really matter anyway. I had pushed him away because I didn't deserve him. Friend or otherwise.

"Friends?" Dad repeated, raising a brow. "Interesting. Tell me more."

"Um, well..." I hadn't thought about how I was going to get around telling Dad that I spent a week alone with Bastian in his mansion. I decided just to go for it. Hopefully, he would just assume that I worked the whole time. "It was just him and me after you left. I mostly worked, but we would eat dinner together sometimes."

"That sounds very cozy," Dad replied. He seemed to take my words at face value and I was glad. I didn't want to get into what kind of friendship Bastian and I had. Just thinking of Bastian hurt. "What about that beach? Did you get any relaxation time?"

"A little- I learned how to paddle-board while I was there." I thought of Bastian again, laughing as he fell off the board trying to teach me a trick. I wished our story could have ended differently, but I had to go home. Jackie waved to me from inside the car as we approached. She had on the cutest little knitted hat and a great big grin. I waved back.

"You glad to be home?" Dad asked, watching me closely. I paused and took a deep breath in of cold, mountain air. It ached in my lungs and my nostrils burn.

"Yeah." I smiled at him, letting the breath out in a slow cloud of steam. "I'm glad to be home with you."

At least that much is true, I thought. I did want to be home with Dad, it was just that I wanted to be with Bastian more.

CHAPTER 24

I plopped the groceries onto the counter and stared at them for a moment, trying to summon the energy to put them away. Usually, I loved putting groceries away. The act of organizing and filling my fridge and pantry always seemed to make me feel ready to tackle anything that might come my way. But not today.

I stared at the sliced cheese and thought of Bastian's grilled cheese. The tomatoes made me think of him. So did the bacon. Everything in my bags reminded me of him somehow and how far away he was. Four days away from him and he was still all I could think about. I wished I could hear his voice.

But he was respecting my wishes and leaving me alone. Just as I had asked. I hated it.

"You okay, Ava?" Jackie asked, coming into the kitchen. She frowned slightly and pushed her short gray hair out of her bright blue eyes. "Want some help?"

I smiled. "That would be great."

She came over and began efficiently taking all the food out

and putting it right where it belonged. Even though Dad was long past needing an overnight sitter, Jackie had been staying at the house. I rather liked her here. Dad and I had moved into this house after Mom died and it had always felt like it was missing something. Now that Jackie was here, I realized that what it had been missing was Jackie. She was meant to be here. With Dad. I was now the piece that was missing.

"Oh, there's some mail for you on the table," Jackie informed me, putting the tomatoes in the sink to wash. "I can finish up in here if you want."

"Thanks," I said, knowing that I hadn't done anything to help put stuff away in the first place. I smiled at her and wandered out to the living room. Dad was sitting in his recliner watching some history show on TV. I shook my head and went to pick up my mail.

In addition to the usual assortment of bills, advertisements, and random coupons, there was a large, professional-looking envelope. I set the rest down on the messy table, deciding to open the interesting envelope first, since whatever was inside of it had to be more fun than an electric bill.

The letter inside was on heavy, high-end paper. It reminded me more of a wedding invitation than actual letterhead, but it was obviously business related. I leaned up against the wall and began to read.

Dear Miss Ava Fairchild,

I am contacting you today to request your professional appraisal services for a piece of art. I have recently acquired two impressionist paintings and wish to sell them. However, due to their historical nature, I am in need of further reference as to the appropriate buyer.

I GRINNED. Maybe this was something that could take my mind off of Bastian.

> *The pieces in question are one by Claude Monet, as well as a smaller piece by Berthe Morisot, both with photos attached. There are several museums and several other interested buyers, but due to a lack of time and knowledge I am unable to determine the best location for this artwork. As such, I am requesting your services.*
>
> *It will take 6-8 weeks to meet with all the museums and possible buyers. All expenses, including airfare, food, and lodging in the various museum locals, is included, as well as payment for taking you away from your business.*
>
> *Included is the list of museums and their locations. I understand that this is a large undertaking, one that will force you to learn about the museums wishing to purchase said piece as well as any collections it may join.*
>
> *Please contact Charlotte Page with any questions. She will follow up with you at a later date to arrange your transportation to New York to view the pieces as well as your international itinerary.*
>
> *Sincerely,*

Sebastian Belrose

MY HANDS SHOOK. I could barely hold the paper as I turned to the next page. A picture of Berthe Morisot's *A Corner of the Rose Garden* painting fluttered to floor followed by one of Monet's *Water Lilies*.

I went to my knees to retrieve it, staring at one of the most famous pictures in art history as well as the one Bastian had claimed as his favorite before looking at the list of potential buyers. The Louvre, Musée d'Orsay, the Marmottan-Monet Museum, and a whole page of others that I couldn't read because my eyes started to blur. I couldn't breathe. This was everything I had always dreamed of. This was the trip my mother and I had spent years hours upon hours dreaming of before she died, with more than we could have ever hoped to have seen.

And Bastian had just given it all to me with a billionaire's all-access pass. He had actually been paying attention to me that night I had told him about Paris. He had remembered.

"Ava?" Dad called, his chair creaking as he stood and then hurried over to where I sat on the floor. "Ava, are you all right?"

I handed him the letter, my mouth opening and closing like a fish and making about as much noise. Dad skimmed the letter, his eyes going bigger with every paragraph.

"Holy mother..." he finally whispered, handing the letter back to me. He grinned and started to laugh. I just sat, still in shock. "It's everything you and your mom used to talk about. You have to do it, Ava."

I let out a sob and quickly covered my mouth. "Why

would Bastian do something so wonderful for me? Why? I don't deserve someone like him."

"Bullshit," Dad contested, wrapping me up in his arms and hugging me tight. "You deserve someone who makes you happy."

"But..." I couldn't wrap my head around it. Why would Bastian do this? I had hurt him. I had pushed him away because he deserved someone better than me, yet here he was, giving me the best gift I had ever received. He still cared about me.

"Aw, honey, that man obviously cares a great deal about you," Dad cooed, as if reading my mind. "This would have taken some time to set up. There's a lot of names on this list that aren't easy to get private access too. He pulled some serious strings."

"But why?"

Dad hugged me tighter. "If I had to guess, between this, the not-so-secret looks the two of you were passing back and forth before I left, and that the two of you spent a week alone in his mansion, I think he loves you."

I had been hoping Dad hadn't caught on that much, but I was a grown woman. I hiccuped and wiped my nose. "But Dad, he's a billionaire. What do I have that a billionaire would want?"

He hugged me tighter. "Everything.

"What?" I sniffled.

"Everything." Dad smiled at me, his green eyes full of love. "You are smart and beautiful. Even as a billionaire, he's still just a man. A man who obviously wants you to be happy."

I looked at the letter. Bastian had gone above and beyond, giving me my heart's desire. And without asking for anything in return. Even far away, he was still making my world better.

"But..." My heart was thrilling and weeping at the same time. Bastian cared for me, but it wasn't asking me to be with him. He was still giving me what I had asked for, but giving me my dreams at the same time. It was a pure act of giving and expecting nothing in return. The only reason to send this letter was to make me happy. Even if I wasn't with him.

"Do you love him?" Dad asked, putting his hands on my shoulders and studying my face.

"I..." I closed my eyes and thought for a moment. The past few days had passed in a gray haze of unhappiness. Just thinking about him made color come back to my world. I nodded.

"I thought so," Dad said quietly. He smiled. "I thought he might be the reason."

"The reason?" I asked. "What do you mean?"

"The reason you've been a different person the past few days. You sounded so happy out on the island, happier than I've ever heard you, but you've just been fading since you came home." He hugged me close. "A father can tell."

"What do I do?" I whimpered. I wiped my eyes with my shirt sleeve and looked at Dad. "He doesn't exactly live just down the street. I can't just waltz on to the island and up to his house to tell him how I feel."

"Why not?" Dad asked. "Go to the island and tell him you love him."

"The auction is by invite only, and I made sure to get myself uninvited. I basically told him I never wanted to see him again." I hung my head in shame. Without a ticket, I would be lucky to get past the security guards at the airport, let alone the ones at the mansion. I had a feeling Bastian would have far more security than just Elijah working for an event as big as this one.

"We'll come up with something," Dad promised. "I want to see you happy. If I have to sell my car to buy you an invite, then I'll walk to the grocery store."

"Thanks, Daddy," I whispered. He hugged me closer.

"Carl," Jackie said, biting her lip and looking at the two of us. "You don't have to buy your way onto the island."

"What do you mean?" Dad asked, his brows coming together.

"The tickets." Jackie motioned to the table and grinned. Dad's mouth opened as he realized what she was talking about and then split into a ear-to-ear grin. He jumped up from the floor and kissed her, full on the lips.

"You are a wonderful woman!" he exclaimed, kissing her again. Jackie blushed a deep shade of crimson, but she grinned.

Dad went to the kitchen table and dug through the pile of mail, murmuring to himself until he found what he was looking for. He handed it to me triumphantly before going to stand next to Jackie.

"Jenny always gives me a ticket to the events I've appraised," he explained as I opened the small white envelope with my aunt's neat handwriting and pulled out the golden invitation. He squeezed Jackie's hand and grinned. "That's how you get into the auction."

"But what about you?" I asked, looking up. "I just got here...."

"I'll be fine. Besides, I have a new ticker." He tapped twice on his chest and then winced at the soreness from the incision. "And I have this lovely lady to look out for me. You go."

I opened my mouth, feeling like I should protest, even if it was halfhearted.

"I've got him, Ava," Jackie promised. "I'll give you hourly updates if you want and I promise to make him eat his vegetables."

"Just daily updates and all the veggies you can get." I chuckled. If she got him to eat something green that was chile, then she was a superstar. Dad hated vegetables. "You're sure?"

"Go," Dad said, a grin filling his face. He put his arm around Jackie. "Go and be happy. You have to find the people that make you happy and keep them in your life."

I stood on shaky legs, hugging them both.

Bastian wasn't Chad. He wasn't out to use me. He loved me. Honest to goodness, love without expecting anything in return, loved me.

You have to find the people that make you happy and keep them in your life.

Dad was right. He was proving it with Jackie. Just because one person left, doesn't mean the next person is going to do the same.

I was an idiot for not seeing it sooner and letting my history with a selfish man cloud my judgment concerning a good man. I was a fool to push him away.

I wasn't going to be a fool for long.

CHAPTER 25

Flying coach sucked.

Flying coach with three layovers sucked even more.

I arrived on the island bleary-eyed and exhausted the next morning after scrambling to get a last minute ticket. I had paid through the nose, but as I took a deep breath of tropical air, I knew it was worth it. I had to see Bastian. I had to tell him how I felt or I would never be able to forgive myself.

I stopped in the tiny airport's bathroom and did my best to straighten my dress and fix the disaster that was my makeup. Sleeping with a stranger's head on my shoulder while my legs cramped under me was not a beauty regime I could get behind. I sighed at the mirror and put on a brave smile. I was here to see Bastian, not to look pretty. It shouldn't matter how I looked. He would still be excited to see me, not my makeup.

I hoped.

I took a deep breath and went to find a cab. The ride back to the mansion was longer than I remembered it.

What if he doesn't want to see me? What if he's found someone else? What if he hates me? The what-if's buzzed around my head like vultures as palm trees and smaller beach houses whizzed by. I shook my head. *What if he's pulled a Mr. Rochester and is now terribly blind and scarred from a fire?* I was going to make myself crazy with questions that I couldn't answer until I saw Bastian.

The cab had to stop about a quarter mile from the house due to traffic. I paid the man and pulled my carry-on bag behind me. The entry to the house was packed with cars that cost more than a standard American house.

I paused in the driveway, suddenly unsure of what I was supposed to do next. I hadn't planned this far, and I certainly hadn't planned for there to be this many people. *And TV reporters,* I thought as I watched a TV crew enter the house.

My original plan of walking up to the front door and knocking suddenly seemed incredibly naive. I looked down at my wrinkled blouse and realized my khaki pants had a nice ketchup stain on them. Bastian was a billionaire. He wasn't going to answer the door. With this many people, it was going to be some security personnel that wouldn't know me from Kate Winslet. I was doomed.

"YOU CAME BACK!"

I turned to see a happy blur of Charlotte speeding toward me, her brown hair flying as she leaped from the front porch and wrapped me up in a giant hug. I didn't know how she managed it in heels, but she did.

"I'm glad to see you, too," I replied with a laugh, hugging her back. She released me and grinned. Charlotte looked great. She had on a sheer, white silk blouse and a black skirt that accented her waist and made her look feminine and in charge at the same time. Something about her face looked happier, too. I wondered if something had changed between her and Leo. I would have to ask later. Now wasn't the time.

"Bastian's going to flip," Charlotte told me. "He's been absolutely no fun since you left. One of the auctioneers told him that you were never coming back and he's been awful since. I knew you'd come back, though."

I dry-washed my hands. I had a feeling I knew which auctioneer had said that. My hands were cold and clammy despite the tropical heat. "Where is Bastian? I need to talk to him."

"I'm sure you do," Charlotte replied with a wink, but then she shrugged. "But he's not here."

"Oh." My heart sank right through my toes and down into the sand. He was gone. I had missed my chance. "Of course. I should have checked before I came…"

"But he'll be back for the gala tonight," Charlotte added. "He's out doing business stuff."

"Oh, he'll be back…" I laughed nervously, feeling relieved for a moment. He wasn't off the island and I hadn't just been through travel hell for nothing.

"You are coming to the gala tonight, right?" Charlotte raised her eyebrows. "It's how we're showcasing everything for the auction."

"Gala?" I pulled out my ticket. It now had a giant fold from being in my pocket all day, and I was glad it was on expensive paper or I would have worn it down to shreds by now. "I totally missed there was a gala on there."

"Do you have anything to wear?" Charlotte asked, eying my very small carry-on suitcase. I shifted my weight nervously. I hadn't brought anything even remotely acceptable to wear to a gala. I had a nice pant suit for the auction, but I had a feeling that the gala was more of an evening gown kind of event.

"Um..." I bit my lip. Maybe I could find something in town. I looked around at the Lamborghinis, Ferraris, and a couple of Rolls-Royces. Even if I managed to somehow find a dress shop, there's no way in hell I would be able to afford anything that would let me even remotely fit in. I was going to stick out like a sore thumb if I tried. This was why I had tried to leave. I wasn't any good at these rich events. I didn't want to embarrass Bastian by showing up as a ragamuffin.

"Oh, good! You didn't bring anything. That makes this so much easier," Charlotte answered for me, a knowing grin crossing her face. She looked like a cat in the cream. "It's always better to work with a blank canvas anyway."

"What?" I was now imagining an Emperor's New Clothes scenario. I was not going naked. I was okay with being a blank canvas, but not a naked or semi-naked one.

"I've got just the designer for you," Charlotte said, looking me up and down and practically cackling with glee. "Oh, this is going to be so much fun!"

I looked at her confused and she just grinned wider. Taking my arm in hers and grabbing my bag, she dragged me into the house. There were people milling around looking at all the pieces up for display before the auction. They stared as she pulled me along, but Charlotte just kept going like they didn't exist.

"I am going to make you the Belle of the Ball," Charlotte promised as we started up the stairs. She turned and grinned, her eyes bright with mischief. "Come with me."

~

THE GIRL STARING at me was wearing a dress that had come straight out of a fairytale. Or a dream. Or both. The girl looked like a princess.

The dress was made of soft gold that flowed over her hips and made the woman in front of me appear lush and slender at the same time. A gold lace overlay started right at her hips and continued down the length of the gown to create a train that was both romantic and stunning. Her dark red hair was pulled back and clipped with a gold comb that matched the dress and brought out the shimmer of the woman's hair.

I swallowed hard and the girl staring back at me swallowed too. I made a face at the mirror and the princess in the amazing dress made the same face back. It was difficult to believe, but I cleaned up pretty good.

The three hours in the hair and makeup chair had done magic, and I was fairly sure that Charlotte had switched out the mirrors in the bedroom with magic ones to make me look this good in a dress. I no longer looked like the small-town girl from nowhere and instead looked like a movie star.

I looked like someone who could be with a billionaire.

"Holy crap," Charlotte whistled, peeking her head in the door. "I do good work."

Charlotte opened the door wider and came in. She was wearing an off-the-shoulder gown with a subtle mermaid tail in royal blue. With her dark hair and eyes, she was breathtaking.

"You look gorgeous, Charlotte," I told her. She grinned.

"What? This old thing?" She grinned. Charlotte looked like she had just stepped out of a fashion magazine. She circled me, evaluating my dress and appearance. She reached up and adjusted the comb in my hair. "Sebastian's going to lose his mind when he sees you."

"You're sure he'll be happy to see me?" I pressed my knuckles against the lace at my stomach. The butterflies inside of me were going mad and for a moment I thought I might be sick. What if he didn't feel the same way about me?

Charlotte sighed. I'd asked her this at least a dozen times while getting ready. "He's been the moodiest, most grumpy man I've ever had the misfortune of being around since you left. He hasn't even gone out paddle-boarding in the mornings. Just keeps talking about the dark."

My heart ached for the pain I had caused. "I'm just nervous. I don't want to screw this up again." I bit my lip and promptly tried to stop. It would mess up the lipstick Charlotte's makeup artist had just spent twenty minutes perfecting.

Charlotte came over and took my hands in hers. "He has been a mess without you. A broody, heartbroken, love-sick mess. He's going to be overjoyed to see you. I promise."

"You know Bastian and I had a fight, right?"

Charlotte reached up and carefully fixed a stray strand of hair. One red lock kept falling out of my up-swept hairdo and falling across my forehead no matter how much hairspray we used."Yes. I know."

She took both my hands in hers. She smiled gently, her eyes meeting mine and making sure I heard her words.

"I said some terrible things..." My lower lip quavered.

"He loves you," she stated. "I know Sebastian. And I've never seen him the way he was with you. He was happy. And this past week..." she shook her head and grimaced slightly. "This past week has been a nightmare without you."

"How could I have been so stupid?" I whispered. My eyes started to water. I had let the man of my dreams go because I hadn't believed in myself. It was the stupidest thing I had ever done. I just hoped he could forgive me.

"Don't you dare cry," Charlotte admonished. "It may be

waterproof mascara, but I will not have you messing up all the work we just did."

I sniffed and looked up, forcing the tears back up. "Sorry."

"Sebastian Belrose loves you. I think he was smitten from the moment he saw you," Charlotte said with a smile.

"I don't think it was that fast. The first moment I was kind of a jerk," I replied.

Charlotte laughed. "This is going to work out. I promise you. Just come downstairs." She smiled and checked the delicate silver watch on her wrist. "You ready?"

I looked over at the movie star in the mirror. No, I wasn't ready. I closed my eyes and thought of Bastian. How he had said I was beautiful. And now I looked it. I could do this.

I nodded, not trusting myself to use words. There was a very good possibility that if I opened my mouth I would try and back out. She took my hand and led me out the door.

The hallway was dark and quiet. I could hear the murmur of a lot of voices and music downstairs. If this went poorly, I didn't think I would survive. I was already planning on how to walk out into the ocean as my backup plan, and I knew that didn't bode well for me.

"Show time," Charlotte whispered as we came to the top of the stairs.

I nodded and let go of her hand to wipe my eyes before she could yell at me for ruining my makeup again. I went to the top of the stairs and looked down at the party.

I saw Chad first. He was standing in a cheap suit trying his best to ingratiate himself with a woman twice his age and wearing a diamond mine around her throat. It was easy to see that he was angling for her money, and by her fluttering eyelashes she was falling for his slimy charms. At least I wasn't the only one. I wanted to back out and run. If

Chad was here, I wasn't sure I could do this. Luckily, Charlotte was standing right behind me and had her hand on my shoulder.

"No running. Bastian's right there," she whispered, nudging me in the right direction.

I saw him and my heart stopped. I had missed him more than I could have ever thought possible. He was by the door, standing with Leo and who I assumed must be Gabe. He hadn't seen me yet, and I let myself admire him for a moment. He was so beautiful.

His suit was crisp and straight and made of some sort of black that seemed to absorb the light. It of course fit perfectly, highlighting the broad strength of his shoulders and his trim waist and even the perfect curve of his ass. He was stunning.

But there was something different about him. He smiled at his guests, but the smile never touched his eyes. If anything, he looked more withdrawn and wound tighter than usual. Leo and Gabe appeared to be carrying the conversation without him.

Charlotte gave my shoulder a gentle push. It was now or never. I took a deep breath, more to remind myself that I should breathe than for actual oxygen, and grabbed onto the bannister. I took one step and then another, my eyes not watching the floor, but instead watching Bastian.

He looked up at the stairs when I was at the halfway point, his blue-gray eyes going directly to mine. A thrill went through me as he did a double take and then a triple take. His mouth slowly opened and hung that way for a good minute.

He walked out of whatever conversation he had been having with Leo and Gabe, leaving them staring after him to meet me at the bottom of the stairs.

"Ava," he whispered, waiting for me to descend the last stair. "You came back…"

"You can't get rid of me that easily." I grinned, my heart pounding in my throat. "Especially when you offer me dream vacations to Paris."

He blushed slightly, the edge of the scar on his cheek going white. "Oh, that."

"Yes, that." I took a step forward, feeling braver by the second. He seemed happy to see me. "Even without that, I couldn't stay away. You didn't have to do that."

"I wanted to." The honesty in his light eyes made my stomach do happy flip-flops.

"That's why it means so much to me," I told him. I couldn't stop smiling. "It's everything. Thank you."

He raised his hand, moving it like he was going to pull me into a kiss, but then he stopped and let it fall. He looked past me and frowned, taking a step back. The light in his expression was now tempered with caution. "Why did you come back?"

I turned to see what he was looking at. Chad. The woman with the diamonds was now flirting with one of his cheaply-dressed friends and he was sipping on champagne that he couldn't afford. I could only imagine what he had told Bastian.

"There's something I need to tell you," I said quietly, biting my bottom lip. I knew I was probably smudging my lipstick, but if my nervous biting hadn't worn it off by now, nothing would. "Something important."

Bastian's eyes darkened with seriousness, but flooded with concern at the same time. He took a step forward, ready to protect me, even from my own words. "Anything."

I glanced back over at Chad. "Somewhere private?"

He nodded and took my hand to led me from the staircase. I could see Charlotte making her way down. Leo's eyes fixated on her and I wondered for a moment what was going on between the two of them. I didn't get to see what happened next because Bastian was pulling me into the next room. We hurried out to the back porch.

Outside the murmur of the music filtered through an open window somewhere, but it was soft and muted. The ocean hummed against the shore, dark water against white sand. I was suddenly incredibly nervous about being alone with Bastian.

He hadn't lost the guarded expression. In fact, as soon as the door swung shut, he dropped my hand and went to the railing to look out at the beach without me. The loss of his touch hurt like a physical wound. The waning moon shone on his dark suit and caught the dark edge of the scar along his cheek.

"Why are you here, Ava?" Bastian's voice was low, but I could hear the quiet anguish in his voice. His hands tightened on the railing making his knuckles turn white.

"I'm here for you." My voice shook. My whole body was shaking. I felt naked even with the beautiful dress and perfect makeup.

He forcibly relaxed his hands from the railing and turned sharply, his eyes catching the moonlight. "Why?"

I swallowed down the fear and turmoil roiling up in my throat. This wasn't exactly the greeting I had been promised by Charlotte.

"I had to see you," I whispered, taking a step forward. He retreated slightly.

"You said that when you left, you were gone." His beautiful eyes were like stars in the night sky: distant and cold. "I was told you were seeing someone. That you had been seeing someone when you came here."

"What?" I shook my head confused. "I wasn't with anyone but you. I don't want anyone but you."

His hard expression flashed with hope for the briefest second before his brows came together again like storm clouds. "Please explain, then."

The breeze off the ocean tugged the loose strand of hair across my face and I carefully tucked it back where it belonged before starting. I was surprised I could talk at all my stomach was so tangled up in knots, yet the words came smoothly.

"When I left, I was sure I didn't deserve you," I started. I looked at his hands, remembering how they felt against my skin. So strong and safe. "I still don't think that I do, but I can't be without you."

I glanced up from his hands. His face was still hard, his expression unreadable. I smoothed the fabric of my dress.

"I'm not worthy of a billionaire. I'm still a little broken and I'm not used to any of this," I motioned to the party behind me, but I looked up and into his eyes. "But, I was wrong to leave. I was wrong to push you away because I was afraid. I guess if anything, it just shows how much I don't deserve you."

My voice failed me at the end and I had to look away.

"And you didn't go home to be with someone else?" he asked. He sounded far more calm than I was. Almost business like. I looked up and into his beautiful, sad eyes and realized that he was using his business voice and face to keep from crumbling.

"No," I replied emphatically. "Who ever told you that was a liar."

"Chad. One of the auctioneers," he said quietly. "He said that the two of you were engaged."

If Chad had been on the balcony I would have thrown him off it and fed him to the sharks.

"*Bastard*," I hissed. "Dirty, rotten, lying bastard!"

Bastian's eyebrows raised and the hint of a hopeful smile crossed his lips. "So, it's not true?"

"No," I nearly shouted. I wanted to scream and cry. "Not even remotely close."

"That's good to hear." Bastian's shoulders relaxed slightly and he lost a little of the guarded look in his eyes. "I was afraid I really had lost you forever if that was the case."

I took another step toward him and this time he didn't shy away. "No, you haven't lost me. I just took a wrong turn for a little bit. You've always had me."

"Why are you here, Ava?" he asked again, but this time his voice thrummed with hope. I was now close enough to touch him.

I touched his cheek, shaking as I traced the scar from his cheek bone to the tip of his lips. The words came simply and more easily than I ever could have expected. They flowed because they were true.

"I'm here, because I had to tell you I love you." I smiled, my heart pounding like a drum. "I love you, Bastian."

His body stiffened and then melted as he reached for me, delicately placing his big hand on the back of my neck, and being careful not to mess up my hair. His blue-gray eyes met mine and sparkled, making me lose my mind with love.

He smiled. It was the smile he reserved for the dawn, and now it was my smile. He pulled me to him and kissed me like he hadn't seen me in months rather than just days. He kissed me like he needed the kiss to survive.

My heart soared on golden wings. Songs would be written about this moment and scholars would look back and say that this kiss was one for the books. It was heaven. Pure and absolute heaven.

He kept his forehead pressed against mine as he pulled away, both of us breathless and shaking.

"I love you too, Ava," he whispered, barely separating his lips from mine. I beamed at him as his face split into a grin that illuminated my world to brilliance. I couldn't stop giggling. I was drunk on my own happiness and love.

"I can't tell you how glad I am that you're here." He was grinning like a schoolboy on the first day of Christmas break. His gray eyes flashed with excitement and joy. When I looked into them, I knew I was where I belonged.

He picked me up, his hands wrapping around my waist and spinning me through the air as if we were dancing on clouds. He set me down, laughing at my shrieks of delight before kissing me again.

This time, he wasn't careful of my hair and I didn't care. The pretty hair was for him anyway. His fingers tangled in it as his mouth searched mine. He tasted so damn good I couldn't stop.

"Don't ever do that to me again," he whispered. "I wanted to come after you so badly, but you had asked me not to... and then he said you were engaged..."

I kissed him, silencing the hurt. "I love you, Bastian. More than anything."

His eyes searched mine, the moonlight catching his tears of joy. I kissed him, closing my eyes and just focusing on how good he felt. How this was the best moment of my life.

"I'm sorry to interrupt," Charlotte announced, peeking her head out of the back door and not looking sorry at all. She was grinning and her mascara was smudged. "But it's time for your speech, Bastian."

"Come with me," he commanded, grabbing my hand

and pulling me back into the house. I giggled and happily followed him, walking on glee rather than the floor. Charlotte high-fived us both as we passed.

Once inside, he guided me quickly to the grand foyer entrance. Bastian waited for a moment at the base of the stairs before snagging two glasses of champagne from a passing server. He handed one to me.

"Now you get to see what all your hard work is going toward." He grinned and pulled me to the center landing between the stairs in the grand foyer. "Come celebrate with me."

I stepped up, willing to follow him anywhere. Upon his ascension to the staircase, the background music died. He grinned once at me and then turned to face the crowd and tap his glass.

The room of celebrities and upper crust society quieted, with every eye turning to look at the staircase. I immediately felt awkward standing on what was now the stage, but it was too late to escape. Moving off the landing or going up the stairs would bring even more attention than just standing there and doing my best to look pretty.

"Ladies and gentlemen, thank you for coming tonight," Bastian called out. The room hummed for a moment as the last of the onlookers settled and turned to watch. "As you all know, I bought this house a very long time ago, but it has never really been mine."

Bastian paused, waiting for the crowd.

"You are all here to bid on the exquisite artwork and furniture, as well as the house itself. I am pleased to announced that Fairchild Auctions and Appraisals has valued the estate and it's furnishings at just over one hundred and seventy million American dollars."

An awed whisper rippled through the crowd and it

made me smile. This was certainly the biggest appraisal I had ever done, and most likely would ever do. One-hundred and seventy million dollars was a lot of money. Even for a billionaire.

"With that, I am incredibly excited to inform everyone that every penny of that money will be going to the Foundling Foundation." Bastian glanced around the room. Most of them didn't know his back story. Most of the people in this room were used to luxury. But Bastian had seen the other side of life. He had seen the children in the system. He had been one of the children in the system.

"They are the people that helped me when I needed it most, and now I'm proud to be able to give something back that will help other lost children like me. In addition to the funds raised by your purchases, I will be donating a matching contribution."

A small gasp went through the room. There would be some foster-children finding their lives getting better because of this. That much money was unfathomable to most, but not to Bastian. I had a feeling that there would be many such benefit galas like this in my future.

"So, please, tomorrow, dig deep and help me give this non-profit organization the funding it so justly deserves," Bastian concluded. He held up his glass and toasted the crowd.

I nearly forgot to raise my own glass and toast. I was blown away. Everything, all of the art, the house, the furni-ture- all of it- was going to charity. To a charity that Bastian believed in. A charity that would help future Bastians. My heart was already full of love for the man and this act made it ready to explode. I didn't know if he could get more wonderful.

Bastian turned and kissed me, claiming me as his own in

front of everyone present. I thrilled, not caring that flashes were going off all over the place. He was mine as much as I was his.

He slowly released me to the sound of applause. I turned to see Leo and Gabe clapping enthusiastically. Bastian flushed slightly, but not near as much as I did. I turned bright red all the way down to my toes. Bastian on the other hand, seemed to swell with pride.

"You are wonderful, you know that right?" I said quietly as we stepped from the landing. He smiled wide. "Why didn't you tell me what this was all for?"

"And risk not seeing the expression on your face right now?" he asked, raising his eyebrows and grinning.

"You're wonderful," I repeated, meaning it completely.

"Save me a dance?" he asked, as someone came up to his elbow, anxious to speak with him about his donation. I nodded and his eyes sparkled. I couldn't wait for my dance. He kissed my cheek one last time before turning to talk with his guests.

A camera phone light flashed in my face as the crowd dispersed. Standing at the base and taking a selfie with me and Bastian in the background was Chad and his friends. I nearly threw my champagne glass at him, but that would have been a waste of good champagne.

"I'll send this little gem of a picture to Ava," I heard Chad inform his friends. Diamond-necklace woman was gone. "Show her just what that billionaire thinks of her. Minute she's off the island, he's got some hussy model hanging all over him. Ava will come crawling back to me with her father's business tucked between her legs."

The two men with him in matching cheap suits laughed. Bastian turned from the man he had been talking with to see my face crumple. I finally understood what Chad had seen in me. He had seen my father's business. That's why he had kept trying to win me back. He hadn't loved me at all.

Bastian's eyes darkened and lightning flashed through them. Chad had told him we were engaged. Chad was a dead man.

Bastian caught Chad's shoulder and spun him around, pinning him to the staircase railing with Bastian's fist wrapped around Chad's bargain-bin tie. With the two of them together, Bastian dominated Chad physically. I had never thought of Chad as small, but he had nothing compared to Bastian.

"Mr. B... B... Belrose," Chad stammered, his face draining of color. He had definitely not been expecting Bastian to have overheard his comment. Several guests were turning to look at what the commotion was and I could see Elijah coming out of the shadows. "I didn't mean any insult to you sir... I..."

"But you did mean offense to her?" Bastian growled, tightening his grip. The scar on his cheek had gone white with rage. I hope he had control of his temper, but part of me hoped that he would just deck Chad. Maybe even break his nose. "You lied to me."

Chad's eyes were getting bigger by the second and flashing around the room to search for help. His two friends had instantly abandoned him. Diamond-necklace was long gone. Chad's eyes met mine, first asking for assistance and then slowly filling with recognition.

"Ava?" Chad squeaked, looking me up and down in shock. I guessed he couldn't believe that I could look like this.

"Hi, Chad." My stomach was in knots, but for the first time, I wasn't going to back down. I didn't need Chad. I didn't need him or what he thought of me. I had myself.

And now I had Bastian. I took a bold step forward. "Crawling back with my father's business between my legs, huh? I am so glad I dumped your ass when I did, you two-timing cheater. I actually pity you."

Bastian released Chad's jacket, smoothing it out and giving him a snide smile. Much of the crowd was staring and listening to every word. Bastian didn't need to hit Chad. I had just hit Chad in the worst possible way. His pride.

Bastian wrapped his arm around me, clearly signifying that I was with him. That I was good enough for *him*. I was good enough for a billionaire. It made me hold my head up high. And everyone now knew it.

Chad stupidly opened his mouth, thinking he would say something clever, but Bastian saw it coming. He lunged, just moving his massive shoulders forward and not even moving his feet, but enough to give the threat of attack. Chad yelped and cowered against the banister while the crowd laughed.

"Shall we, Ava, my love?" Bastian asked loudly, holding out his arm for me to take. "I'd like to introduce you to Jack Saunders and his wife. I saw them in the drawing room and I know they'd love to meet you."

"That sounds wonderful, dear," I cooed, knowing that Chad would be crying at this missed opportunity. Not only was I dating a billionaire, but he was introducing me to his billionaire friends. How was that for not good enough?

My skirts swooshed against the marble tiles as Bastian led me out of the room. I walked like a princess, finally letting myself feel like one. Bastian treated me like a princess because I deserved to be treated like one.

"The lunge wasn't too much, was it?" Bastian asked as we rounded the corner into what I thought was the drawing room.

"Not at all," I told him, kissing his cheek. He must have

shaved right before the party as he still smelled of his after-shave cream. "I thought it was perfect."

Bastian smoothed the stray strand of hair away from my face. His eyes were soft and full of love just for me. Everyone else in the room melted away. "You're perfect," he whispered. "I'm so glad you're here."

"Me too." I beamed up at him. He smiled back and kissed me, soft and sweet, but full of promise. For a moment I wondered if one of the upstairs rooms were empty...

"Bastian!" A masculine voice called out and Bastian released me from his kiss. "Great party."

Bastian looked over at the voice and smiled before turning back to me. "Now, I'd like you to come meet Jack and Emma."

"For real?" I asked. I had been sure the offer had been just meant as one more parting blow to Chad. "I get to meet Jack and Emma Saunders?"

"Yes," Bastian answered. He shook his head like I was asking if we were having wine later. He had every intention of introducing me to his billionaire friends.

"Just one more question," I said, pulling on his sleeve. Bastian stopped and waited. "How late is this party supposed to go tonight?"

He grinned, joy bubbling in his eyes. "Until after sunrise, my love."

EPILOGUE

It's dark outside. The stars twinkle and the gray promise of dawn has started. The sun will rise in exactly 9 minutes. I know this because I have had the hour and minute circled on my calendar for the past six months.

"Your mother would be so proud of you," Dad whispers. He's said it at least fifty times already today, and a thousand more yesterday, but I still smile. I wish she could have been here for this. There is an ache in my heart for her, but I know that she's here in spirit. She wouldn't have missed today for the world.

"Five minute warning," Charlotte announces, stepping into the small room where I've been getting ready. "Sunrise in seven, but we have to get you down there."

Butterflies alight in my stomach. I press my palms against the smooth satin of my dress, trying to tell the butterflies to settle once again.

Dad clears his throat. He stands in front of me and takes my hands in his. Tears make his eyes glisten and I can tell that he's holding his emotion back. I hug him, pulling him close. He wraps his arms around me, holding his breath. I feel like a little girl for a moment, cradled and safe with my father.

"Your mother asked me to give this to you on your wedding day," Dad says, slowly releasing me. A tear trickles down his cheek and I know I'm about to start bawling at any moment. He reaches into his suit jacket pocket and pulls out an envelope. "She made me promise."

My hands tremble and it's taking everything I have not to cry. Charlotte hands me a tissue.

"It's okay," she whispers. "There's a reason they make water-proof mascara."

The envelope is wrinkled and there's a small tear in the corner, but my name is on the front in my mother's hand. I trace the letters, imagining her writing it and smiling. I open it.

 Dearest Ava,

I wish I could be there today to cry at your wedding. Instead, I will be watching you from above and loving you with all my heart. I love you so much and I'm so incredibly proud to have called you mine.

Love you more than words

-Mom

I DAB at my eyes and I don't dare look over at Dad because I know I'll lose it. There's something else in the envelope. I shake out a thin silver chain with several petite charms dangling from it. There's a replica of the Eiffel Tower, a paintbrush, a heart, and tiny angel.

I smile and turn to Dad. His cheeks shine in the pale light as he helps attach the delicate bracelet to my wrist. It's perfect.

"It's time," Charlotte says quietly. She hands me another

tissue and takes my used one. "It's a good thing I stocked up on these."

I chuckle. I was right to pick her as my maid of honor. She certainly has become my best friend in the past year. Though, Bastian and I did have a small squabble over which one of us got her, I had won the argument since he had Gabe and Leo.

Charlotte and my best friend from high school walk out the door. Dad offers me his arm and I thread mine into his. He smiles and guides me out the door and out onto the sand.

The sky is alight with pink clouds and golden promise of the coming dawn, but I don't see it. I don't see the ocean's beauty reflecting the colors of the sky or the people I love standing on the beach. There are three men waiting, but I just see Bastian.

He's wearing a light gray suit that matches his eyes. His face splits into the biggest grin I have ever seen as I approach. I'm not nervous anymore. I'm not scared. I'm excited and incredibly happy. I don't care about the rest.

"Who gives this woman to be with this man?" The minister asks.

"I do," Dad replies. His voice cracks slightly. I turn to say goodbye to him. He hugs me close and kisses my cheek before carefully placing my hand in Bastian's.

"Take care of her," Dad says quietly.

"Always and forever," Bastian assures him. Dad smiles at us both and then steps back to join the small crowd gathered on the beach.

The world fades away as I look into Bastian's eyes. The words come easily. I've already made the promise to love him forever. I made that promise a long time ago without ever having to say the words out loud.

The sun starts to rise. Yellow gold light spills across the ocean, starting our new life together with the dawn. Bastian's eyes sparkle with joy and his scars seem to fade into the light.

"Do you take this woman to be your lawfully wedded wife?"

"I do." Bastian's voice is calm and controlled, but his hands are shaking in mine.

"Do you take this man to be your lawfully wedded husband?"

"I do." I don't falter. I don't have to think. I want Bastian to be mine forever. I want to be his forever.

I promise my heart and soul to him as Bastian promises his to me. I hear someone sniffle. Charlotte is using the tissues she is supposed to be holding for me. There are more words and more promises, but the meaning is all the same.

I love him. He loves me.

"By the power vested in me, I now pronounce you husband and wife!"

A cheer goes up from the small crowd on the beach. A bright pink cloud slips in front of the sun and allows a single ray of perfect golden sun to shine on just the two of us. It's our own personal dawn as Bastian cups my chin in his hand and draws me to him. The kiss is sweet, but with just enough heat to promise more later.

The sun is now up, making the world sparkle with color and promise. The ocean is bluer now, and the sand whiter. This is the dawn of a new day and the start of our new life together.

Bastian squeezes my hand tighter in his and I can't stop smiling. My face already hurts from smiling so hard, but I know I won't be able to stop. I don't want to stop. I'm happier than I ever could have imagined.

Bastian leans forward and kisses me again. This time it is just for the two of us, a sunrise kiss that promises a lifetime of joy. I kiss him back, knowing that we have a lifetime of sunrise kisses before us.

Escape With Me: A Midlife Love Story

"I gave it all up to be happy. I'd give it all up again for you."

They say life begins after 40, but Cassie ain't feelin' it. Divorced and feeling trapped by her job, she wants to let loose for her friend's tropical beach wedding. She decides to let her hair down and get a little unpredictable. That's when she meets a handsome bartender, Wyatt.

Despite a few grey hairs, Wyatt's the liveliest man that Cassie has ever met. She knows that there's got to be more to his life story than just being a bartender, but this is just supposed to be a vacation fling. And after sunny days spent breaking all the rules on the beach together, Cassie realizes that nobody has ever listened to her the way that Wyatt does.

His carefree life is enviable, his kisses are intoxicating, and she can almost imagine a life with him. But all vacations come to an end. And when Cassie invites him to visit her hometown, Wyatt reveals that he can never go back. Not to her town. Not to America. Not to civilization.

Cassie leaves, confused and heartbroken, wondering just who she got herself involved with. Suddenly, her predictable life gets turned upside down when she sees her picture splashed across the Internet. And when the tabloids come looking for the mature woman who found the lost billionaire, she has no idea what to do...

...until he comes back.

Escape With Me: A Midlife Love Story

ABOUT THE AUTHOR

New York Times and USA Today Bestseller Krista Lakes is a thirtysomething who recently rediscovered her passion for writing. She is living happily ever after with her Prince Charming. Her first kid just started preschool and she is happy to welcome her second child into her life, continuing her "Happily Ever After"!

Thank you for supporting an indie author. Anything you can do, whether it be writing a review, or even simply telling a fellow reader that you enjoyed this, helps me out immensely. Thanks!

Krista would love to hear from you! Please contact her at Krista.Lakes@gmail.com or friend her on Facebook!

Further reading:

Bad Boys and Babies
　　Family Doctor's Baby
　　The Billionaire's Baby Arrangement
　　Crime Boss Baby

Kinds of Love
　　A Forever Kind of Love
　　A Wonderful Kind of Love
　　An Endless Kind of Love

Billionaires and Brides
>Yours Completely: A Cinderella Love Story
Yours Truly: A Cinderella Love Story
Yours Royally: A Cinderella Love Story

The "Kisses" series
>Saltwater Kisses: A Billionaire Love Story
Kisses From Jack: The Other Side of Saltwater Kisses
Rainwater Kisses: A Billionaire Love Story
Champagne Kisses: A Timeless Love Story
Freshwater Kisses: A Billionaire Love Story
Sandcastle Kisses: A Billionaire Love Story
Hurricane Kisses: A Billionaire Love Story
Barefoot Kisses: A Billionaire Love Story
Sunrise Kisses: A Billionaire Love Story
Waterfall Kisses: A Billionaire Love Story
Island Kisses: A Billionaire Love Story

Other Novels
>I Choose You: A Secret Billionaire Romance
His Every Desire: A Billionaire Seduction
Wolf Six's Salvation: A Shifter Love Story
Burned: A New Adult Love Story
Walking on Sunshine: A Sweet Summer Romance
An American Cinderella: A Royal Love Story
Mr. Darcy's Kiss: A Contemporary Pride and Prejudice

www.ingramcontent.com/pod-product-compliance
Lightning Source LLC
Chambersburg PA
CBHW050344190726
48284CB00007BB/2147